The Sizzling Fascination of Seduction . . .

Agnes felt heavy and light at once, her head spinning with anticipation and her body yearning for a respite from desire. At their own direction, her hands worked Edward's tunic above his waist, and her fingers mapped his tautly muscled body.

"Oh, yes," he said. "That's it exactly." He reached around her and scraped aside a stack of books. Then he pressed an index finger into her cleavage and drew a line to her navel.

"What are you about?" she asked.

"A poor idea." But the gleam in his eyes spoke of excitement.

He's a doctor, she mused, and so much more. A teacher. A scholar. An inventor. And the man who owned her heart. "Tell me your idea."

"I warn you. What I'm thinking is out of the main."

"A place to which I aspire. Tell me."

"I'd very much like to rip this garment off you. . . ."

Please turn the page for praise for Arnette Lamb's marvelous romances. . . .

CHIEFTAIN

"Powerful, emotionally intense, sexually charged, *Chieftain* typifies Arnette Lamb's storytelling talents."

—Kathe Robin, *Romantic Times*

"Excellently written and powerfully moving. . . . All-in-all, another superb read from the pen of a master storyteller."

—Harriet Klausner, *Affaire de Coeur*

BORDER BRIDE

"Vintage Arnette Lamb. This irresistible tale warms your heart, tickles your funny bone, and delights your senses."

—Kathe Robin, *Romantic Times*

"Deep and sensuous . . . sexually stimulating and very fast-paced. Its theme is love heals the human heart. You will bask in its afterglow."

—*Rendezvous*

BORDER LORD

"All that a historical romance should be: fast-paced, funny and hot-blooded . . . one of the best of the year."

—*Detroit Free Press*

"An excellent tale of high adventure. . . . Ms. Lamb has written a choice story filled with humor and a special understanding of human motivation and love."

—Sherrilyn Kenyon, *Affaire de Coeur*

Books by Arnette Lamb

Highland Rogue
The Betrothal
Border Lord
Border Bride
Chieftain
Maiden of Inverness
A Holiday of Love
Betrayed
Beguiled

Published by POCKET BOOKS

ARNETTE LAMB

Beguiled

POCKET STAR BOOKS

New York   London   Toronto   Sydney   Tokyo   Singapore

This book is a work of fiction. Names, characters, places and incidents are products of the author's imagination or are used fictitiously. Any resemblance to actual events or locales or persons, living or dead, is entirely coincidental.

An *Original* Publication of POCKET BOOKS

A Pocket Star Book published by
POCKET BOOKS, a division of Simon & Schuster Inc.
1230 Avenue of the Americas, New York, NY 10020

ISBN: 0-671-88219-8

First Pocket Books printing May 1996

10 9 8 7 6 5 4 3 2 1

POCKET STAR BOOKS and colophon are registered trademarks of Simon & Schuster Inc.

Cover art by Danilo Ducak

Printed in the U.S.A.

For
Lina Levy
An extraordinary artist, who has brought so many of
my characters to life in her beautiful cover paintings.

Thanks to both Alice Shields and Pat Stech for the gift of their time and their expertise.

Beguiled

1

Edinburgh, Scotland
Summer 1785

FURTIVE MOVEMENT BROKE THE SOLEMN STILLNESS OF THE
moment. On the edge of her vision Agnes MacKenzie
spied a form darting in the shadowed aisle between
the columns and the stained glass windows at the side
of the chapel. Beside her, her just-married sister,
Sarah, penned her vows in the family chronicle, the
Book of the MacKenzies. The scratching of the new
nib on the old vellum echoed off the stone walls of
Saint Margaret's Church.

The dark figure moved past the confessionals and
neared the chancel.

Agnes tensed.

The quill was passed to Sarah's new husband, Lord
Michael Elliot. Behind Agnes the congregation murmured approval.

Who was creeping soundlessly in the shadows? All
of the clerics, their attendants, and students stood at
the altar before Agnes.

The ceremony lost its reverence. Her protective senses, born of guilt and nurtured by years of training, stayed fixed on the progress of the uninvited guest.

Her father, Lachlan MacKenzie, the duke of Ross, began a prayer asking God to watch over Sarah and Michael and to bless the grandchildren they would give him.

Agnes thought of the one lost sheep in the MacKenzie clan. Regret and heartache over her part in the tragedy weighted her soul. With effort, she rose above the distressing subject of her younger sibling and steered her attention to the danger slithering along the far wall. Danger, yes. Agnes could feel it in her bones. Trouble was like a smell to her, like a foul odor prefacing a foe, another tangible adversary she lived to hunt down and conquer.

Who lurked on the periphery of this joyous occasion but was too cowardly to show his face?

A quick intake of breath sounded behind her. Turning, Agnes looked over her shoulder and scanned the occupants of the church—family members, long-time friends, and newly made acquaintances. Only one other head was unbowed for the prayer, and the worried expression on the face of the earl of Cathcart told Agnes that he, too, felt the danger.

Their gazes met. Anxiety flickered in his eyes. He stared past her.

The melodious cadence of her father's voice faded.

Agnes craned her neck, and her attention stayed focused on the front pew where Lord Edward Napier, earl of Cathcart, sat with his children. Befitting her life's work, the little ones were Agnes's prime concern. The lad was about eight, the girl no more than four years old. The younger sat quietly on the lap of a granny-faced nanny. The lad's hands were clasped in

2

prayer. His bowed head bore a crown of auburn curls the exact shade and texture as that of his noble father.

In a protective gesture, the earl drew his young son closer to his side but continued to stare at the spot where the intruder lurked. The defensive maneuver struck a chord of understanding in Agnes.

A chorus of "amen's" signaled the end of the prayer.

The shadow took form. A hooded black robe hid the features of a gray-bearded man. He stood near one of the trunk-size columns that framed the chancel. Sharp angles appeared beside him.

A mason sent to repair one of the vaulted arches, his tools in hand? Surely not, not during a wedding ceremony.

"Agnes, 'tis your turn to sign." Sarah's gaze turned cunning. "What's amiss?"

In spite of her apprehension, Agnes knew she must not fly with her imagination. Not unless a true threat existed. Overreaction on her part could spoil the most important day in her sister's life.

"You look . . . troubled," Sarah said.

For now a light reply would allay Sarah's suspicions. Agnes forced a smile and whispered, "I *am* troubled. I'm the only virgin left among us." By "us" Agnes referred to herself, Sarah, and their sisters, Lottie and Mary. "Give me the quill."

Sarah's suspicion faded, replaced by the most radiant feminine smile Agnes had seen since the morning after Lottie's wedding.

"You'll find your dashing Highlander, Agnes."

Love and marriage had no place in Agnes's life, not until she righted the one great wrong of her youth. But to mention that sad day would taint this happy occasion.

With one eye on the hooded man, Agnes scratched

3

her name beneath the signature of David Smithson, the other witness and husband to Lottie. That done, Agnes performed her last task in the ceremony. She picked up the Book of the MacKenzies while the family Bible was placed on the pedestal. As head of the family, Lachlan began making the proper entry. None would take offense at the order in which the books were presented; religions came and went, but Highland custom held sway.

Agnes felt the weight of the heavy chronicle, with its ancient wooden bindings and thick vellum pages, but she refused to be distracted. Once the ceremony was over, she'd find out who lurked against the wall and why. She'd also learn why the presence of the intruder troubled the earl of Cathcart.

She'd met Edward Napier the evening before. A widower and resident of Glasgow, he had come to the wedding at the invitation of the groom. Papa had been impressed with the Glaswegian nobleman; he had said that thanks to the earl's many scientific achievements, Scotland would step boldly into the next century. Sarah, whose thirst for knowledge was unequaled in Clan MacKenzie, had been effusive in her praise of the earl, had even asked him to present a lecture in science at Edinburgh's orphanage school. He had agreed, time permitting.

Cathcart had been polite to Agnes, but reserved. In retrospect his aloofness smacked of apprehension.

Did he know the intruder?

His part in the ceremony concluded, Lachlan MacKenzie closed the family Bible. The bride and groom turned toward the congregation. A cheer went through the crowd. Agnes stayed where she was. In the shadows light glinted on pointed steel. Looking back, she studied the occupants of the front pew. The nanny had disappeared. In her childish boredom, the girl swung her legs and gazed at the vaulted ceiling. Her brother toyed with a wedding souvenir. The earl's attention was still focused on the robed man.

Suddenly the earl's eyes grew large. He shot sideways, shielding his children.

A keening whistle sliced the air. Awareness ripped through Agnes. Sharp angles. A crossbow.

Her reflexes worked like lightning. Holding out the heavy book, she lunged to the right.

The arrow thudded into the wooden bindings and slammed the book against her chest. Pain exploded in her shoulder. Knocked off balance, she set her jaw for the impact to come. Then she was falling, the vaulted arches and stained glass windows cartwheeling in and out of view.

She hit the stone floor hard, and as blackness gripped her, she heard the sound of her father's voice.

"Agnes!"

Pushing his new son-in-law aside, Lachlan Mac-Kenzie fought the fear clawing at his gut and made his way to Agnes. Had she tripped? Nimble-footed Agnes? Impossible. Had she fallen ill before she could make a graceful exit? An absurd notion. Agnes was in her prime, healthy and high-spirited.

Before he could reach her, he saw the earl of Cathcart pluck his children from the pew and put them beneath it. As he moved to cover Agnes, Cathcart pointed to the side of the church. "He's there!" he yelled. "A robed man with a crossbow! He's shot her."

Shot! Fear pumping through him, Lachlan didn't break stride as he called to his sons-in-law. "Michael! David! Agnes has been shot. Go after that bowman!"

Changing directions, the young men gave chase. The crowd converged on Agnes, slowing Lachlan's progress. Familiar voices formed a mosaic of sound.

His grandchildren cried. His daughters screamed. His friends spoke in outraged whispers.

He shoved his way past the throng and to Agnes's side.

She lay in a heap of yellow silk, the Book of the MacKenzies covering her from breast to hip. A crossbow quarrel protruded from the wooden bindings. With sickening dread, he knew the arrow had passed through the book and pierced her.

Ripping off his coat, Lachlan called out to her. "Agnes?"

Her eyes drifted open, and as if drawn, she sought out the earl of Cathcart and his children. "Protect them," she begged in a pained whisper.

Pushing her hair from her forehead, Lachlan spoke quietly. "Are you hurt badly?"

She reached for the frightened children, who were huddled beneath the pew. "'Twas meant for them, Papa, and the nanny's gone."

"The devil with Edward Napier and his servants. How badly are you hurt, lass?"

She swallowed with difficulty, and as he watched her throat work, he saw blood seep from beneath the book, pool at her collar bone, and soil her jade necklace. Dread robbed him of breath.

Pity the bastard who'd fired the shot, for his life belonged to Lachlan MacKenzie. A slow, painful death awaited the villain.

Through a fog of anger he heard the earl of Cathcart say, "The quarrel's embedded in her flesh, but it's missed her heart and lungs."

The clinical explanation enraged Lachlan. "I should rejoice for that?"

A hand touched his shoulder. His wife, Juliet, knelt at his side. "Have a care, my love, and tell me what happened."

Anger gave way to fatherly angst. "'Twould seem that trouble has again found my firstborn."

"Worry not." Juliet cupped Agnes's cheek, but Lachlan knew her words of comfort were meant for him as well. "We'll take care of you."

Agnes bit her lip, but her eyes shone with rare trust.

Again the voice of the earl. "'Tis not a mortal wound, but the arrow must come out."

Straining, Agnes looked at the stubby arrow. "The fletchings are English," she said.

Tough, unreachable Agnes, thought Lachlan. Why couldn't she be like other young women her age? Why did this sensitive and loyal woman risk her life for others, then make light of her own injuries? For years, he'd indulged her, but now Lachlan intended to quell her penchant for danger.

Knowing the pain he was about to cause her, he grasped the quarrel and tugged. He met resistance.

Agnes winced as the barb tore at her flesh.

"Sorry, sweeting."

"Move aside, Your Grace," said Cathcart, his attention focused on Agnes. "I'm a doctor. I studied here in Edinburgh."

Lachlan searched the man's face, hoping that he spoke the truth. Edward Napier's achievements were legend, but medicine was not known to be among his considerable accomplishments.

"The children, Papa," Agnes pleaded. "Protect his children." Her elegant features, so like her noble mother's, turned angelic in entreaty. "Promise me you will."

Lachlan would promise to turn Puritan to save her. "Aye, lassie. You have my word."

"I can protect my own children," said the earl. "But if that arrow doesn't come out now, you'll lose the use of your arm."

Flattening himself on his belly beside Agnes, Cathcart peered under the book. After examining the spot where the arrow impaled her, he smiled reassuringly. "'Tis not too deep." Catching Lachlan's gaze, he said, "Pull—very gently and do not twist it. I'll lift the book. Lady Juliet, hold her hand."

Juliet reached for Agnes and said, "'Twill be over before you can make the MacKenzie war cry."

Agnes set her jaw. "I'm ready."

Lachlan grasped the wooden shaft. The fletchings prickled his palms. At the first tug, Agnes moaned.

"Easy, love," Juliet murmured, still speaking to the both of them.

"Do it, man!" Cathcart urged.

His stomach sour with worry, Lachlan pulled the arrow free.

The earl cursed and shoved the book, with the arrow running through it, into Lachlan's hands. Like an evil invader, the bloodied tip of the quarrel protruded from the book. Lachlan tossed it aside.

Agnes's yellow gown was stained crimson. Her skin glowed pasty white.

Cathcart grasped the bodice of her dress and ripped it, pulling the sleeve away. With a gentleness that should not have surprised Lachlan, Cathcart explored the wound. Using the skirt of his kilt as a bandage, he stemmed the flow of blood.

Agnes sucked in her breath.

Cathcart murmured soothing words of encouragement, and as Lachlan watched, the distinctive black-and-white tartan of the Napiers literally ran red with MacKenzie blood.

Agnes's blood. His golden-haired, once precocious child had yet again endangered herself for another. And all because she could not let go of the past.

Impotent rage coursed through him. Noise from the

onlookers rose to a deafening roar. He must end her foolish quest. But how? He could not treble her chores or take away her pony. Banishing her to the country wouldn't work; he'd tried that before and paid the heavy price of a year's estrangement.

Again fabric ripped. "Here," said Juliet, handing Cathcart a length of white petticoat. "God bless you, Lord Edward."

Cathcart took the cloth and pressed it over the wound, but his intense gaze never left Agnes. "Breathe slowly," he told her. "The pain will ebb. Do you understand? Will you trust me?"

She nodded, her nostrils flaring, her lips pursed in agony.

Lachlan pierced him with an accusing gaze. "Was the assassin sent for you?"

"Hold this." Cathcart shoved the now bloodied wad of satin into Lachlan's hand. "I'll carry her." He scooped her into his arms and turned to the cleric. "Lead the way to your chamber. I'll need boiled water, and send someone to the Dragoon Inn for my medical bag."

The clergyman whirled, surplice fluttering, and headed for the side of the chapel.

"Lady Juliet," said Cathcart. "I'll need plenty of bandages. And bring a clean sleeping gown."

To Agnes Juliet said, "Shall I send them with Auntie Loo?"

Resting in the cradle of Cathcart's arms, Agnes struggled to keep her eyes open. "Yes. Show her the arrow. I need her."

To his children Cathcart said, "Christopher, Hannah, you can come out now. You're to go with Lady Juliet and mind yourselves."

They scrambled from beneath the pew. "You'll make her all better, will you not, Papa?" his son pleaded, a protective arm around his bewildered sister.

"'S'bad," the girl said.

"Will you make her better?" his son demanded.

"Of course I will." He started to move away, but stopped. "Come, MacKenzie, and keep the pressure on that wound."

Taking orders was foreign to Lachlan. The sight of another man tending his daughter . . . ripping her clothing . . . holding her possessively robbed him of logic. "Give her to me."

"No." Slightly taller than Lachlan and slimmer in his youth, Edward Napier no longer appeared the esteemed scholar and respected statesman; field general better suited his manner. "She grows weaker by the moment."

Cathcart spoke the truth, but Lachlan balked.

"Please, Papa," Agnes begged. "There isn't much time."

Her eyes were now glassy. Lachlan's fear returned with a vengeance. "Time? What do you mean?"

Perspiration dotted her brow, and her head lolled against Cathcart's shoulder. On a sigh, she said, "The arrow was poisoned."

As he cleansed the star-shaped wound that marred Agnes MacKenzie's shoulder, Edward Napier struggled between anger and gratitude. The duke's daughter was either the bravest or the most foolhardy woman he'd ever met.

But she had saved his life—at the risk of her own.

The unselfishness of her act moved him in a way that was new. Gratitude didn't begin to describe his feelings; he'd need time alone to explore what was in his heart. The event was too vivid: the sight of the crossbow aimed at him; the fear for his children; the image of Agnes MacKenzie moving into the path of danger; the horrible sound of the quarrel bringing her down.

"Are you well, Lord Edward?" she asked. "You look as if you might swoon."

He banished the memory but knew it was only temporary, for he'd never forget her bravery, her generosity.

"Never mind about me." His voice caught, and he had to clear his throat. "How are you feeling?"

Fatigue rimmed her warm brown eyes, and her skin was as pale as snow on ice. She gave him a valiant smile. "I've been better. But your children are safe now."

He had spoken briefly with her the evening before, and Edward recalled every word of their conversation, for at the time the casual exchange had been a welcome respite from the troubles that had plagued him of late.

"Are you done?" demanded the duke of Ross.

"I doubt he'll ravish me, Papa."

Edward summoned patience. Most men in the duke's position would have forbidden another man— even a physician—to touch a female relative. No matter how unskilled, a female healer was the preferable choice in the circumstances. Necessity had forced MacKenzie's hand, and now that Edward had ministered to her, the duke reverted to propriety.

To spare his wife and his other daughters, MacKenzie had barred them from the room. Under the father's watchful eyes, Edward had cleansed and stitched the star-shaped wound. The arrowhead had missed her clavicle. No bones were broken, but she'd have a powerful array of bruises on the morrow.

If the arrow tip had been poisoned, as she believed, the poison was weak. That or the act of traveling first

11

through the wooden bindings of the heavy book and the layers of thick vellum had somehow worn away the potion. Yes, that theory had merit.

"Well, Cathcart? You've seen enough of my first-born. She's half naked, for God's sake."

She was half naked for her *own* sake, but Edward didn't point that out to the worried duke. Instead he counted to ten and gave her a reassuring smile.

"Did you hear me?" roared the duke.

"I'll be done as soon as the bandages arrive."

The door opened. Edward looked up and blinked in confusion at the sight of the unusual woman entering the room. She wore a fashionable if plain gown, and her thick black hair was upswept and coiled at the crown of her head. In bearing and fashion she typified the style of Scotswomen of the day. In heritage and complexion she bore the striking features of the Orientals.

She bowed from the waist. In one hand she held the blood-stained quarrel, in the other she carried a valise. In perfect English she said, "I am Auntie Loo. I've brought the bandages you requested and a gown for Lady Agnes."

His patient tried to rise. "Come quickly," she said. With the heel of his hand, Edward held her. "Stay where you are or you'll rip those stitches."

She grunted, and the distressed sound again roused her overprotective father. "Stop yelling at my daughter, and take your hand off her breast."

Edward took no offense. He hadn't noticed her breasts. Well, he had noticed, but not in a disrespectful or lustful way. She was injured. He was helping her.

A basic truth dragged at his conscience. The assassin had been sent for him. Had he remained at home in Glasgow, the bowman would have sought him there. Agnes MacKenzie would be unharmed and making merry at the wedding feast. But strong reasons had compelled Edward to make the journey. The groom, Michael Elliot, was Edward's friend, and he had wanted to share in the joyous occasion. Christopher and Hannah deserved a holiday, and until moments ago, the excursion to Edinburgh had been good for Edward's family.

Reluctantly, he stepped back as the woman named Auntie Loo examined the wound. Satisfied, she waved the arrow before Agnes. "There wasn't enough poison on the barbs to kill you."

"'Twas monkshood." His patient huffed. "Tell me that when my limbs turn to useless stumps and my tongue rots in my mouth."

The duke cursed. The women paid him no mind.

From within the folds of her dress Auntie Loo produced a small stone bottle. "The ache in your heart will hurt you more than this latest wound."

Stubbornness lent the Lady Agnes a queenly air. "So you say. What do you know about it?"

The woman tisked, but her eyes twinkled with mischief. In broken, affected English, she said, "Golden One too strong for Englishman's death powder. But Chinaman's poison send you to the harpers. This potion make you rest and call up your demons." She waved the bottle, and with a crooked, loving smile, said, "More better you lose one skinny arm?"

Perspiration beaded Agnes's forehead. "Then I couldn't cover both of my ears against your nattering—in any dialect. I will not drink that mind-stealing concoction."

Auntie Loo stared pointedly at Lachlan. Reverting to the King's English, she said, "Your oft foolish daughter will live to trouble you again, my lord."

Wringing his hands, the duke paced. "Nay, she will

trouble me no more. Her outlandish behavior is at an end." He gave her a stern glare. "You're coming home with us to Tain, and I'll not let you out of my sight until a husband catches your fancy."

She rallied her strength for what Edward suspected was an old argument. "Never," she swore. "You cannot force me to live with you. You cannot force me to wed."

Uncomfortable at witnessing their strife, Edward fished out the bandages and began wrapping the cloth around her shoulder. Too caught up in his anger, the duke did not notice that Edward was again ministering to his patient.

"That's where you are wrong," MacKenzie spat. "I forbid you to put yourself in danger again."

"That's where *you* are wrong."

"Agnes," he said on an expelled breath. "I indulged you when you begged to go to China to learn those foreign fighting skills."

Foreign fighting skills? To what was the duke referring?

She glanced at the woman named Auntie Loo. "Where I saved a member of the royal family."

He went on as if she hadn't spoken. "I also allowed you to travel with Burgundy."

"Where I foiled two attempts on the life of his heir."

Edward had heard the tale. According to the French duke, Agnes MacKenzie, with only a knife for weapon, had brought down two would-be assassins. She didn't appear so formidable now, and if he hadn't seen her in action, Edward wouldn't have believed the tale. It baffled him that this beautiful woman was capable of so much daring.

MacKenzie threw up his hands. "You nearly

drowned pulling that gin-soaked beggar from the Thames."

That rescue was news to Edward.

"She was only a babe," Agnes said. "Her mother fed her the vile drink apurpose. She would have sold her own child to any man with an unholy urge and a copper."

MacKenzie paused and pointed a threatening finger at her. "I'll cease your allowance. You'll have no funds to continue that futile search. Your sister is dead."

Like the shadow of the moon eclipsing the sun, the light faded from her eyes. Tears pooled, but she blinked them back. "Nay. Virginia lives, and I will not forsake her."

"Virginia is dead, and you must get on with living."

She stiffened. "I tell you, I will find her."

The duke eyed her with cool regard. "Without money?"

"I'll earn it myself."

MacKenzie chuckled, but the sound held no humor. Edward decided that the duke was goading his daughter into disobedience. A now familiar stubbornness engulfed her, and her expression mirrored her father's belligerent stare.

"Why can you not be like your sisters?" said the duke.

"Like Mary? Pregnant without benefit of marriage?"

"What?" His face turned crimson.

"You didn't know?"

"I know that she loves Wiltshire."

"Then you'll have me be like Lottie, who pries into everyone's business?"

"Lottie is a good wife and mother."

"Then like Sarah, who is not my blood sister."

"Who told you that?" her father demanded.

15

"Sarah did."

"We are not speaking of Sarah, Lottie, or Mary. We are discussing your sedentary future in Tain."

"Nay."

"Then I'll betroth you to Revas Macqueen."

Revas Macqueen was the richest and most devout bachelor in Scotland. Although not yet thirty, the Highland earl epitomized the old patriarchal chieftain.

Lady Agnes huffed in mock laughter. "You'd sell me to him?"

"I'll give you away to the first man with the wherewithal to control you."

"Do," she spat, "and you shall never see me again."

Anguish and determination made a battlefield of Lachlan MacKenzie's expression.

Guilt swamped Edward, for he was to blame for the enmity between the duke of Ross and his unconventional firstborn daughter.

Edward leaned over her. "I order you to rest." Watching her, he admonished the duke. "As her physician, I insist that you leave her alone for now. She's not going anywhere."

"As your better, I command you to hold your tongue."

"Leave off, Papa."

Edward had enough. "Stop! Both of you."

A change came over the duke of Ross. He squared his shoulders, tipped back his head, and stared down his regal nose at Edward. "You overstep yourself, Cathcart. Should you do it again, you'll be very sorry."

Not since his first year at Oxford had anyone spoken so disrespectfully to Edward. His pride smarting, he gazed at the beautiful and brave Agnes MacKenzie.

"Do not let my father bully you, Lord Edward."
Her friendly tone belied the tension in the room.

Edward had ceased practicing medicine in noble
circles for precisely these reasons. The poor appreciated his help; the ruling class disdained him for his
efforts in treating the person—above and beyond the
illness.

"Stand aside, Cathcart."

Agnes murmured, "My father thinks himself a
king."

Her strength and determination drew Edward like
iron to a magnet. "Then it follows that you are a
princess."

"Without a kingdom at the moment. Have you
room in Glasgow for an exiled Highlander?"

"I forbid it, Agnes MacKenzie!"

Her smile grew radiant. "Please, Lord Edward?"

His guilty conscience reigned. "Very well."

The duke turned livid. "You cannot live unchaper-
oned in his household. Think what it will do to your
reputation."

"Auntie Loo and the earl's honor are enough chap-
eron. Isn't that true, Lord Edward?"

Now that the danger had passed and his patient
would recover, Edward had second thoughts.

"I do so *love* Glasgow," she said.

"If you step one slippered foot into that city, I'll
betroth you to Macqueen."

As if her father hadn't uttered the dire ultimatum,
she said, "Take me with you, Lord Edward."

"But I cannot come between you and your father."

Lord Lachlan slapped the table. "Well said,
Cathcart."

"You can, and you must take me with you."

"Why must I?"

"Because you owe me your life."

2

"PISCINARIAN!"

"Weasel brain!"

"Hannah! Christopher!" Lord Edward glared at his children. "Behave yourselves."

To hide a smile, Agnes used her free hand to pick up her teacup. She sat with the earl and his children at a corner table in the public room of the Dragoon Inn. Three days had passed since the attempt on his life, and this luncheon was the first outing he had allowed her. In further compliance with his instructions, she had fashioned a sling from cotton cloth to cradle her right arm against her breast. The wrapping eased the pain in her shoulder, and she could use her left hand as well as her right.

"'Tis your fault," Christopher grumbled.

"'Tis yours," Hannah argued.

Until moments ago, the Napier children had behaved surprisingly well. Now they were restless and eager for dessert.

Hannah wore a pink satin gown fashioned with small panniers and puffed sleeves. The ensemble was stylishly feminine, with one outrageous exception: a man's cravat, tied in intricate loops, cascaded from her neck. Her father, dressed in his tartan kilt and black velvet coat, and her brother, garbed in a brown frock coat and knee breeches, wore identical scarves. How interesting, Agnes thought, that the earl indulged his daughter. Had he tied the scarves himself?

The children squirmed. The earl glanced at the front doors. He'd done that often since Agnes joined them. He should have chosen the table in the far corner, between the kitchen and the side exit. She'd apprise him of that later.

Christopher wadded his napkin. "You've botched it now, Hannah."

"Have not."

"Both of you will stop bickering or forfeit your dessert."

The lad dropped his fork. "She started it, Father. She kicked me."

"He pinched me with his crepit thumb." Turning and holding the back of her chair, the four-year-old Hannah scrambled to her feet and pulled up her dress. Twin bruises the size of a lad's thumb and fingertip marred her chubby thigh. "See?"

Murmurs rumbled from a table nearby, but the earl didn't seem to care that others were observing him in the act of disciplining his children.

How uncommon and welcome.

"Sit down, Hannah." He closed his eyes and took a deep breath.

Agnes choked back laughter. The earl's eyes snapped open, and he stared at her, startled.

Words failed her, and with alarm, she worried that he might change his mind about taking her with him. He had not mentioned it today, and her father had been present during his brief doctorly visits. She must not give him any reason to withdraw his offer. Leaving Edinburgh in his company posed her best escape from her father. Once they were settled in Glasgow, Edward would come to appreciate her expertise. For now she must appease him.

She scanned the diners. Her sister Lottie occupied a table with the mayor of Edinburgh, but they were blessedly out of earshot. Two clergymen sat near the hearth and cast disapproving glances at both the earl and Agnes.

"Have we mortified you, Lady Agnes?" The earl popped a last bite of bread into his mouth.

"Mortify me? Impossible. My family is quite large," she began by way of honest explanation. "We often bickered and usually embarrassed our parents. Yet we were welcome at table."

That got Christopher's attention. "What if the king came to visit you?"

Agnes pretended to ponder it. Putting down her cup and keeping a straight face, she said, "Then I would have sat close by His Majesty and discovered if he talks with his mouth full."

Hannah erupted with giggles. Christopher guffawed. The earl made an admirable effort to contain his laughter. He failed, and when humor overcame him, Agnes felt her heart tumble in her breast. Edward Napier didn't laugh often, she was certain of that. But what man could with an assassin on his heels? Agnes would ease his burden and in the doing gain a respite from the guilt that weighted her soul.

When he'd mastered his mirth, he said, "I'm glad you can speak kindly of the duke of Ross."

The duke of Ross. The battle between Agnes and her father had been years in the making, but no matter their difficulties, she loved him deeply. A final resolution would come; she lived every day of her life with that goal in mind, but the separation was pure torment.

Quietly, she said, "He's the best man o' the Highlands."

A hush fell over the table. Into the silence Lord Edward said, "I cannot argue that, nor would I try. But I am encouraged to know that all of us poor Scotsmen *below* the Highland Line have a prize of our own at which to aim."

At his engaging remark, her melancholy fled. "Are you the best man o' the Lowlands?"

"Oh, nay," he said, but his expression told a different tale. "I'm average on the most successful of days."

And she was a goose without wings. Edward Napier, the brilliant and forward-thinking scholar, was also a bit of a rogue. The subtle challenge in his eyes begged her to trade quips. The urge to play his verbal game thrummed through her. A part of her longed for the distraction of a courtship, but she'd answered that call once before and regretted it to this day. Like others of life's best distractions, Edward Napier would have to wait.

Practicality forced her to turn the conversation to Hannah. "That's a lovely neckcloth."

Wiggling with glee, the girl slid her brother a coy look. "Papa made it all tied up—for me."

"'Tis silly," spat Christopher. "A lassie cannot wear a man's clothing—"

With only a stern gaze, the earl silenced the boy, but in that glance passed a wealth of communication. Christopher succumbed to good manners.

The earl turned to his daughter. "Sit down, Hannah."

"'S'Christopher's fault."

"You put my toad in the laundry basket."

"You took all the letters." Her bottom lip quivered, and she sent her father a beseeching look.

His features softened, and he reached for her. "You're tired, aren't you, Button?"

Her head bobbed, setting her ringlets and her cravat to bouncing.

Button. Yes, thought Agnes, admiring the sweet-faced, dark-haired Hannah. The name suited her perfectly. She must favor her mother; the earl's angular face and strong, square chin were anything but buttonlike.

He kissed her forehead. "Bid good day to Lady Agnes, and I'll have Peg take you upstairs."

In the absence of the nanny, a local girl named Peg had cared for his children. The woman's sudden disappearance from the church was one of dozens of things Agnes intended to question him about.

"Christopher, finish your food and say good day."

"Oh, please no, Father," Christopher begged. "You said if we didn't pick our noses or spill our cider, we could take our whole meal with you and Lady Agnes."

Suddenly alert, Hannah yanked her thumb from her mouth. "I want lemon cake."

"You promised," said her brother, a whine lifting his voice. "I get clotted cream on my cake."

"Very well. Would you like clotted cream, too?" he asked the girl.

She shook her head so vigorously, her black ringlets slapped his face. "I want . . ." Now that she had his attention, she took full advantage of it. Agnes knew the ploy well; as a child she'd often used it herself. "I want . . . partridge pie."

22

Humor danced in his eyes. "On lemon cake? How thoroughly individual of you, Hannah Linnette."

She basked in his praise. "I want May posies and angel bugs, too."

"You'll spend the night retching in a pot," said Christopher.

Hannah stuck out her tongue at him. "And toy soldiers."

"Not *my* toy soldiers."

The girl giggled and flung an arm toward Agnes. *"Her* toy soldiers."

Christopher sighed dramatically and turned baleful eyes to Agnes. "You must give them over to her, my lady, else she'll pout until your ears ache."

"No, she will not." The earl put Hannah into her chair and lifted his arm to attract the serving girl. "There'll be no pouting at the table." To Agnes, he said, "Will you have cake, my lady?"

"Yes, with a new carriage filled with rose petals on top."

He laughed again. His children chortled.

When the serving girl arrived, he instructed her to bring dessert. That done, he addressed his children. "We haven't even inquired after Lady Agnes's health."

Nodding, Hannah said, "She got hurt in church and fall down."

"Our father made her all better."

Although the children addressed the adults at the table, they spoke to and through each other. Beneath the squabbling lay genuine fondness. Agnes thought it sweet that they conversed so easily. However, she did not condone their being kept ignorant of the danger. Their father should explain the circumstances, prepare them.

"Not all better," the earl corrected.

"Oh, but I am, and by tomorrow I'll be as fit as a Flandersman."

Hannah looked curiously up at her brother. "What's a Flanerman?"

"'Tisn't a person, but a witty rejoinder Lady Agnes made. You know, 'tis the same way the Lady Georgette speaks when she wants Father to have a look at her finances."

"Why, thank you, Master Christopher." To the earl she said, "Finances?"

"A gentleman serves where he may. As your physician, I forbid you to travel for a fortnight."

"But I'm hale and hearty."

Authority gave him a hawkish air. "I've seen soldiers take to their cots for a week with a slighter injury."

"I'm perfectly capable of travel." To prove her point, she wiggled her fingers.

The earl moved aside his plate and reached for her. Then he thought better of it. Glancing yet again at the door, he said, "Later, I'll need more substantial proof of your recovery."

His movement and something in his tone put her on alert. Or was it simply the sound of his voice? According to Papa, Lord Edward was chancellor of Glasgow University. Scholars flocked to his lectures about the coming age of machines. He certainly exuded authority.

She balked at the possibility that he might treat her as an inferior. She must stand on even ground with him; only then would he trust her completely. "Granted, I cannot arm wrestle or ride a horse."

He stared pointedly at her coiffure and the army of buttons that marched up her dress front.

"I have a companion to help me, Lord Edward.

Surely you recall meeting Auntie Loo. She sees to my personal needs, and I assume responsibility for her." Agnes's companion possessed the wealth of a princess, but he needn't know that.

"My compliments. She is obviously skilled and certainly patient." He gave her a silent nod of approval, then spoiled it by saying, "Perhaps after the children have retired, you will speak of the few activities you can perform. That shouldn't take long."

A slight exaggeration didn't truly count as a lie. Misrepresentation better suited her intentions. No matter her methods, ending the subject of her health and gaining a commitment as to their departure for Glasgow was foremost on her mind. The man himself, although roguishly attractive, held no place in her rush to leave Edinburgh.

Yielding a bit seemed prudent. "'Tis for certain I cannot carry my luggage, but I expect you have a porter for that."

Engrossed in her neckcloth, Hannah murmured, "He's bossy, our porter is."

Christopher rolled his eyes. "Mr. Boswell's his name. Everybody calls him Bossy, but he doesn't order us around."

Agnes didn't doubt that. "Then I shall pack only one valise and have everything else sent to Glasgow later."

Hannah discovered the game of blow the cravat. "When are we going home?"

"Tomorrow, Button."

Tomorrow? They couldn't. Not without her. Swallowing apprehension, Agnes put on a smile. "How lovely. We can stop in Murcat's Field and see the heather. Perhaps your father will allow us to take lunch there."

"I know how to build a fire," piped Christopher.

Hannah screwed up her face. "Fire will burn me."

"Ah, here's dessert," said Lord Edward. "We'll discuss our plans privately, Lady Agnes."

"With pleasure, Lord Edward."

The children sat as straight as soldiers as the serving girl placed plates of cake smothered with clotted cream before them. The lure of conversation proved a poor second to dessert, and the children ate in silence. Enlisting their support to gain the father's approval did not trouble Agnes; this family needed her.

She said, "Tell me what you like best about your home, Christopher."

"We have a new foal in the stable—a filly. Hannah has books with drawings."

The girl was busy raking her spoon over her plate to scoop up a last bit of cream. "You took the letters," she murmured.

She'd made the puzzling statement earlier, but before Agnes could inquire about it, Christopher said, "Our cook will serve you pease porridge whether you have a taste for it or not."

"Blah!" Hannah scowled.

"Excuse me a moment, my lady." Lord Edward rose, extended his arm toward the stairs, and stared at his children. To Agnes's surprise, they said their good-byes without protest. Watching them walk away, Hannah's small hand tucked into Christopher's, Agnes remembered holding her sister Virginia's hand just so. A pity she'd let it go.

The earl handed his children into the care of a nursemaid, conversed with her briefly, then stood at the base of the stairs and watched them ascend. Preoccupied, his brow creased in concern, he strolled toward Agnes. The need to ease his troubled mind rose inside her. As he moved closer, other women in the room paused to stare at him. Whispers of feminine approval drifted on the close air, but he didn't notice.

By the time he resumed his seat, Agnes felt a sense of pride at being in his company.

"Now," he began in his no-nonsense physician's voice. "Take your arm out of the sling and let me see how strong you are." He held up an index finger. "I want you to squeeze it as hard as you can."

Her shoulder was sore, but not enough to prevent movement, certainly not the don't-lift-a-finger kind of movement he suggested. As she slipped her arm free, she felt his gaze. Curling her fingers around his, she gave a gentle squeeze.

"You're weak."

Her special prowess lay in her agility. Cunning did the rest. "Strength is a relative term, my lord. Are you making a reference to my gender or a professional opinion on the state of my health?"

With his other hand, he felt her pulse. "Both I suppose."

Chang Ling, the master who'd taught her the fighting ways of the ancient ones, had also schooled her to control her emotions. Calling up his teachings, she tightened her grip.

Lord Edward's hands were large, but not square or overly callused, and his fingers were long, graceful, and vaguely reminiscent of those of a violinist she'd met in Paris. It was odd that she should think of that engaging Frenchman now. Her sister Lottie was quick to say that she'd love her own husband, David, even if he had warts on his nose and crippled limbs.

"Surely you can do better than that—unless the pain distracts you."

She was distracted—by him. The realization gave

her pause. Lord Edward Napier was attractive enough with his cool gray eyes and his noble bearing. But it was more than that. Good looks aside, something intangible drew her to the troubled earl of Cathcart.

"Are you sleeping well?"

Banishing unnecessary thought, she concentrated on the task at hand. She squeezed harder. An instant later, the tip of Lord Edward's finger turned deep red, but he gave no sign that he was in distress.

"One thing is certain." His voice dropped. "You have either an affection for a gentleman in this room or your injury causes your heart to race." He touched her forehead while his eyes searched the room. "Do you perspire from heat or from a personal discomfiture?"

She'd sooner walk to Glasgow than answer him. Putting on a false smile, she withdrew her hand. "I fail to see why it matters. I'm on the mend."

"Based on what Lord Lachlan told me, I choose the ambient temperature rather than a romantic entanglement."

Did she appear incapable of romance to others? Is that what father had meant? Her success or lack of it was her own concern, and neither the Highland rogue nor this Glaswegian nobleman would make her lament her life's choice.

She returned her arm to the sling, and the ache in her shoulder eased. "I'm curious. Tell me exactly what my father said."

Absently, he touched the iron trivet. When it rocked in place, he picked it up and examined its wooden legs. "His Grace was quite forthcoming." From his waistcoat pocket he produced a metal object no bigger than her little finger. Releasing a hinge, he unfolded a tiny knife and began shaving away at one of the trivet legs.

"That's an ingenious tool."

He shrugged. "You spent over a year in China, engaging in all sorts of unfeminine pursuits. His grace swears that your hands are deadly weapons, with or without a pistol or a blade."

"What else did he say?"

He put down the trivet and tested it. When it didn't sit evenly, he again went to work on the legs. "He grieves because you harbor too much blame for events beyond your control. He says you will not let go of the past."

A stillness came over her. "Did he tell you why?"

"Nay." Again, he tested the trivet; it no longer rocked. He folded the knife and returned it to his waistcoat.

The simple answer, combined with the subtle finality of finishing his repair on the serving piece, told Agnes that he preferred to leave the subject alone.

That suited her perfectly. "Are you satisfied that I'm strong enough to travel?"

He laughed ruefully. "I'm satisfied that you are *stubborn* enough to travel."

"I'll be fine, you'll see."

His level stare pierced her. "You'll be jostled for two days in the carriage."

Praise the saints; he had relented and was giving her fair warning of how difficult the journey would be. "I'll bring along a blanket and a pillow to use as cushions."

"Then you do admit that you have pain?"

Placating him should put the matter to rest. "I have more respect for you than to lie. Yes, there is pain and soreness, but 'tis not unmanageable. Only the itching."

"A good sign. The wound is healing. I'll remove the stitches in a day or two. 'Twill hurt."

"When do we leave for Glasgow?"

He was sorting it out; she could read his indecision. To give him time, she sought to placate him further. "I've been stitched up before."

"Where?"

"At home in Tain."

Thinning patience tightened his smile. "Where on your person were you stitched up? A hand, a finger?"

"A lady wouldn't mention where—not in mixed company."

"A lady should speak freely to her physician. How did the injury occur?"

"My sister Mary pushed me down. I fell onto a broken butter crock, bottom first. I took supper standing."

"How old were you?"

"Eight as I recall, and an excellent retaliator."

"What did you do to her?"

"While she slept, I trimmed the hair on the right side of her head."

"Were you punished?"

"In a way. Sarah and Lottie cut their hair to match Mary's."

"So you were odd lass out."

"For that occasion. When do we leave for Glasgow?"

"Christopher and Hannah are curious children. I have encouraged them to be that way. They have not traveled often, and this journey did not turn out as I planned. The carriage will be confining, and if you grow annoyed with them—"

"Rest assured, my lord, my tolerance is infinite where children are concerned. At what time shall I be ready?"

"At daybreak, and I'll not wait for you."

"I always rise before dawn. 'Tis done then."

Now that she had the commitment, she broached the subject that had troubled her since that fateful moment in the chapel. "Who is trying to kill you and why?"

Weariness settled over him; he looked around the room as if the answer lay there. "I haven't the slightest notion, and believe me, I've pondered it long and hard."

Not from an objective perspective. "Did you recognize the bowman?"

"Nay."

"Have you insulted a powerful peer of the realm?"

A wry smile lightened his expression. "Only your father."

So, she thought, this troubled earl possessed a true sense of humor. Another point in his favor. "Someone in your family wishes you ill."

"Impossible. I have only one immediate relative, a first cousin who lives in the Canadian Territory. He prospers in the fur trade and wishes me well of the title."

"A dismissed student or a sultry one, wanting revenge over failing marks?"

"I have not taught a class proper in years. I only lecture on two or three subjects."

"Have you dishonored—albeit unknowingly—a woman?"

"I believe I would know if I had behaved improperly with a woman. I have not."

A touchy subject for him, considering his umbrage. "An investment gone sour?"

Proudly he said, "With Michael Elliot as a partner? Nay, none of our investments has gone badly. He has an excellent mind for business."

"Are there other ventures?"

"My only constant participation in commerce is a

textile mill in Glasgow. My family has operated the business for centuries."

"Does it prosper?"

"For the most part."

The vague answer pricked her curiosity, but she'd delve into his commercial dealings later. "Any unexplained accidents?"

"There was a fire, but such misfortunes are expected in mills. Cotton is highly flammable, and while there are as many windows as I can provide without cooling the air overmuch, we must use open flames."

"How did the blaze start?"

"'Twas a commonality, a lantern left unattended in the night."

"Any other *misfortunes?*"

He shook his head, but his attention was suddenly drawn to the entrance. Agnes turned, and the door swung open. Arm in arm and grinning like newlyweds, the duke and duchess of Ross entered the room. Juliet gave Agnes a discreet wave of acknowledgment but moved toward the stairs, preventing Lachlan from noticing that Agnes and Lottie were in the common room.

Lottie noticed, too, and for a moment Agnes thought her sister might foil their parents' plans; but good behavior held sway, and Lottie gave no indication that she saw the duke and duchess of Ross.

"Your parents have taken rooms here?" Edward asked.

For an afternoon lovers' tryst, Agnes decided. With so many children in their household, the duke and duchess had always snatched moments of privacy where they could.

Straining to hide a blush, she said, "He's probably going to scold her."

"Scold her? He looks smitten."

They disappeared up the stairs and Agnes relaxed. "Pardon me, but it's a private jest."

"You have an odd way of scolding in Clan MacKenzie."

"Aye, we do."

"Tell me more about Lord Lachlan's scolding."

Before Agnes could speak, Lottie approached their table. Tall and regal, the countess of Tain commanded the attention of every occupant in the room, even the clergymen. She wore a stunningly creative day gown of yellow silk. The color complemented her auburn hair, and the sapphires at her throat and earlobes enhanced the deep blue of her eyes.

Edward rose. "Good afternoon, my lady."

"Good afternoon to you, Lord Edward."

She offered her hand. Agnes remembered the times years ago that the four sisters had practiced that graceful gesture.

"Will you join us?" Edward asked. "Lady Agnes was just explaining to me the MacKenzie way of scolding."

"Nay, she was not," Lottie said. "Agnes doesn't know you well enough. But I trust that she will?" Lottie sent Agnes a saucy wink, which meant she approved of the earl of Cathcart. "I must decline your invitation. But I felt compelled to tell you how delighted I am that you and my sister have become acquainted."

Agnes almost huffed in disbelief, but all things considered, Lottie was putting her best foot forward. Then she spoiled it by staring pointedly at Agnes's bound-up arm and saying, "How are you today, Lady Fearless?"

"At peace, Countess, for I mind my own business. A practice foreign to you."

Lottie arched one brow and her expression turned

cool. It was a look that sent servants and family alike scurrying for safety. All except Agnes.

Turning that haughty gaze to Lord Edward, Lottie said, "Will you and your children take tea with me today, my lord? My children would like to say good-bye to yours."

Lottie was up to mischief, of that Agnes was certain.

"Why thank you, Lady Lottie," said the earl.

"Good," she said with finality. "And should you wish to know the tiniest thing about Agnes, I'll gladly provide it."

Agnes laughed; she was impervious to Lottie's meddling ways. "I haven't had a secret since the day you learned to speak—none of us have. Now off with you."

Lottie glided from the table and left the inn.

"You have an interesting family."

"You are too kind, my lord."

"You still haven't explained what you meant when you said that your father was going to scold Lady Juliet."

"When I know you better."

When next Edward saw the duke of Ross, both the situation and the mood were very different.

The men stood eye to eye in the entryway of the house his daughter Sarah had vacated for her honeymoon. To say the duke of Ross was unhappy was a monumental understatement. Tall and broad, Lachlan MacKenzie was handsome in that rugged Highland way.

"Your Grace," Edward greeted him. "How is Lady Juliet?"

"Upstairs, troubled over Agnes's leaving. You will not change your mind?"

Rather than answer, Edward thought it best to toss the question back to the duke of Ross. "Only if you are able to change her mind."

"She is my firstborn and long out of the nursery. Even at three and twenty, she carries a guilt so great 'twould bring ten soldiers to their knees. My poor, dear Agnes."

"Did I hear my name?"

She glided into the room, the very vision of Highland womanhood. Over a gown of forest green linen she wore a MacKenzie plaid, draped shawl-like, with one end tossed over her injured shoulder. Wearing it that way concealed her arm, which was bound securely in the sling.

"Aye, lassie," said her father, his powerful arms crossed over his chest. "I was telling Napier that you can bother a man to madness."

She faced her father squarely. "You'll not lay the blame on me for your ill humor this morn'."

As he watched Lachlan MacKenzie gaze down at his daughter, Edward could see into the man's soul. There he found fatherly love in all its painful glory. He knew the feeling well, experienced it every time he looked at Hannah and Christopher.

Sympathy for the duke made Edward say, "I think you should reconsider your decision, Lady Agnes."

She caught his gaze. "Are you reconsidering your offer?"

He didn't try to hide his reservations.

"I see," she said. "Must I remind you that there is a compelling reason for you to keep your word?"

"'Twould seem I must be reminded."

In a manner more direct than any woman he'd ever seen, she said. "You owe me your life."

The duke cursed. Edward wanted to. Instead, he did the only thing he could. He nodded in agreement.

Lady Agnes lifted her chin and faced her father. "If we part badly, 'twill be your doing."

"Go with Juliet to Tain, or come with me to London," said the duke.

Her brown eyes brimmed with regret. "You know I cannot. Mary needs you. I can take care of myself."

"So you say."

"Hug me, Papa."

His shoulders sagged, and he held out his arms.

She rushed into his embrace. "I love you."

"Oh, lassie mine. I love you more than spring."

"Sarah is spring to you. I have always been the fall."

The duke of Ross squeezed his eyes shut and drew in a ragged breath. "If you harm yourself while in Napier's service, I'll marry you to Auntie Loo's father. You'll never again clap eyes on another Christian soul."

"Oh, Papa, the emperor thinks I'm bad luck. He will not have me, and you know it well."

The emperor of China? Taken aback, Edward could but stare at these unusual people.

With a last, fierce hug that surely must have hurt her shoulder, Lord Lachlan turned her around so they both faced Edward. If she felt any discomfort, she hid it well.

A warning glittered in the duke's eyes. "Dishonor her, Napier, and I'll save your enemy the trouble of killing you. And you," he said down to her, "I expect you to write to me every Saturday. I'll send a messenger to collect your letter. I shall be in London with Mary. Should you neglect your duty to your family, I'll come to Glasgow to find out why. Do not use that injury as an excuse. Your penmanship is as poor with either hand."

She grimaced in mock outrage. "I'm wounded."

His look was pointed, challenging. "Aye, Agnes MacKenzie. You've hurt yourself for the last time."

Undaunted, she touched his cheek. "Farewell, Papa."

The duke again turned his stern gaze on Edward. "Trust her with the safety of your children, Napier, and follow her advice. She is clever in ways you cannot imagine, and she is wise beyond her years."

By the time the carriage stopped for the night in the village of Whitburn, Agnes would have argued that point. She felt as if she'd been run over by a carriage rather than conveyed in one. Hannah had stretched out in the seat beside her and fallen asleep, her head on Agnes's lap. Since her right arm was useless, Agnes had strapped her knife to her left thigh. Because of Hannah's added weight pressing on the weapon, Agnes's leg tingled with numbness.

Lord Edward had donned a cape and plumed bonnet and chosen to ride his own mount for the duration of the journey. A pair of heavily armed outriders had led the way out of Edinburgh; a second pair of escorts, equally armed, brought up the rear. When they'd passed through the west gate and entered the farmlands, the earl had relented and taken Christopher on the horse with him. Unfailingly fair, as only a good father can be, he'd also given Hannah a turn.

In the facing seat, Auntie Loo was answering another of Christopher's queries about her culture. This one involved the wrapping of noblewomen's feet.

"But your feet are average," the boy said. "And your father is the emperor."

"My mother would not allow it."

The driver, a young Glaswegian named Jamie, yelled, "Whitburn ahead."

He might have announced their arrival at the pearly gates, so eager was Agnes to rest.

Hannah stirred.

"I'll carry her," said Auntie Loo as she reached for the girl.

A post horn hung below the inn's symbolic sign bearing a badger and a bird. Smoke streamed from a nearby smithy, and merchants' stalls and clerks' benches dotted the main thoroughfare.

Jamie opened the door, and Christopher hopped out. The earl reached in to hand Auntie Loo down. As Agnes stepped from the carriage, her left leg buckled. Edward caught her. "Have you torn those stitches?"

"Nay, my leg's gone wickety from sitting for so long."

"Shall I carry you?"

"No!"

He started at her sharp denial. "No?"

"I meant to say, thank you, but 'tis a minor discomfort." She stomped her foot. "I'm getting better as we speak."

"I'll have the innkeeper send you a hot towel. Put it directly on your shoulder and leave it there until it cools."

"I'll be asleep by then."

"Then I'll awaken you, for I intend to have a look at those stitches."

3

"FATHER, DID YOU KNOW THAT LADY AGNES HAS A collection of knives?"

Edward fluffed the pillow on the narrow bed his son would occupy. The only accommodations at the inn acceptable to Lady Agnes had been a spacious upstairs suite with a parlor in the center and two bedchambers on each side. He smiled at both the memory of her reasons behind choosing the accommodations and this latest bit of information about her penchant for sharp objects.

"No, I did not know, but let us hope she never gets angry with us."

"Oh, Father," the boy chided in exasperation. "'Tis a hobby, like collecting fast horses or country estates, but more manageable."

The explanation was too adult, too proudly said. "Did she tell you that?"

"Aye, 'tis the MacKenzie in her. She has a score 'n' more of blades, but none of them like your palm knife." Christopher buttoned his sleeping gown and sat on the edge of the bed. "I told her 'twas your invention and there's none to be had but yours and mine." He frowned, looking very much like portraits of Edward as a child. "I wish I had brought it with me."

"There's time enough to show her your knife when we get home."

"She has a castle full of sisters and one brother. He'll be a duke when he grows up."

"I hope you were polite to her today."

He blinked in surprised innocence. "Ever so, Father, and Hannah, too. We must be mindful of the family reputation."

Hearing his own words recited earnestly made Edward proud. He ruffled his son's already mussed hair. "Good. Now say your prayers and go to sleep."

Christopher knelt beside the bed and steepled his hands. Edward started for the door.

"Father, why is Lady Agnes coming to live with us? Will she be our nanny?"

An answer eluded Edward. Describing Agnes Mac-Kenzie defied conventional explanations. She had been exhausted when they arrived in Whitburn, but she had rallied long enough to interview the innkeeper and select rooms "that suited their purposes" as she phrased it. Like a general on campaign, she had taken control of the situation and seen to the needs of everyone in their traveling party.

Added to that, Edward was intrigued on a more basic level. Agnes MacKenzie was the embodiment of every man's dream.

"Will she, Father? She'll be the bonniest of nannies."

Bonny. An understatement only a child would utter, for Agnes MacKenzie could make an archbishop ponder his vows. But there was more to her than physical beauty; she possessed strength of character, and she demanded respect. The acquiescence of the mighty Lachlan MacKenzie stood as proof of that.

"What's wrong, Father?"

You owe me your life.

The truth of that declaration worried Edward more than the presence of the woman herself bedeviled his scruples. What if she were hurt again in his defense? He banished the morbid thought and extinguished the lamp. "Nothing, son. Lady Agnes will be our guest."

Christopher began his prayers, but stopped. "Father?" Poignancy crept into his youthful voice. "Did you and Mother ever come to Whitburn?"

Edward knew where his son was headed. Christopher understood that his mother was in heaven. After his nightly prayers to God, the lad always spoke to his mother. For some strange reason, he thought his mother could hear him only if he were physically in a place where she had been.

Edward was relieved to say, "Aye, we stopped here every time we traveled to Edinburgh."

"Good, for I've much to say to her tonight."

The old loneliness filled Edward, for he had loved his wife deeply. She and her older sister had died of a shipboard illness after a visit to her family in Boston. Only half a dozen of the crew had survived. The dead had been buried at sea. Hannah had been one year old at the time. Edward had insisted that Elise leave their new daughter with him and Christopher in Glasgow, not for any possessive reasons; Edward had simply thought that Elise deserved a holiday from the cares of motherhood.

Time had healed the wound and eased the guilt, but

the troubles of late had started him to thinking about the past.

"Are you sad, Father?"

Edward masked his concern. "Not at all. Sleep well."

As Edward pulled the door closed and entered his own sleeping chamber, he said a silent prayer, asking God to watch over everyone in the growing Napier household. Things would be better at home in Glasgow; he wouldn't need to be constantly on alert for assassins.

Why had someone tried to kill him? He hadn't the faintest notion. But like a great shadow of doom, the truth of the matter hovered around him.

Someone wanted him dead, and it frightened him to his soul.

Mindful of his duty to examine his new patient, he went into the private parlor that separated the four sleeping chambers. The room was empty. The sound of feminine voices drifted from Agnes's adjoining bedchamber. The door stood ajar, and yellow lamplight poured through the opening. Agnes was telling a story to Hannah, who should have been asleep. Edward had sent the child to bed with the retiring Auntie Loo over an hour ago.

Hannah's trilling laughter brightened his mood. Other than hired nannies and an occasional indulgent moment from a visiting noblewoman in Glasgow, his daughter had not often enjoyed female companionship. Loath to interrupt them, he slowed his pace and dawdled in the parlor.

Feminine articles dotted the room. Hats and cloaks hung by the door. A pair of Agnes's gloves rested near his traveling pouch. Not in years had he seen his possessions nestled with articles of feminine attire. Oh, his mistress hung his clothing in a special place, but this innocent mingling of personal items reminded him of his life with Elise. A carefree couple, they had often packed up their young son, left the servants at home, and taken off for Carlisle or to a favorite inn near Paisley.

Hannah had been conceived on a balmy summer night with only the stars as witness. It was odd that he would recall that event now; he hadn't thought of it in years. Nor had he felt so lonely.

Desperate to put it aside, he peered inside the adjoining room and froze at the sight of Agnes MacKenzie.

She sat up in bed, a mountain of pillows at her back, a well-worn copy of *Humphry Clinker* in her left hand, Hannah fast asleep in her lap. Agnes wore an Oriental robe of red satin, elaborately embroidered with peacocks. Her honey blond hair was braided and draped over her shoulder.

Her smile gladdened his heart. "Come in," she whispered.

His throat grew thick, but he managed to utter the first thought in his mind. "You look . . . different."

She closed the book and put it aside. He moved to take Hannah, but Agnes stopped him. "Let her stay here and sleep with me. She's frightened—being in a strange place."

He tried to ignore the alluring vision of Agnes MacKenzie and his sleeping daughter. "How do you feel?"

"Much better." She caressed his daughter's head. "Hannah put a good spell on me. 'Tis powerful magic, she assured me. Upon our arrival in Glasgow, I should be well enough to climb into the manger and see the mouser's newest litter of kittens."

Edward entertained the urge to keep his distance. He was still pondering the thought as he sat down on the edge of the bed. "She's a sound sleeper. I doubt our talking will wake her."

"She's a delightful lass."

The smell of exotic blossoms filled his senses, and he knew that Agnes MacKenzie had acquired both the garment and the unusual fragrance in China. "How do you truly feel?"

"There's stiffness, but I'm making progress."

"Christopher tells me you collect knives."

"My contribution to a MacKenzie tradition."

"Begun with?"

"The first one out of the cave. He collected clubs."

Her candor disarmed him. "Do you all hoard weapons?"

"Oh, nay," she said, as innocent as a child. "Lottie doesn't have to. She was born with a razor-sharp tongue."

Edward remembered the elegant and efficient countess of Tain. With the duke and duchess of Ross attending the wounded Agnes, Lady Lottie had taken charge of the MacKenzie brood. She had also taken Christopher and Hannah under her wing. Edward had spent an edifying few hours in her company. "If I'm remembered of it correctly, the countess assured me that you were beyond reformation and could not be trusted in polite society."

"The word 'polite' left Lottie's vocabulary long before *we* left the nursery." Her expression turned pensive. "But there's no one better in a crisis."

"Tell me about the Lady Mary. Michael Elliot swears she's the finest artist on the isle."

Agnes raised her eyes to the beamed ceiling. "Sarah's new husband is correct, but poor Mary fell in love with a man who belittles her devotion to art."

"And her political views."

"According to the earl of Wiltshire"—Agnes stiffened her neck and lowered her voice—"a woman hasn't the intelligence to comprehend the deep subject of politics, or the soul to paint with the skill of the great masters."

"Let us hope he has a change of mind soon, else her child will be branded illegitimate."

Absently, she combed her fingers through Hannah's hair. "'Tis not so heavy a cross to bear."

Abashed, Edward said, "I'd forgotten."

"As do most people worth counting. What other family secrets, besides Mary's condition, did Lottie tell you?"

"A doctor would recognize Mary's 'condition' without a word from Lottie. She did, however, tell me all of your secrets."

"*All* of them?" Her finely arched eyebrows rose. "From your tone, 'twould seem you think of me as notorious."

"What I think of you will be *my* secret. But I'll tell you this, you have an interesting family, to say the least."

Fondness glimmered in her eyes. "Aye. Tell me how you came to know Sarah's new husband."

"I met him in India about twelve years ago. I went there to learn more about the cotton industry. For centuries the Napiers have dealt in textiles—I now manage our Glasgow mill. Elliot convinced me to invest in the East India Company, and together with Cameron Cunningham, we've done very well in the trade."

"'Tis a small world. Cameron promised to marry my sister Virginia—when she grows up."

"The lost sister."

"She is not lost, only misplaced. I'll find her."

Remembering the friction between Lord Lachlan and Agnes, Edward thought it best to change the subject. "I hope you do. Now let's have a peek at that wound."

She parted the robe enough to show him her injury.

The star-shaped wound flitted into focus, but his attention was drawn to the thin shoulder strap of her white silk gown. Against the pale fabric her skin glowed like ivory satin.

"It itched frightfully all day," she said, "but the hot towel you sent up took care of that. Thank you."

Hannah squirmed; Agnes soothed her with soft words.

Edward forced himself to concentrate on the wound. He found the surrounding area bruised but only slightly swollen. "The muscles adjacent the clavicle and the covering tissue are healing nicely. Your powers of recuperation are remarkable."

"How remarkable?"

She was mocking his professional speech; she'd done it several times in Edinburgh. Her father had been present during those visits. But the duke wasn't here now, and thank the saints for that small favor.

Edward caught her gaze. "Most remarkable—like that of a healthy child or an animal in the field."

She tensed. "An animal?"

"Aye," he said with zeal. "Vixens are the most adept."

"Thank goodness." She huffed with disdain. "You could have compared me to a cow."

"Only were I daft would I liken you to a bovine."

Apprehension flashed in her eyes. "Tell me about your other patients."

Satisfied that he'd made a subtle point, he relaxed. "I only treat the poor, for they do not mock me."

She radiated confidence. "I did say that you overburdened my injury. You would not listen."

"'Tis better said that I underestimated you." Actually he'd underestimated his own attraction to her. "You come from good stock."

"So my mother says."

"Your mother? I was speaking of the MacKenzies."

"The duchess of Enderley swears that my heartiness comes from her kinsmen, Clan Campbell."

Edward was shocked to learn the identity of her mother; he hadn't expected her to be so forthright. But why not, considering how bold she was. "Bianca Campbell gave birth to you? She must have been very young at the time."

"And very much in love with Lachlan MacKenzie. 'Twas a flourishing malady in '61."

She spoke candidly about what would have been a scandal in any other family. But the ducal MacKenzies had managed to hold themselves above gossip. Almost above, for the duke's four illegitimate daughters had made their own mark on society. "No more so than the season you shared with your half sisters at court. They say you lifted the value of every Scots maiden in the marriage market."

"None of us found husbands there."

She had not mentioned her father's role, but everyone knew that MacKenzie's lassies could select their own mates. Edward had to admit that Sarah had chosen well in her pick of Michael Elliot. "No, but you turned the Hanoverian court tapsal-teerie."

"They needed a bit of excitement. Too starchy and boring, those Germans."

Again his attention moved down. The robe had slipped aside, revealing the darker outline of her areola through the silk. As he watched, it puckered, making a tent of the fabric. He glanced up at her neck, and her pulse quickened. She turned her head to follow the line of his vision, and their cheeks touched. The slight drag of his stubbled jaw rasped against her smoother skin, sending currents of sensual friction to his loins.

Her lips were a quarter turn away, and without conscious thought, he moved closer. The first touch of her mouth on his only whetted his appetite for more. The kiss was tender but not tentative, yet something in the intimacy told him that she had not anticipated it and was as surprised as he.

In the blink of an eye, spontaneity turned to earnest discovery, and Edward laid into the kiss. Startled, she grew still. "Shush." He whispered the word, and to his delight, she yielded, moving beneath him in a graceful, if unskilled, effort to deepen the exploration. Like a midnight fog obscuring the stars, need clouded logic, and as he thrust his tongue between her lips, he noted that Agnes MacKenzie was a woman who could free his mind of all thoughts save those of her.

Too soon to suit him, she pulled away. "I will not fall in love with you, Edward Napier."

The words sounded like a pledge, letting him know that she'd uttered it before. In doing so, she made the mistake of grouping him with men he'd never met. She didn't know Edward well enough to box him in with a horde of swains eager to clap hands on her dowry and gain favor with the powerful duke of Ross.

Pride stinging, Edward said, "Love?"

She acquiesced beautifully. "Perhaps you're just grateful to me for saving your life."

A slap would have hurt less. "What I feel for you at the moment is desire, base and raw."

That statement fixed her attention, and she studied him so closely, Edward almost looked away. She lost the advantage when she said, "Then you would feel the same for a milkmaid?"

They were sparring words on dangerous ground. To end the battle, he said, "Were you a milkmaid, I'd learn to monger cheese."

He might have patted her head, so quickly did she settle down. "I think perhaps—" she hesitated, then grudgingly said, "I did encourage you."

His manly control restored, Edward spoke from the heart. "A treasured invitation, to be sure, but one I should have declined sooner. My apologies."

As fast, her ire returned. "You are sorry? Didn't your father tell you that a gentleman never apologizes for being attracted to a woman?"

"Aye, but my father never had a patient of your like."

"He was a doctor?"

"To barnyard animals."

"You despicable rogue—"

He put his hand over her mouth. "Careful or you'll awaken Hannah."

She relaxed, and he withdrew his hand. "Be careful yourself, or I'll find another physician."

Weariness weighted him. "You should not have been injured at all."

"Are we back to that, Lord Edward?" She laid her hand on his arm. "Please, put it behind you. I have no regrets, and rest assured, I would do it again."

Rather than soothe, her touch provoked him to say, "I should have left you in Edinburgh."

She glanced down at the soundly sleeping Hannah. "The safety of this angel should be reason enough to keep me."

He remembered the fierce argument between her and Lord Lachlan. "That and your father's threat to banish you to China."

"Speak no more of the duke of Ross. Tell me about Napier House and your life in Glasgow."

"You'll find it dull and parts of my home ancient."

"In the carriage today, Christopher told me you were an inventor of machines. Where is your laboratory?"

"In the old dungeon. I'll put something on this and then let you get to sleep."

He treated the wound with a soothing salve, applied a bandage, and bound her arm to her chest. "That should do it."

"Have you a balm for bruised pride?"

Would she never leave it be? He felt like a lad called to task for finishing his studies too quickly. "Will you please forget my unfortunate choice of words?"

"Certainly. If you will forget the kiss."

He hadn't played a courting game in years, and certainly not with a woman as bold as she. "You're setting another verbal trap, and I refuse to stumble into it. I should not have kissed you. I enjoyed it. I wish I had not."

"Will you promise never to kiss me again? Honestly?"

"That depends on how long you stay in Glasgow."

"There's no mystery to that. I'll stay until I find the man or woman who is trying to kill you."

"A woman?"

She yawned. "Women are more than capable of murder or its solicitation. Surely you've read about the Borgias, and everyone accepts the guilt of Lady Notorious of Kent."

In a fit of anger, the Kentish lady had poisoned all of her in-laws. "I'll ponder it tomorrow." He leaned down and kissed Hannah's cheek. "Sleep well, Button."

Speechless at his tenderness and unfeigned affection for his daughter, Agnes closed her eyes. But she would not sleep, not until Auntie Loo awakened at the prearranged hour of two o'clock. Then Agnes would sleep for a few hours. From this day forward, until the assassin had been captured, neither of the children would be left alone. Staying awake posed no difficulty for Agnes; awareness of the kiss lingered, and she wanted to explore the feelings a little longer.

The next morning as Agnes lay on a canvas pallet beneath the Napier carriage, checking for signs of tampering, she was thinking about the intimacy. She was attracted to the earl of Cathcart. What woman would not find him appealing? But more was involved than admiration. She felt a rare comfort—even a promise of companionship in his presence.

Why? What set Edward Napier apart from other men who had courted her? She didn't know but suspected his vulnerability was the cause. That or the fact that she'd temporarily lost sight of her own mission: finding Virginia. On a favorable note, she could more easily conduct her inquiries from Glasgow. But she must forewarn him that if news of Virginia reached her, she'd leave immediately.

With a last inspection of the undercarriage, she satisfied herself that no one had tampered with the conveyance. Elbowing her way under the vehicle had been easy; getting out proved much more difficult. After several tries, she gave up and called for Jamie, the driver, to help her.

The pallet began to move, and she was pulled free, not by the driver but by Lord Edward himself. A very disgruntled Lord Edward.

From her vantage point, being flat on her back, he looked too imposing. He wore riding boots, the distinctive Napier kilt, and a tailored frock coat. Were she a hand's length closer, she'd have an unobstructed view of his manly assets. She fought a blush at the unladylike thought and looked away. Staring at his bootprints in the soft earth, she noticed a band of wear in those impressions. From experience she knew that stirrups had caused the marks on the soles of his boots.

Encouraged by this small example of her special insightful gifts, she again gazed at him, only to find him surveying her unconventional attire. Before her eyes his sheer exasperation turned to outright fury.

He reached for her.

Prudence made her yield her hand.

Through clenched teeth he said, "A wise choice, Agnes MacKenzie."

His tone sparked her defiance. To prove her fitness and capability, she pushed herself to her feet and even did a little hop. With her free hand, she dusted the leather breeches she had donned for the dirty job of examining the carriage.

"You cannot even dress yourself in proper clothing, and yet you crawl about on the stable floor."

"I've only begun, and these clothes are perfectly suited to what I was doing."

"You cannot possibly be well enough to toil 'neath a carriage."

"Have you ever treated a woman with a bowshot wound?"

"Of course not."

"Then explain to me how is that you know precisely at which rate I or any other female heals from such a wound."

"I know because you are weaker physically."

"Weaker? I'd cherish seeing you give birth."

"Have you given birth?"

In most circles the question would be considered slanderous, but she'd broached the subject herself. "Nay, but I held Lottie's hand through the daylong ordeal. Travail you call it. Ha! 'Tis a flowery word coined by men to describe a tribulation they cannot fathom."

"Fathom this, Lady Agnes." He pointed a finger at her. "If I ever again see you on your hands and knees while you are under my domain, I will save your father the price of passage and personally put you aboard the next ship to China."

He'd sprout gills and fins first, but telling him so would only heighten the dispute. She'd risked her life to save his. The challenge of finding his enemy beckoned, a task she was more than qualified to meet. Her father could curtail her movement, but he would not send her to China. What this Glaswegian nobleman would do was a mystery as interesting as the identity of his assassin.

A graceful retreat was her only option. "You see me at my most foolhardy, Lord Edward."

"I'll be the judge of that."

Good intentions fled. "May I suggest you concern yourself with helping me find out who tried to kill you?"

He threw up his hands. "Driving a man to madness only scratches the surface of your abilities. Curse me for thinking Lord Lachlan exaggerated."

Agnes couldn't help but say, "He often does."

"Not about you." Lord Edward pivoted and yelled, "Jamie! Saddle my horse."

If he preferred a mount to the carriage, who was she to argue. She grasped his arm. "Have the farrier examine the harnesses."

"Why?"

She gave him a crooked smile. "Because I doubt you'll want me to do it."

"Your intuition grows by the moment."

The subtlety in his reply surprised her. The muscles in his arm felt like steel beneath her hand. "Why are you so angry?"

He looked at her and sighed. "I do not know."

At least he was honest. For her part, she thought it best to change the subject. "I'll summon back the farrier."

"How do you know that he will not sabotage my mount?"

"Because he is trustworthy. He belongs to a respectable guild, and his wife thinks well of him. She also bakes the best oatcakes I've ever tasted."

"You know the farrier and his wife?"

"As of half an hour ago, aye."

"You interviewed him—in his home? This morning?"

"Of course. I always rise before dawn."

"You are no ordinary female, Agnes MacKenzie."

"Why, thank you, Lord Edward."

His expression grew blank, but an instant later he again became the determined earl of Cathcart. "Go and ready yourself. It'll be nightfall before get home."

That said, he strolled toward the sorrel gelding that Agnes had earlier admired.

Twenty minutes later, as Agnes secured her hat she heard footfalls in the private parlor. From the quick pace and lightness of the steps, she knew that children were approaching her door. She didn't need her sister Sarah's mathematical mind to suspect who was coming to visit.

A knock sounded. "Come in," she said.

Christopher pushed Hannah through the door before him. The girl's determined expression told Agnes that they'd come with a mission in mind. She'd seen it often on Lottie's face, because Lottie couldn't hide her feelings.

Christopher's eyes did meet Agnes's, but then he searched the room until he located her traveling bag. "We came to see if you're ready to go." Moving toward it, he said, "I'll carry this."

"Thank you, but I can manage it myself."

"Oh, but I must. If you carry it, my father will send you someplace faraway."

"Stay with us," Hannah pleaded.

"Did your father send you here?"

"Nay, and I was hoping you'd say we happened upon each other and I was . . ." He shrugged.

"Merely being a gentleman?"

Nodding vigorously, he said, "Yes, exactly."

"'S'good. 'S'good." Hannah clapped her hands and chirped, "Then Papa will be happy."

Considering how angry the earl had been at their last meeting, Agnes awaited his good humor. "What if we each carry a handle?"

Christopher stared at his boot tips. "Any compromise on the matter will be seen as disobedience."

"Your father said that?"

"Aye. I think you should know that he always gets his way."

"You discussed it with him?"

"Of course." Squaring his shoulders, he looked very much like his sire. "I argued my point most fiercely."

An exchange she hoped to witness one day, for it reminded her of discussions she'd had with the duke of Ross. "Where is your father now?"

"He's offering the farrier a position in our stables at Napier House."

She took great satisfaction in the news. With that came the realization that even unbeknownst to one another, the Napiers worked as a team. An admirable practice, she had to admit, and one she'd grown up with.

Pleased with herself, she allowed Christopher to act the porter.

He hefted the bag to his shoulder and motioned them toward the door. "On the way home we'll play every game we know."

Hannah was taking her third turn at "What's in the big dipper" when the carriage approached a horseshoe-shaped drive that was lighted by at least a dozen post lamps.

"Haggis and hashes!" the girl declared.

"There's no food in the sky. You're a Piscinarian!"

"Dishclout."

"Capricornified!"

"Cribbage face!"

"Haud yer wheesht!" Agnes stared out the window and counted to ten, hoping they would obey. Their good behavior had ended at the gates of Glasgow. Nudging had turned to pinching; separating them had brought on the name-calling.

The carriage slowed. They passed a brick column bearing a shield emblazoned with a hand holding a crescent, a heraldic symbol Agnes recognized as that of the Napiers. Against the night sky she could discern the shape of an ancient stone tower rising behind the elegant Georgian entrance.

When the children remained silent, she relaxed. The conveyance stopped, then rolled backward a bit. They had arrived.

As stoic as a statue of the mother of Khan, Auntie Loo opened the carriage door.

Jamie helped them down. A stableman held the reins to the sorrel gelding, now riderless and lathered. Agnes spied Lord Edward. Surrounded by a group of important-looking men, he stood before the open front doors of the estate. One of the visitors drew her attention. She recognized his chain of office as that of the Constable of Glasgow. A tidy porter who wore a fresh bandage around his head stepped into the circle of men.

Something was wrong. The constable was speaking to Lord Edward. She could almost hear him curse to himself, so violent was his reaction to the news. His jaw tight with restrained anger, he glanced through the opened doors, then looked to the injured servant.

Agnes hurried up the steps and to the earl of Cathcart's side. His troubled frown worried her more than the presence of the authorities. "Is something amiss, my lord?"

Rather than answer her, he said, "Lady Agnes MacKenzie, may I present our good constable, Sir Oliver Jenkins."

"Sir Oliver."

"'Tis an honor, Lady Agnes." Bristling with excitement, he swept off his hat, made a courtly bow, and motioned for his minions to do the same. Replacing his hat, he said, "Would you be of the Saint Andrews' MacKenzies?"

Out of the corner of her eye she saw Lord Edward shift his weight to one booted foot and stare into the lane, as if searching for someone. Absently, she said to the constable, "Nay, my father is the duke of Ross."

His earlier enthusiasm paled. "You're one of Lord Lachlan's lassies?"

"Aye, what has occurred here?"

"A burglary," said Lord Edward, his words dropping into the polite conversation like the banging of a temple bell. "Mr. Boswell will escort you to your rooms." Catching the servant's gaze, he added, "The blue apartments, Bossy. Keep the children close to you for now, and put a guard outside their door when you retire."

Mr. Boswell nodded and moved into the foyer. "Aye, my lord. This way, my lady. Hannah and Christopher."

Innocent of the proceedings, the children skipped up the steps and queried Boswell about his injury. A refusal to follow them perched on Agnes's lips, but another glance at Edward Napier stifled the words. Restrained anger simmered beneath his facade of civility, and she was reminded of a man poised to do battle with his sworn enemy.

"Go along now," he said.

Not "Go along, Lady Agnes" or "Excuse us, my lady." The absence of protocol gave further proof of his distraction. She'd get settled in her room and wash her hands and face. Then she'd find him and learn the details. Or perhaps she'd ask the fellow named Bossy. But no matter the source, she'd learn the particulars about the burglary.

"Thank you, my lord."

As Edward watched her leave, he chided himself for bringing her here and again placing her in danger. First thing tomorrow he'd send her back to the duke of Ross. He had his own demons to deal with now.

He removed his cloak and handed it to the housekeeper, Mrs. Johnson. Sadness wreathed her face. "'Tis a gift of the Almighty himself that you and the wee ones wasn't here, my lord."

Putting on a smile he didn't feel, he patted her arm. "Worry not, Hazel."

Then he asked the constable to show him what had occurred.

The tour began with a broken window in the old wing and ended in Edward's study. The destruction he found there, and the threat it carried, chilled him to the bone.

4

THE PORTER, MR. BOSWELL, PROVED AS TIGHT-LIPPED AS he was polite, and to Agnes's dismay, she left her room with only one more piece of information than when she'd arrived. In keeping with their routine, Auntie Loo had retired for a few hours. Agnes would sleep later or not at all. Even as a child, three or four hours' rest a night had been sufficient for her. At the moment she couldn't have slept had she tried; trouble awaited her. Convincing Edward Napier of the danger posed an additional problem.

Making her way down the lighted corridor that led to the main staircase, she organized her thoughts and arranged her plans. A few elementary precautions would help secure the family living quarters, which would form the center of an ever-widening circle of protection around the Napiers. The concept and execution were as basic to Agnes as brushing and plaiting her hair for the night or writing letters to her father on Saturday.

No children would be ripped from the Napier family, unless God himself called them home. Safeguarding the innocent was her special ability; employing it was her salvation.

Buoyed by the challenge ahead, she tested the banister and found it secure, then started down the marble stairway. Tomorrow she would order a carpet and better the odds against serious injury, should an accident occur on the stairs.

In the entryway she peered through the leaded glass panels that flanked the front doors. One of the men she'd seen earlier guarded the residence. Turning left, she found herself in an odd portrait gallery. Beginning with a carved wooden rendering of its first chieftain and continuing in chronological progression, Clan Napier was immortalized on the wall. Unusual about the wall was a sampling of textiles, from exquisite medieval tapestries to a more modern panel of woven silk, that mingled with portraits of past earls and countesses of Cathcart.

Agnes wished her half sister Mary were here. Mary'd make a fuss over William Hogarth's depiction of Edward's grandfather, especially the dogs in the painting. She'd also covet the old wooden frames and lament over the poor workmanship of carpenters of today.

Were her sister Lottie the mistress of this house, she'd make a grand occasion of escorting guests down the gallery. She'd provide an endearing story about each person depicted. Sarah, the more scholarly of Agnes's sisters, could name the raw materials used to create the paints and site their place and time of origin. Uninterrupted, Sarah would supply an account of the painter's contribution to his craft, as well as the artist's impact on his contemporaries.

Mary would fume at Sarah over the general use of the male pronoun and name a dozen female artists more talented than the one under discussion.

Fondness filled Agnes; she had been blessed with three good-hearted, honest women for sisters, and they loved each other dearly. Oh, they had and still did prank among themselves, but in the matters that counted, the children of Lachlan MacKenzie were loyal to a fault.

Thoughts of Mary and the coil she'd made of her affair with the earl of Wiltshire troubled Agnes more each day. Too stubborn to yield and too infatuated to go their separate ways, Mary and her nobleman were destined to make a scandal of their love. But until Mary solicited help, Agnes would not intervene. As matters stood, Agnes was needed here in Glasgow.

The last of the portraits intrigued her, for it depicted a young Edward Napier. Rather than the traditional painting of the family heir pictured astride a favorite hunter or posing stiffly beside the hearth, the current earl of Cathcart was surrounded by books, a telescope, and dozens of drawings, some spread out and some rolled into tubes. The birdcage in the background was empty, the little door open. An intriguing detail, Agnes thought, but not so intriguing as the man himself.

He'd aged a decade or more, and time had clearly been his ally, for maturity enhanced his masculinity and added character to his exceptionally handsome appearance. Only the expression in his eyes had not changed. She saw intelligence, confidence, and a gleam she remembered well.

Agnes recalled the kiss but tried to forget the

feelings it had inspired. Romance was not an option for her now. But as soon as she found Virginia and reunited her with her beloved, Cameron Cunningham, Agnes would find a man of her own. For the time being she had a greater purpose, and finding the earl's study was her immediate concern.

She heard approaching footsteps. Not looking away from the portrait, she said, "Is there much damage, my lord?"

He stopped. "How did you know 'twas me?"

Turning, she pointed to his footwear, but the bruises on the knuckles of his right hand drew her attention. He'd removed his coat and rolled up his sleeves. "Your left boot squeaks, and you walk in a casual gait, as if you belong here."

She took great joy in his surprise, for it softened his expression. His mouth was slightly parted, just the same as when he'd kissed her.

In disbelief, he asked, "You listen for and derive information about the sound and the velocity of a man's footfalls?"

Embarrassed, she pushed aside her romantic musings. One day soon he'd appreciate her special skills: Better men than the earl of Cathcart had belittled her abilities. All of them had lived to thank her.

She shrugged. "Aye, 'tis an easy way to detect an intruder."

"What if I had been an intruder?"

How much should she tell him? Considering her injury and his insistence on making too much of it, she decided on a lie. "I'd call for help."

"That's good to know." He chuckled softly. "I feared you'd try to capture him by yourself."

Hopefully the occasion would not arise, at least until her wound healed completely. "I'd never try that." She wouldn't simply try. She'd do it. Surprise was a woman's first weapon, because men did not expect to meet resistance from the fairer sex.

"Were you looking for me?" he asked.

"Yes, my lord. Bossy was struck from behind. Whom do you suspect?"

"Whom does Bossy suspect?"

Sarcasm didn't come naturally to Edward Napier. Loyalty from his servants did. Two very good signs. "That was all he would say. Have you determined where the vandal entered?"

"Yes, in the old wing."

Getting information from him was harder than making Auntie Loo angry. But Agnes was up to the task. "May we go there?"

"Surely you'd rather retire." He flexed his fingers, but his attention was focused elsewhere. "'Tis late."

Another lie and a truth would skirt the issue and, perhaps, loosen his tongue. "I napped in the carriage today. I couldn't sleep now, even if you commanded me to."

A quirk of humor lifted one corner of his mouth. "A wasted effort in any event."

That he could smile told her much about his mild temperament—either that or he was a very good actor. And where had he gotten those abrasions on his hand? If she didn't know better, she'd think he'd been in a tavern brawl.

Again she glanced at his portrait. "I obeyed you this morning at the stable in Whitburn."

He held up both hands, as if warding her off. "I'd as soon forget our shouting match."

And the kiss, she thought morosely. He'd made it clear that the kiss meant nothing to him—a view she would adopt, too. "As would I. Tell me about the damage."

His gaze sharpened and anger flickered in his gaze. "Better you should have something to eat. Mrs. Johnson braised a hare with turnips and carrots. Her bread's exceptionally fine, and there's always fresh, cold milk."

Agnes's stomach rumbled, but she ignored it. "I had hoped for a tour of your home first." She extended her hand. "Show me where the vandal entered." Only a poor host would refuse her, but he was clearly considering it. "Please?"

"You cannot expect to see much. 'Tis black as pitch."

He too was proving an expert at skirting the issue. But Agnes was determined. "Lantern light will do."

"I will not allow you to involve yourself. You may have foiled an attempt on the life of Burgundy's heir, but I shan't put you in danger. The brigand could still be on the grounds."

"With a guard stationed outside?" Tossing her head, she laughed. "Come. Show me—unless you've caught him." And bashed in his face in the doing, she added silently.

His demeanor changed, as if he were recalling an unpleasantry, which she suspected was the case. Why else would he have bruised knuckles?

"Nay. He's not inside the estate proper." After fetching and lighting a hand lantern, he took her through a formal parlor with groupings of brocaded chairs and tables with carved thistles for legs. The cold hearth of a marble fireplace was hidden behind a tapestry screen. A standing clock struck the half hour before midnight.

Nothing was out of place.

A peaked lintel, topped on either side with sculptures of a lounging Pan, framed the entrance to an older wing. As the light illuminated the room, Agnes felt thrust into a museum of the Elizabethan Age. Heavy furniture of Jacobean mahogany dominated the room. A matching pair of standing candelabrum flanked a table containing an onyx and pale pink alabaster chess set. A collection of silver and brass pomanders sat atop a low table in the center of the room.

Deeper into the building, the earl ushered her into another wing of older origin. Replete with standing suits of polished armor, battle axes, and hanging tapestries larger than a wading pool, this room was a testament to the Age of Chivalry. The flagged stone floor was scattered with small woven carpets, probably products of the Napier looms. A door in an inwardly rounded wall must be the entrance to the old tower she'd seen from the street.

"The vandal entered here." Across the room, he moved aside one of the tapestries and revealed a broken window.

Nothing else was amiss.

The rough-hewn bookshelves contained a number of valuable items. The price of the illuminated manuscripts alone would support a dozen common thieves for a year and more. The twisted pewter candlesticks would buy a wagon and a team of horses.

Why hadn't any of these treasures or the ones in the next room been taken? What and where was the havoc the intruder had wreaked? She'd find out. "Have you considered replacing the window with mullioned glass?"

Suddenly attentive, he glanced from the gaping window to her, then back to the window. "Aye, all the way 'round." He let the tapestry fall into place. "I'll summon the glazier tomorrow and a locksmith to secure the ground level windows. Although it pains me to make a prison of my home."

She knew grudging respect when she saw it, and respect from Edward Napier felt especially fine. "'Twill not be forever, my lord. Only until we find out who and why."

"I like your confidence, my lady."

"As did Burgundy and the others."

He busied himself with straightening the tapestry. "Christopher and Hannah behaved well on the journey?"

Light conversation was not what Agnes had in mind. "They behaved very well until he called her an odd name . . . Capricorn something."

"He's only begun then. He's made a science of employing big words. Wait until he accuses his sister of being a Hugotontheonbiquiffinarian."

Baffled, Agnes shook her head. "Where did he learn such great words, and what do they mean?"

"From his tutor last year, a student at the university. I cannot recall the meanings exactly, but I think they were societies of some sort. Christopher only brings it up to bedevil Hannah because she cannot read as yet."

"It works."

He shrugged and began rolling down his sleeves. He'd clubbed his hair at the nape of his neck, but some of the wavy strands had worked themselves free of the tie. "'Tis his poor behavior of late." He raked a stray lock back behind his ear. "He'll grow bored with it eventually and take up something else. Last year he swore only to speak French during meals."

"Did he succeed?"

"Quite admirably until he couldn't think of the word for chocolate cake."

"He got no dessert?"

"No, and petulance overcame him when Hannah was served. He was sent to his room."

"My sisters and I carried on our poor habits at once, and not two of them alike." At the thought of those happy and carefree days, her spirits brightened. "'Tis a wonderment that my father didn't sell us for slaves."

"I doubt he would have done that. Is it true that he took you from your mothers and raised you himself?"

Love for her father filled Agnes. "Yes, until we were six. Oh, we'd had dozens of governesses, most of them more interested in laying claim to our father than to teaching us. But then a Colonial named Juliet White came to Kinbairn."

"Lord Lachlan married her."

Juliet's influence had left its mark on Agnes, and for that she was proud. On the day Agnes met Bianca Campbell, the woman who'd given birth to her, Juliet had been at her side. "He did, but we all reaped the benefits."

"A delightful woman," he said. "A match and more for the Highland rogue. Life here will surely be boring to you."

Even wearing modern clothing, he looked at home in the ancient surroundings. Were he to don the plain clothes of the Dark Ages, he would have dominated the room. In any era or wearing any style, Lord Edward Napier commanded female admiration.

"How can life be boring while someone is trying to kill you?"

"Trying is the operative word."

Uneasy with her growing attraction to him, she turned and opened the door to the tower. Stale, musty air rushed out, and a mass of cobwebs ripped from their moorings. Peering inside, she could see an arch-shaped pattern of moonlight streaking across the dusty floor. Overhead a vast wooden wheel of aged and spent candles marked this tower as the bedrock of

Napier House. Other than discarded stools and chairs and some kind of spinning machine, the room was empty.

"You'll soil your dress."

Yes, but she'd have a peek anyway. The tower was probably the safest part of the estate. To be sure, she'd come back for a closer inspection and bring a torch to deal with the current inhabitants.

"Tell me about the tower. How many rooms?"

"Three, one on top of the next."

"How many entrances?"

"Just this one. There's a door leading to the battlement on the top floor, but no ladder to reach it."

Satisfied for now, she closed the door and returned to her immediate mission. "May we walk a bit? I'm rather stiff from sitting in the carriage for so long, and I'm not sleepy in the least. Unless 'twould be an inconvenience for you?"

Good manners dictated that he oblige her. He grasped the lantern. "No, of course not."

Even had he declined, she would have gone to her room, waited a while, then come downstairs to continue her inspection. Tomorrow morning she would put her opinions to paper. After that she would visit the harbormaster, as she always did when in a port city, and look for information about Virginia. But Glasgow was unique, for it was home to Haskit Trimble, an unusual man with exceptional abilities, many of which he'd passed on to Agnes.

Later in the day, she'd present her suggestions to Lord Edward. This family was in danger, and she intended to help them, with or without his consent.

They retraced the path they'd taken to the old wing, but instead of entering the formal parlor, he swung the lamp toward a hallway to the left.

As they walked, she said, "My father swears that I

prefer the night because I was born on the shortest one of the year."

"Midsummer's Night?"

"Yes, but please don't feel obliged to indulge me. Retire if you like. I promise not to bang a drum or inconvenience the staff." But she'd inspect that tower tonight.

"Everyone's abed, my lady."

Perspiration glowed on his forehead, and his face bore the shadow of a stubble. She recalled the feel of his skin brushing gently against hers. For how long must she remember? The answer came easily: until she thought of his response. *Love?* he'd scoffed. *'Twas desire, raw and base.* To perdition with him and his vulgar honesty.

"Auntie Loo said you had bad dreams," he said in his doctorly tone. "Is that why you do not sleep for long?" When she did not answer immediately, he added, "'Tis not uncommon, nor is it a sign of a serious malady."

He shouldn't be so attentive, not about personal matters. No doctor on earth could ease her sleepless nights; only the return of Virginia MacKenzie could. "Auntie Loo exaggerates—when she's not making trouble."

"Should you have a change of mind and want my professional help, please ask."

A change of mind would occur—on the day she was reunited with her sister. Knowing his offer was sincere, she said, "Thank you."

He led her into a wide corridor typically Georgian in style. "How did an Oriental woman who speaks the King's English come to be your friend?"

He probably wouldn't believe Agnes's explanation, and if he did believe, the odds were good that he'd judge her unfairly or call her unfeminine. Most of her kinsmen did. A pity, for among the Orientals the ancient skills Agnes practiced were revered as artistry.

But she couldn't tell him another lie. Not tonight. "I saved her father from an assassin. According to custom in his country, he owes me his life. Since he could not give it, he gave me Auntie Loo."

"She is a slave?"

"A well-fixed one. Her allowance is greater than mine."

"Did you take a crossbow quarrel for the emperor of China?"

He sounded irritated, but she knew it was only bruised male pride. "'Twas not nearly so dramatic, for I didn't suffer the smallest bruise."

"But you will not furnish the details."

"Certainly," she chirped. "When I know you better."

"So you've said before. On the day we become friends, we will have much to discuss."

He hadn't said if but when. Was their expected friendship a foregone conclusion or a polite slip of the tongue?

His voice dropped. "You were foolish to move into the path of that arrow."

He was entitled to his opinion. "I thought the book would stop it."

"'Twould have taken a powerful book to halt the trajectory."

Only a scientist would phrase it that way. "It is a powerful book," she said proudly. "'Tis filled with the chronicles of Clan MacKenzie."

He chuckled. "How remiss of me to forget your great Highland heritage." Swinging the lamp toward a door, he said, "There's the library. Does the wound pain you tonight?"

"Only a wee bit, but I think you stitched me up with itch weed."

Bemusement suited him well. "Here we have the music room and beyond it an audience suite for the day Hannah masters at least one musical instrument."

"Christopher has no liking for music?"

"Manly adventures are his watchwords. That door leads to the east receiving room. It's also the entrance nearest the stables. We leave our muddy boots and wet cloaks there."

"I shan't be entering there until I'm well."

"A hole 'neath your clavicle is nothing to scoff at."

She slid him a cheeky look. "Not unless I were trying to anger my physician."

Now that he was smiling, she decided to broach an important subject. "What other damage was done— in your study?"

"Why do you wish to see the vandal's leavings?"

"Because it will tell us what he wants."

"Above my demise?"

"Aye. The more we know about his purpose, the quicker we will find him."

His brow furrowed, and his mouth tightened in indecision. "Will you persist until I agree?"

She sighed and gave him her most self-effacing grin. "To be honest, the odds favor that, my lord."

Blowing out a breath, he exuded impatience. "Are all of the women in your family as spoiled as you?"

"All except Mary, but she's more stubborn than the rest of us. She's an independent thinker, too."

"Pity the earl of Wiltshire then," he murmured as he pushed open the door to his study. "Here we are."

They had walked a path in the shape of an inverted U, but square at the corners. According to her inner compass, the west outside wall of this room should face the tower.

She stepped inside, and as she surveyed the destruction, apprehension overcame her. The innocent smell of aged leather bindings and newly applied furniture wax mingled with the almost oppressive odor of the intruder. This assassin was well paid and determined, else he would have helped himself to the many treasures in Napier House. Instead, he'd aimed his assault directly at the earl of Cathcart.

A quarrel had been shot into the high back of the earl's chair, the fletchings identical to those of the weapon used in Edinburgh. Another arrow pierced the tapestry firescreen emblazoned with the heraldic shield of the Napiers.

Keepsakes in the room had also been targets. Books were torn from the shelves, the pages ripped from the bindings. Rugs were upturned, and upholstery split. But no glass was broken, and none of the heavy furniture was upturned. The silver canisters hadn't been opened; neither had the marquetry boxes or tobacco containers been disturbed. The intruder had been quiet in his work, and whatever he sought was larger than a humidor.

Pushing aside the pain of sympathy, she laid her hand on Lord Edward's arm. "What was he looking for?"

"Money? Valuables to pawn?"

"Nay, else he would have taken the treasures in the old wing. Or the silver canisters there on the mantel." She could feel his frustration and knew that anger simmered beneath the surface of it. Turning, she implored him with, "Please think, my lord, and think objectively about every person you know. Whoever did this was looking for something. For what?"

He doubled his fist and pounded his chair. When he

reached for the quarrel protruding from the upholstery, she yelled, "Nay. Let me."

Hurrying to his side, she grasped the stem and
gently worked the arrow free. When separated from
the shaft, the arrowhead itself would bear the mark of
the craftsman who'd made it. She already knew that
the fletchings were English, and by sending a courier
to London with one of the quarrels, she could have it
examined by a knowledgeable expert, thus gaining a
history of the weapon. Having the quarrel intact
bettered the odds of learning its origin. But she'd wait
until the messenger returned to present the findings to
Lord Edward.

Behind the chair she noticed an indentation in the
wainscot wall that matched the size of the earl's
doubled fist. Tiny splatters of blood marked the spot.
She touched it, then glanced at his bruised and
abraded knuckles. "I wish it had been the assassin's
jaw you bashed."

"As do I," he said. "But I'd rather refer to him as a
would-be assassin, if it's all the same to you."

"It's very much the same to me," she said, and felt
the air grow heavy between them. Light from the lamp
behind him threw his features into shadow. The rich
auburn of his hair glowed as red as fine claret. He
loomed beside her, a powerful figure of a man bedeviled by an unknown enemy.

He stared at his hand, but Agnes knew that his
attention was fixed on her, and the pull of his masculinity set her heart to racing. A similar occurrence had
led to a kiss that neither of them had planned. Had he
truly meant those harsh words? Were his feelings
toward her solely based on lust? His expression spoke
of more tender feelings, and she fought the urge to
lean into him and learn the answer.

Much as she hated to end the sensuous moment,

she feared where it would lead. Her fingers tightened on the quarrel. "Shall I have Auntie Loo doctor your hand?"

"Nay, I've suffered worse mishaps in my laboratory. A little soap and—" He looked up and their gazes locked.

He licked his lips in a manner that she might have deemed seductive, were the circumstances different. Yet the potential was there. Lord, how she wanted to explore it. "Soap and . . . ?"

Giving himself a shake, he broke the spell. "Soap and a salve 'tis what it needs."

She took two steps back. "Where is your laboratory?"

"In the dungeon."

"Where is the dungeon?"

"Near the entrance to the tower door. A tapestry covers the entrance."

"What damage did you find there?"

"None. The door is heavy oak and the lock proved impenetrable."

The would-be assassin was no thief, she'd decided that, but now she knew that he was not a lockpick, either. A dire bit of information, for it proved to her that the man was a killer without conscience or scruples.

She stifled a shudder at the thought. A thief could be bought for a higher price. The same was true of a vandal. This enemy was deadly serious, and he had only one agenda: the death of Edward Napier.

"What of interest would he find in your laboratory?" she asked.

"Nothing of import to anyone but me. But I'll tell you this, our heathen has put himself in exalted company by assaulting the door to my laboratory. It withstood the will and might of Robert the Bruce."

Lowland Scots of her acquaintance were, by comparison, passive in their heritage. Or was it because the Highland MacKenzies put clan before God if their loyalty was at stake? But as she watched Edward Napier, his vehemence grew as fierce as that of any Highlander she'd ever known.

She'd ponder the matter later; for now she walked to the window and pulled aside the drapes. As she had suspected, the mass of the tower loomed in the darkened sky. A garden or maze covered the ground, filling in the U shape of the building. Was the assassin now crouched in the shrubbery, his crossbow cocked and aimed to kill.

She jumped back and moved to retrieve the quarrel in the firescreen.

"Nay!" he shouted, his voice again cracking like a whip. "It stays where it lies until I find the bow and the man who shot it. Then I'll bury both in unconsecrated ground."

Startled, she stared at him in confusion. Left unchecked, his anger continued to rise. In his wrath this scholarly Lowlander resembled the great chieftains of the Highlands, long known for their power to wreak terrible retribution upon their enemies.

"'Tis later still, my lady, than when last I brought it up." Giving the room a final inspection, he motioned toward the door. "I'll walk you upstairs."

"But I'm not ready to retire."

"Come." Thoroughly distracted, he tipped his head toward the door.

He could have been herding a cow, so careless was his regard for her. What had overcome the scholarly nobleman? Feminine wiles begged for a go at challenging him. Demurring, she said, "Please?"

That got his attention, and the fire in his eyes gave her a shiver. His voice dropped to an ominous rumble, "Any compromise on the matter will be seen as . . ."

She remembered what Christopher had said. "Disobedience, my lord?"

"Aye, and you will not like the punishment."

The will to yield to him set off sparks of excitement, battling wonderfully with her need to prevail. She felt alive and eager to stay in his company. "Frankly, I'm taken aback by you, my lord."

"As am I vexed by you, Agnes MacKenzie." Pointedly he added, *"Not* of the Saint Andrews' branch."

The constable's words, but coming from Edward Napier, they sounded the perfect light foil for these dire straits, and Agnes laughed. "You needn't see me to my room."

He closed his eyes, and his shoulders shook with silent chortles. "A prudent decision was there ever one."

The truth dawned on Agnes. "You'd rather be alone."

Alone, Edward thought? Giraffes would graze in Glasgow before he'd prefer his own company to hers. Tumbling naked with her there on the rug before the hearth held great appeal. With the slightest effort, he could see a pile of discarded clothing. He could feel her soft skin against his palms and his lips. He could hear her purrs of contentment.

"Are you all right?" she asked.

Absolutely not. He stood three strides from an honorable kinswoman of the most decent of Highland clans, and he could think of little beyond suckling her breasts and tasting her sweeter parts. A lusty beast raged within him.

"My lord? What has come over you?"

She was delightfully baffled, an interesting aspect to an altogether exciting woman. "Nothing for you to worry about." He could have laughed at that. Instead he added the truth, "There's nothing for you to worry about . . . tonight."

"Good." She moved toward him, a radiant smile on her lips. She wasn't pinched in at the middle, but sleek and graceful in her femininity. "I wouldn't want you to think me a poor guest."

Now she was pushing the limits of his patience. The vixen. Oh, but a part of him liked her playfulness, and he almost growled with satisfaction. Agnes MacKenzie was a prize, but only for the man who could manage her.

The next morning he decided she was more trouble than she was worth.

Dodging a pair of maids carrying brooms and buckets, Edward went in search of Mrs. Johnson. Small in stature but great in her girth, his cook-cum-housekeeper sat at the worn oaken table, a bucket of leeks before her.

"Morning, my lord," she murmured, her head down.

"Morning, Hazel. Why are maids tromping through the parlor at this time of day?"

She slapped one of the field onions onto the table. "May I speak frankly, my lord?"

"When have you not?"

"Meaning no disrespect for the Highland MacKenzies, but your houseguest is most peculiar."

He had a different opinion, but one that her father also shared.

"She has odd ways, the Lady Agnes does." Mrs. Johnson's nose twitched in disdain. "Not in her appearance, mind you. She's a beauty to rival her famous sister Mary—that painter in London. But the Lady Agnes is a puzzlement."

Edward snatched up a scone. "How so?"

"I came upon her in the kitchen before dawn. She was cleaning up the mess she made winding torches."

"Torches?"

"Aye, for the tower, where she spent most of the night laboring like a scullery maid. Turn me out to sweep the streets, but I think she means to occupy it." From her apron pocket, she produced some papers. "Gave me this. 'Tis an order for carpet for the stairs and a draft to pay for it."

He examined the document. "Carpet for the stairs. Why?"

"You'll be needing a wizard to learn the why of it, my lord. She's also taken Bossy and the carriage off with her."

"I'll deal with her."

Edward did not learn the answer to the question about the new carpet, but over the course of the morning and early afternoon, he discovered that a stair runner was the least of the changes Agnes MacKenzie intended to make in his household. Her visit was turning his life into a Tobias Smollett novel. Was this what Lord Lachlan had meant when he said trust her with your safety?

"Where is Lady Agnes now?" he demanded hours later.

"She's here."

She hurried into the room, a vision in crimson silk. Bossy trailed behind her, his arms laden with packages.

With her free hand, she pulled the pin from her plumed hat and swept it off. Her hair was twisted into a fashionable coil and secured at the crown of her head. The style accentuated her slender neck and delicate chin. She'd been outdoors for too long; her cheeks and nose were pink from the summer sun.

Admiring her, Edward questioned the reasons behind his anger and knew that unbidden desire was also at the heart of his displeasure.

He leaned against the large foyer table. "Your father sent an ax-bearing Highlander. He's in my stables."

"He's one of father's many messengers. He'll stay in the stables, and I doubt you'll notice him. He's to take my letters to Papa. Another messenger will bring Papa's letters to me. The duke of Ross demands that we communicate regularly with him. Is something wrong, my lord? You look vexed." Alarm flashed in her eyes. "Has there been trouble? Are the children harmed?"

"The children are fine." Edward waved toward an array of baskets and flowers that filled the parlor. "I'm surprised that every noble family in Glasgow has sent you a basket of fruit or baked goods. Their eligible sons have sent you flowers and love notes of dubious origin. Six maids are scouring my tower. By way of a minion, the parson promises to be a regular visitor during your stay."

"Good. I had hoped they'd get started as promised."

She'd invited guests to his house without permission? What would she do next? Plan a harvest ball? "What will the parson get started doing?"

"I was speaking about the cleaning girls. They're from the orphanage and need the work. The tower's a fright. Has Trimble arrived?"

"There's an Englishman who calls himself that quaffing beer in the pantry. He insists you summoned him but refuses to say more until he sees you."

She moved to leave. "Then I'll see him now."

"Wait." Was she trying to anger him?

"Is there something else?"

"Yes. You've received invitations to dine from two dozen of Glasgow's best families."

Obviously unaware of his discomfort, she strolled to the large table and began inspecting the contents of the baskets. "I did not encourage this attention, if that is what's troubling you. Please do not think that you must escort me, my lord. They would have sent the invitations had I taken rooms at Farley House. You're my host, not my guardian."

Thank heaven for that. Windsor Castle couldn't accommodate her callers. "Pity that fellow," he murmured under his breath, thinking that Lachlan Mac-Kenzie was a man deserving of sympathy. Edward couldn't imagine governing three more like her.

As if baffled, she shook her head. "How did they find out so quickly that I was here?"

"The banker you visited spread the word . . . after you gave him a draft of above one thousand pounds for work being done in my home, even as we speak."

She hefted an orange, then put it to her nose and breathed deeply. "I'm sure you were planning to make similar changes and haven't gotten 'round to them. You'll reimburse me. I had intended to discuss the matter with you, but you were abed when I left."

He felt as if he were speaking English and she Scottish, so disjointed was their conversation. "I'm delighted to know, at this juncture, that you considered consulting me."

"As I said, you had not arisen."

She made boldness sound so reasonable. "A Commodore Lord Hume has sent his regards. His ship is docked fourteen miles away in the harbor. Have you been to the docks?"

"I visited the harbormaster." She turned to his housekeeper.

At her dismissal, Edward fumed. "Keeping in mind as you ventured there, that as your physician, I would disapprove of so much activity?"

Facing him again, she blinked in confusion, and he knew without a doubt that Agnes MacKenzie seldom followed the orders of another. But then, Edward had had fair warning; he'd seen her with her father. "Riding in a carriage?" she asked. "I've spent the last two days in a carriage."

"Which is why I ordered you to stay abed today."

"Yes, of course." Again she turned to Hazel. "These are for you, Mrs. Johnson." She handed her a large canvas bag. The sides bulged and an umbrella handle stuck out from the top.

Flustered, Mrs. Johnson wrung her hands. "You shouldn't have, my lady."

Lady Agnes patted the cook's shoulder. "The duchess of Ross would have my hide did I not thank you properly for putting up with Auntie Loo and me. Will you please tell Mister Trimble that I'll be with him shortly."

"Of course. You're very kind. Very kind, indeed, my lady."

At that point, she poured on the Highland charm. "I promise not to be too much trouble to you, Mrs. Johnson."

Completely disarmed, Mrs. Johnson did two surprising things: she curtsied twice and left the room without a word to her lord.

A knock sounded at the door. Bossy answered it and returned with another basket. Lady Agnes sent Edward an apologetic look and, with her unbound arm, lifted the cloth. Frowning, she read the accompanying card. "Hoots!" She dropped the paper as if it were aflame, same as her cheeks. "I'm so sorry. 'Tis for you, my lord."

The scent of a familiar perfume drifted to him, and he could guess what was in the basket. Judging from the depth of Lady Agnes's embarrassment, his mistress had intended the contents for him alone.

"If you'll excuse me." Head down, she fussed with her hat. "I'll fetch the quarrel and give Trimble his instructions."

They both needed time to regroup, but Edward wasn't done with the meddlesome Agnes MacKenzie. "Speak with your Mr. Trimble, but I want to see you in my study in fifteen minutes."

5

Carrying the basket containing fresh bread, a silk neckcloth he'd forgotten, and a message from his mistress, Edward went to his study to await Lady Agnes. On scented paper, the note read, "Welcome back, darling. I've missed you dreadfully."

It was no surprise that his houseguest had blushed; he felt embarrassment for her himself. She had every reason to assume the basket was for her, but he couldn't find the words to ease her humiliation.

He had no experience with maidens who shunned tradition. The university was closed to women, as were scholarly circles. Men ruled the church. Women didn't even rule at home, but if he objectively examined his own behavior toward his houseguest, questions arose.

He'd scolded her. He'd interrogated her. He'd criticized her every move. In the circumstances, any man of his acquaintance would have done the same. Why, then, did he feel uncomfortable? Because Agnes Mac-Kenzie was an exceptional female. Again he saw her moving into the path of that arrow, and his belly tightened with fear.

Trust her with the safety of your children and follow her advice, her father had said to Edward. What of the safety of his heart? In less than a week she'd turned his life around, literally and figuratively. She challenged his every rational belief and took him to task for his every normal move.

Then there was the kiss. When his lips had touched hers, his world spun on its axis and fundamental needs ruled. More bothersome was the knowledge that she was as affected and equally uncomfortable with her reaction to him.

What could he do about it?

He couldn't send her away; he owed her his life. Worse, budding feelings for her sparked to life a part of him he thought he'd buried long ago. When he delved within himself, he discovered that his reasons had little to do with obligation and less to do with gratitude. Desire stood at the forefront of his emotions, but close by was attraction of another, more basic kind. He remembered the most tormented of her father's opinions of her. The duke of Ross had proclaimed his firstborn, "a deep thought to ponder." Edward agreed, and with contemplation came excitement. After five minutes in her company, he felt enlivened, tempted to let loose the reins of propriety and see how far the attraction would take them. But their passion would cool, and what then? What would a well-traveled, headstrong Highland lass find of interest in a widowed scholar whose great quest was the perfection of a low-pressure steam engine?

Dizzy from the dilemma, he tore a hunk from the loaf of bread and turned his attention to the puzzle she'd presented last night. She believed the intruder had been searching for something, and if Edward viewed the damage in the room through her eyes, he must concur.

But what did the man want? Edward's journals and the documentation of his university projects had been a target, but those works were published and easily acquired.

The placement of the two quarrels held a deadly message and maybe a clue. Agnes had said the fletchings were English, and that might be true, but Edward knew in his heart that the assassin was a Scot. An Englishman wouldn't violate the Napier shield, for as a race the English had no common allegiance. Wiltshiremen did not stand shoulder to shoulder against their neighbors from Dorset. So why, unless he was Scottish, had the assassin assaulted the symbol of the Napiers?

An assault on his clan. The notion sounded absurd to Edward. In both his lifetime and his father's, the Napiers had enjoyed a peaceful association with other clans and with the English. Not since his grandfather and the other Scots had faced the Jacobite rebellion of '45, had the allegiance of the Napiers been brought into question.

Brought into question. Put that way, it sounded rather benign. Certainly not a "rattling to life of the auld hatred," as his grandfather had described the great clan war.

Rattling to life of the auld hatred. Edward now understood what his grandsire had meant, for every time he looked at that quarrel desecrating the family crest, anger rumbled inside him.

"Am I interrupting, my lord?"

Lady Agnes stood on the threshold, a sheaf of papers in her left hand. Her right was bound in a sling cut from the same cloth as the lavender dress she'd donned. From the odd bulges in the sling, he knew she concealed a number of things, but he was too involved in the woman herself to ponder it. Her embarrassment had passed; his need to admonish her had waned.

The parting words of the countess of Tain came immediately to mind. Lady Lottie had said, "God never made a better woman than Agnes. He just forgot to make her a mate." Even with Lottie's heartfelt words to warn him, Edward couldn't stop himself from wanting to be the man to woo and win Agnes MacKenzie.

"Nay." He got to his feet and welcomed her into the room. "I was thinking about something your sister, the countess of Tain, said to me."

Her brown eyes twinkled with mischief. "Then I stand before you, a pleasant respite from Lottie's wicked tongue."

She looked fresh and fit, an odd description for a female who had spent the night rummaging through the tower and the day traipsing around Glasgow. To outward appearances, no stitches bound a wound in her shoulder. "You're not curious?"

"Originality has never been among Lottie's accomplishments, but let me guess. Since you are young and an earl, and you are smiling, I suspect she told you something far too personal. Did she say that contrary to common belief, male children spring from the wombs of Lachlan's daughters?"

During their lengthy meeting in Edinburgh, the countess had spoken those very words to Edward, citing her own two sons as proof. Uncomfortable with his own feelings, he borrowed another of Lottie's opinions. "She said you were a duke's daughter and spoiled for it."

She tipped her head and gave a little huff. "Lottie's either with child or without her husband's graces then. She knows the peerage from the most recent ducal by-blow to the last Hanoverian hopeful. In her quest to find me a husband, she reserves that particular remark for eligible dukes, and never would she mistake your rank. Pay Lottie no mind."

"She's a matchmaker?"

"A poor one, but she hasn't the wherewithal to do anything else except save Tain from mediocrity." Striding to his desk, she placed a sheet of paper before him.

Glancing at the neatly penned page, Edward was reminded of her father's statement that she wrote as well with her left hand as her right. The duke had been correct, but Edward noticed a very interesting aspect of her penmanship. She fashioned words plainly, without looping scrolls or flowery symbols. She even forgot to dot the *i* in dancing master.

That suited to perfection her unconventional ways.

He read the entire page, which contained an odd mix of occupations, and his confusion grew. "What is this?"

"'Tis a partial listing of people you and the children see on a regular basis. I should like to speak with each of them privately. Except your banker." She toyed with the edge of the sling. "I know that Robert Carrick is trustworthy."

That explained the dancing master's name on the list, and it also reminded Edward of why he'd asked her to come to the study. Strange that he should forget her intrusive actions. "How do you know my banker?"

"From Cameron Cunningham. He patronizes the establishment on occasion."

Edward had known Cameron Cunningham for over

five years. Employing patience, logical arguments, and well-placed bribes, Cunningham had convinced the king to rescind the ban on bagpipes and tartans. He was a true Scottish hero, and every Scot, above the Highland line and below, owed him a debt of gratitude. Today he owned a fleet of merchantmen, most of which had been built here in Glasgow. With Michael Elliot as the third partner, Edward and Cameron had established the first dependable China silk run out of Glasgow. Edward had adapted the machines in his mill to spin and weave the silk, and the profits were substantial.

But Cunningham had never mentioned Agnes MacKenzie. They were close in age and better than a decade younger than Edward. Agnes had mentioned Cameron, but Edward had forgotten the gist of the conversation. "How well do you know Cameron?" Edward asked.

She reached under the sling and scratched the wound. "I have sailed the world with him." Paper rattled.

"You have?"

"With whom else would I travel, save a family friend?"

"He hasn't mentioned it to me."

"Cameron is the very soul of discretion. His father and mine are longtime friends. He is also very close to one of my sisters."

The subject had not come up between Cameron and Edward. And what, other than paper, did she conceal in that sling? "Which of your sisters?"

Lifting her chin, she looked him in the eye. "Virginia."

The lost sister. The daughter believed dead by the duke of Ross. The source of the rift between Agnes and her father. Feeling an outsider in the volatile issue, Edward thought it best to let the uncomfortable subject pass.

As he glanced at the list, he again remembered her father's assurance that Hannah and Christopher would be safe under her guard. The word *others* at the bottom of the page confused him more. "Who are these unnamed others?"

"The nanny, Mrs. Borrowfield."

Her disappearance from the church had worried Edward, for he feared she had fallen prey to the assassin. "Did Christopher tell you about her?"

"Only her name and that she barged into his room overmuch."

"My son values his privacy. A lad will at his age."

"My brother used to set traps for any who ventured into his private domain." The joy of happy memories shone in her eyes. "A pot of coal dust perched over the door frame was his favorite."

"How old is your father's heir?"

"Kenneth is Christopher's age." She grew distracted. "Where is Mrs. Borrowfield, and why did she leave the ceremony in Edinburgh?"

"I do not know. After caring for you in the church, I returned with the children to the inn, but she'd left without a trace."

"She took her belongings and nothing else?"

"Only what was hers, and no one at the inn saw her leave."

"What of her belongings?"

"She hadn't many. She'd only been with us since March."

"May I examine her reference?"

Edward found it in an undisturbed drawer in his desk. Lady Agnes read the letter, then held it up to the light. But she did not comment.

Her gaze slid to the basket. "I'd also like to talk to your mistress."

He drew the line of propriety. "Nay."

"You needn't worry that I'll tell tales, my lord. I'm only thinking about your safety and the children's well-being. I'd simply like to speak to your mistress and learn if her motives are pure."

Edward laughed.

Agnes frowned.

Seeing her so discomfited pleased him. "Purity," he replied, "is hardly a quality one seeks in a mistress."

This time her maidenly blush had a different and decidedly physical effect on him. But before he could savor the yearning she inspired, she recovered her composure. "Enlighten me, my lord, as to your *standards* for choosing a mistress."

Realizing she wanted to play, Edward stifled his desire and obliged the tantalizing minx. "A proper mistress must be agreeable."

"Like a well trained horse, my lord?"

Edward couldn't remember the last time he'd had so stimulating a conversation, especially with a woman who stirred his interest to dangerous levels. "A mistress should cater to the tastes of her provider."

"Like a talented cook?"

Taste in food was a far cry from the delights he had in mind, but he couldn't bring himself to broach the vulgar. Instead, he decided to test the limits of her generosity. "Aye, would you care for bread?"

"Certainly. How kind of you to share the bounty." With a surprisingly agile left hand, she tore off a piece of the bread and tasted it. "Delicious."

Why had he expected jealousy or prejudice? Why was he disappointed for the lack of it?

Giving him a hum of satisfaction, she said, "Now

that we've exhausted the expectations of that position . . ."

Choking with laughter, he pretended to cough.

"Do you or do you not wish to find this villain?"

She looked so flustered, he was forced to relent. "Yes, and the magistrate has set about to do that."

"You don't want my help?"

"I'd sooner let a bull loose in my laboratory than argue with you." He turned up his palms in surrender. "With one exception, my life is yours to explore."

"Good. Will you indulge me in a wee bit of Highland tradition?"

He'd probably indulge her in his own demise, so captivated was he by her. "Of course."

From within the bulging sling she withdrew a napkin-size square of the MacKenzie tartan plaid. Pinned to the cloth was a smaller golden version of the MacKenzie clan badge. She moved to the firescreen and draped the colors and the symbol of her family over the damaged image of his family crest.

Edward felt off balance watching her perform the simple show of clanship. He'd heard of such pledges, but never had he witnessed one. Peace reigned among his kinsmen, and he spent his time as chieftain attending weddings, christenings, and funerals.

"This assures you of the resources and the sanctuary of Clan MacKenzie, should the need arise."

She spoke as if he were the pupil and she the teacher instructing him on Scottish custom. The insult stung his pride. "I know its meaning."

"I did not think—" She turned her back on him and stared out the window.

"What didn't you think? That as a Lowlander I am ignorant of the way pledges are put forth? Were the Highlands a day's ride from England, I doubt your people would be so smug."

Her features sharpened. "I thought—" She stopped on a sigh. "'Twas not my intention to insult you."

Even cloaked in polite words, the message was clear: Agnes MacKenzie would keep her own counsel when it suited her. He balked at being closed out, and words of challenge begged to be spoken. In a sentence he could strike their disagreement anew. Or he could learn something about her. "Trust comes hard by you, does it not?"

"In these time, aye." She waved her unbound hand. "We have children in this house to protect." Making a fist, she pounded the windowsill. "We have an enemy—an assassin—to rout." Almost at a march, she moved toward him, her eyes glittering with confidence. "We cannot make light of what has happened or wish it away."

"We? Speak for yourself."

"Very well, I will. Give me three days, and I'll make your home so secure, a hungry midge couldn't find its way inside."

With expert subtlety, she had turned the disagreement into conversation and ebbed the flow of strong emotions between them. He'd have none of it.

The sound of workmen tromping down the hall added irony to the discussion and fueled his resolve. He folded his arms. "Midges I can tolerate. 'Tis the other comings and goings that I resent."

"Such as?"

"In the east receiving room there's a human ladder who calls himself Gabriel. He carries a child on his shoulders. The boy is attaching hooks to the wall. I find that odd."

"As well you should, my lord," she chirped, as proud as could be. "Those workmen are following my orders. 'Tis an idea of my own invention. We'll thread sturdy string through the hooks, tie one end to the doors and the windows and the other end to a bell. Each bell will ring in a different tone and sound. If a door or window is opened . . ." The lift in her voice invited him to finish the thought.

Her mind worked in the strangest, most clever way. Granted they were speaking of dangerous matters, but she managed to make Edward feel as if he were playing a game. Bemused, he said, "If the door is opened the bell rings."

"Alas! Every home should have such an alarm."

Alarms were going off in Edward, and the warning had nothing to do with strings and windows and bells. "Another of your special talents?"

"His grace of Burgundy thought so." She appeared positively coy, with her pretty mouth pursed and her attention focused on the smoothly buffed fingernails of her free hand.

He ached to touch her and discover if her excitement were tangible. "Mrs. Johnson believes you mean to occupy the tower."

"Why not? 'Tis the safest place to be. There's only the one ground entrance, and the fishtail slits are too narrow for a bowshot from any angle, any place, save midair in the courtyard."

So much for wooing and winning.

"Please, my lord, hear me out." At his nod, she continued. "I still believe the children should be told about the danger, and I've a partial remedy—should you remain decided that they should not."

His children were too young to deal with an assassin. "I remain so decided."

"A move into the tower will take away the advantage of surprise when we are most vulnerable—at night. We'll only sleep there." She touched his arm. "Hannah and Christopher will have a merry time of it. Auntie Loo will help. We'll even dress for a day in surcoats and tunics and have a plain meal at the hearth."

She made it sound adventurous and practical at once. He liked the idea of seeing her in a tightly laced bliaut, her hair unbound in maidenly fashion. "Must I grow a beard?"

Startled, she blinked in surprise. "You'll join in? You'll play the medieval lord?"

"Of course. Why should you have all the fun?"

She grew serious. "You're wise to give yourself this peace of mind, my lord, unless you'll tell the children about the danger?"

"Nay. I'll not have them know."

"In that event—" She fished into the sling once more. "Let's give them these." She pulled out a pair of whistles, one strung on pink ribbon, the other on a strip of leather. "We cannot watch them every moment of every day, or they will grow suspicious, especially Christopher. He's very bright."

Nearing total bafflement, Edward marched to the firescreen and touched the MacKenzie brooch. The metal retained her warmth. "Any other precautions we should take?"

"A pair of peacocks in the courtyard?"

Curse the Highlands that bred her, for Edward was beginning to understand the way her mind worked. "To serve as watchdogs?"

She fairly bubbled. "Pretty ones without fleas."

Life in the old wing offered a closeness to her, and he liked the idea well. But he must first establish boundaries. "My laboratory stays as it is. I want no changes there. No alarms. No bells. No meddling. No snooping, and no cleverly worded excuses after the fact."

She tucked the whistles back into the sling. "How can I change a place I have not seen?"

He gave her a big grin. "Precisely."

Her expression grew wary. "Have you medical experiments down there?"

Laughter almost choked him. "I design new machines and try to better the ones we have. I am a scientist, not a practicing doctor."

"I could argue that point." She demurred beautifully. "You're a very good doctor."

"In search of a very good patient."

"And meeting with futility?"

"I couldn't have put it better."

She opened her mouth to respond, but hesitated. At length she grew serious again. "What in your laboratory would interest the assassin?"

Edward missed the playful side of her, but it would return. She was too friendly to keep a distance for long. "My pursuit in the design and building of machines is a private one, apart from my university work."

"Then your experiments involve your mill?"

"Yes, but 'tis better said that the whole of industry will benefit when I've perfected my work."

"Who will not benefit?"

"No one. 'Tis simply progress."

"Your mill will become more prosperous."

"Of course. 'Tis not missionary work I do, or the dabblings of an eccentric nobleman."

"I know that, my lord. Even my father, when his temper left him, praised your work. Will you take me to the mill?"

"If I do not, will you go on your own?"

"What do you think?"

"I *know* that concession is becoming my watchword."

" 'Twill not be for long, I promise. Then you can return to your peaceful life." She extended her hand.

"Now come and see what progress we've made in the tower."

He thought she had a good point, but he wasn't about to admit it. He couldn't remember when she'd gained the advantage or how; yet the discussion was over, and he'd conceded to all of her plans but one. He would not, however, be led down his own hall.

As he guided her toward the old wing, he broached a subject that fit the congenial mood. "Will you accept the mayor's invitation to dinner?"

She stopped and let go of his hand. "Have you read the invitations that came to me today?"

Her expression could melt ice and blister stone at once. The right to inspect her correspondence was his by law. The rule of common courtesy called for better behavior. Respect for her urged him to offer an explanation. "Nay, I did not intercept your messages. The mayor's wife sent me a note to say that she was quite eager to have you to table. To that end, she encouraged me to use any influence I may have with you."

"So you're trying to persuade me on her behalf."

Looking down at the crown of her head, he noticed that golden pins secured the heavy coil of her hair. Each of the precious ornaments was embellished with a tiny thistle and enameled in lavender.

"Are you encouraging me, my lord?"

She had thistles in her hair. The traditional symbol of Scotland, worn by a very untraditional woman. "'Tis the neighborly thing to do . . . in the Lowlands."

"Do you wish to escort me?"

He knew better than to answer that. "Do you wish to be escorted?"

"Only if you promise to take no other meaning from it."

Other meaning. Straightforward Agnes MacKenzie was dallying with words. An interesting occurrence, having her yield the conversation to him. With relish, he accepted the task. "You mean will I assume that you harbor an affection for me if we do all of the normal things that accompany an evening out together."

"Aye, that is what I mean."

Now she was direct again, but she'd waited too late, and he intended to put her on the run. Urging her to begin walking again, he said, "That will include handing you to and from the carriage. Am I to assume that I'd be required to perform that small service?"

Grudgingly, she said, "Yes, and you're a troll to belabor it so."

He felt lively inside and fought the urge to skip down the hall. "Part of my duties would also require me to help you on and off with your cloak."

"A gentleman would perform that simple courtesy out of habit." She sounded grumpy.

He felt divine and couldn't resist putting an innocent twist on his next words. "Will you want me to fetch punch for you?"

Her mouth pursed with humor. "I despise punch."

"What of cutting your meat? You cannot wield both knife and fork with one hand."

"I've managed so far."

"And lost half a stone of your weight."

"I am not gaunt, nor am I a cripple."

"Good!" He made a show of being relieved, but his mind was momentarily lodged on the body beneath that alluring dress.

"You're wearing an interesting expression, my lord. What are you thinking?"

Savoring lustful thoughts about her was becoming a

habit. "I'm thinking that I should suggest that the mayor's wife serve a stew."

"Stop making a jest of me."

"Me? You're doing a fair job of it on your own."

"We are newly met, and a woman cannot be too careful."

"Nor too prissy."

"Prissy or not, may I remind you of the bell on the east door, so you won't wake the household, should you return late from a visit to your mistress."

The line between right and wrong with her became hazy. They should not discuss his mistress. It was wrong in any man's rules. But with an insight that gave him great joy, Edward knew his association with Agnes MacKenzie would be like no other he had shared.

"I'll be so quiet when I return from visiting my mistress, even you will not notice." Actually he had not planned to see her until the assassin had been found. Now he thought of ending the association completely. Could he make love to one woman with another on his mind? He didn't think so.

"Shall we make a wager of it, my lord? Ten pounds?"

"Not money. For my forfeit, I expect you to explain that business about scolding in your family."

"Done, and if you visit your mistress and forget about the bell on the door to the east wing, you must show me your laboratory."

He had intended to show it to her anyway, not that he thought his scientific endeavors would be of interest to her.

"We have a bargain."

The pounding of hammers grew louder as they approached the old wing. "Did Burgundy allow you to disrupt his household in this fashion?"

"His grace did not share a residence with his children."

Edward noted the slight scorn in her tone. "A practice you disdain?"

"Yes, but regardless of my opinion, 'twas better than draping his estates in mourning for the loss of his son."

She could bite, and Edward smarted. "That's a wretched thing to say, Agnes MacKenzie."

"The truth often is." Satisfied at his reaction, she walked faster. "Please remember that the bowman reached Glasgow hours before us."

"What makes you think I've forgotten it? My house is under guard for intruders, and you've brought in a dozen strangers—hardly an act of prudence."

"I hoped you would trust me to hire honest workmen and maids. Gabriel and the others came highly recommended."

He remembered the farrier in Whitburn, a man soon to be in Edward's employ. "In that regard, I do trust you."

"Good. We must take away the assassin's every advantage and lessen his opportunities."

The woman was relentless. "Will you please remember in whose home you reside? Jamie said he drove you to the docks. What were you doing there?"

She stopped in the Elizabethan wing. "Asking questions of anyone who might have information on the whereabouts of my sister. I do so in every port city I visit, because—well, that's the best place to look."

"What if you had located her?"

Her smile was bittersweet. "Then I would now be offering my apologies and saying farewell to you."

What had her father said? That she shouldered a guilt too great for ten men to bear. Edward understood, but that would not prevent him from speaking his mind. Holding the dust curtain that had been draped over the door, he said, "You overstepped yourself by ordering the carpet without my permission."

Pausing on the threshold, she said, "The stairs are dangerous, and Hannah bragged about skipping down them. If he hasn't already, Christopher will eventually discover the fun to be had sliding down the rail. The laundry maid could slip, any of the servants could have an accident."

"I insist on reimbursing you."

"I assumed you would." Again she delved into the sling. "Here's an accounting of the materials and wages for the workmen. If you like, you can put the money into Carrick's bank on my behalf."

Edward took the list. She had saved him time. With her help, he could return to his work. The contracts with suppliers in India who furnished spooled cotton to his mill must be renewed soon, unless he perfected the new engine. When that occurred, he could buy raw cotton and spin it here in Glasgow, thereby saving an enormous amount of money and time.

In the old wing, all of the furnishings had been moved against the walls and covered with heavy cloths. The tapestries had been taken down, revealing the corridor that led down to his laboratory. The door in the convex wall that led into the tower stood ajar, and light poured through the opening. In his childhood the tower had been his favorite place to play, and the prospect of occupying it again brought back fond memories.

The smell of freshly cut wood filled the air, and a layer of sawdust coated everything, even clung to the damp stone walls.

"Starting at the topmost level, the carpenters are building staircases to replace the ladders."

He couldn't help saying, "I hope you thought to order carpet—for safety's sake."

"Mockery will be repaid in kind, Lord Edward. 'Twas a good idea, and only nicked pride keeps you from crediting me for it."

"I'll save my pride for greater issues, if you please. Did you climb the ladders in the tower?"

She grew still. "Ladders, as in more than one? Nay. I touched only the one ladder."

But the tower had two levels above this one and a battlement on top. He'd wager ten hours of time working on the steam engine that she'd lied or at least stretched the truth. He knew the way to find out. "I presume my telescopes were removed from the roof."

"Telescopes?" She frowned. "I saw only pigeons and wayward gulls up there. The cobwebs were so thick—"

"Aha!" He pointed a finger at her. "So you did climb the other ladders."

She knew exactly when to retreat. "Well, to your way of thinking, I'm certain I was foolhardy. Believe what you want, but I was careful. I do not relish injuries."

She moved beneath the hole in the ceiling and peered at the workmen on the floor above. A saw grated loudly and hammers banged like flat drums.

"Have you decided who will sleep where?" He could offer a suggestion that was sure to make her blush again.

"I think that Hannah and Christopher should occupy the middle chamber, with a partition between them for privacy. Auntie Loo and I will take this chamber. You'll have the uppermost room, to be close to your telescopes."

Lord, there was sauce in her tongue. Much as it

pained him, he held to the intimate subject of sleeping arrangements. "The children will take the top chamber. You and Auntie Loo will take the middle. We'll have our meals and such in here. I'll sleep on the cot in my laboratory."

"Will you be comfortable there? Can you rest well on a cot?"

"Aye, I've done so many times."

"Shall we summon Auntie Loo and the children and tell them the good news?"

A crash sounded above, and before Edward could reach for her, a block of wood plunged through the opening and crashed into her shoulder. As he pulled her out of the way, her knees buckled.

"I've got you, Agnes."

"I'm fine, truly." She tried to pull away but didn't have the strength. "You needn't make a fuss."

As he watched, she valiantly fought a swoon. Lowering her to the floor, he removed the sling. With half his attention on her eyes, he pulled the bodice of her gown off her shoulder. The bandage was clean, unbloodied. She hadn't torn a stitch, but the crown of her shoulder would be bruised anew on the morrow.

"Now you will rest." Tossing the fabric sling at her, he said, "Cover yourself." Then he swept her into his arms and hurried out the door.

"You needn't carry me," she said through her teeth.

"Haud yer wheesht!" he said, and headed for the main staircase.

"I cannot grasp why you must continually be so tiresome—especially in Scottish. I'm fine."

"And I'm the bellman of Glasgow. Take notice, you and your special abilities are going to bed for what remains of the day."

Her eyes narrowed. "Are you always such an ungrateful wretch?"

"Nay, on occasion I'm grateful."

"Ha! A twist of my words."

Now that she was out of harm's way, he let himself grow angry. "Spoken by a true novice of the sport of twisting words."

"You're a knave."

"For treating you as an equal?"

"Equal? An odd description for one who is being carried against her will. You're a boring cave dweller."

Edward laughed. "What refinement in the face of defeat. Resign yourself, or I'll tie your good arm to the bed."

"You never would."

He did feel rather primal, and he liked it.

Noises sounded in the foyer. As he passed the entryway and turned to climb the stairs, Mayor Arkwright's wife stepped through the door. The parson and a smartly dressed military man followed.

Edward froze.

"Sweet Saint Ninian!" Agnes exclaimed, then warbled, "Good day, Commodore."

"What are you about, Lord Edward!" huffed the mayor's outraged wife.

Agnes sent him a knowing look and whispered, "You should have let me walk. Equal indeed."

As quietly, Edward said, "May we keep our disagreements between ourselves?"

"Who would care?" The sling slipped and fluttered to the floor, leaving her shoulder and too much of her breast exposed. "When word of this folly gets out, a disagreement between us will be old news."

"Explain yourself, my lord," declared the officer.

"I . . . uh . . ." He glanced down at her. "I was . . ."

Her brown eyes glittered with retribution. "Lord Edward is conducting a scientific experiment. I'm only helping him. Do tell them what it's called, my lord."

An acceptable explanation eluded Edward, but he had to try. A coolness swept over him. "I'm doing a study on the relative properties of silk when put to the test of the gravitational pull."

His guests gaped. Edward held his breath. Agnes fairly gloated.

In the uncomfortable silence, the officer said, "Lady Agnes, is that a bandage on your . . . ?" He couldn't quite name the place.

Relief swept over Edward. "Yes. Lady Agnes has injured herself and being her doctor, I—"

"Being my doctor, Lord Edward feels obligated to examine me."

"Please be quiet," Edward urged. "You're making it worse. Mayor Arkwright's wife looks ready to swoon."

Lady Agnes must have believed him, for she relented. "Nothing untoward goes on here, Commodore. I've hurt myself 'tis all."

Knowing opinion was going against them, Edward asked Mrs. Johnson to show the guests into the parlor. Then he lifted Agnes higher into his arms and carried her to the stairs.

In her room, he lowered her to the bed. "We've done it now," he said, more to himself than to her.

Straining to see the damage to her shoulder, she said, "I'll change my gown and speak with the commodore."

"Absolutely not. I'll manage Hume and the others. You stay here."

"I hope Lord Hume doesn't tell my father. They are old friends, you know."

Edward hadn't thought of her father; he'd been preoccupied with her. "They should have waited for an invitation. Now everyone will think I've seduced you."

"Rubbish."

Her sharp tone set him on edge. "Why do you say that?"

"Because I'd rather lie with a toad."

6

CURSE HER FOOLISH TONGUE AND BRAND THE MARK OF
idiot on her brow. In one sentence, spoken in anger,
Agnes had alienated the earl of Cathcart. For three
days, she'd paid the price. She'd suffered his cool
replies. She'd accepted his absence at meals. She'd
damned herself a shrew and worse.

To her surprise, he had placated the pastor and the
mayor's wife. The commodore, he'd taken to dinner
at his club. Sponsoring Hume for membership had
assured him of the man's loyalty and silence.

Agnes had worried over nothing.

Lord Edward had also made wicked with a sentence. He'd sent her a message declaring, "You'll have
to beg me to remove those stitches."

Enough was enough.

Her mood was sour. The itch in her healing wound
made her want to scream. With a slight pressure, she

rubbed her hairbrush over the spot and shivered with relief.

Her other agony was not so easily assuaged.

The mix of it was, she'd intentionally insulted Lord Edward's seduction. The habit was old, ingrained, and she'd had no choice. The attraction between them was almost tangible, but their ways of dealing with it were vastly different. He'd been honest after that first kiss. Desire, base and raw, had inspired him. Her reaction was more tender, dangerously subtle, and it frightened her. So she'd struck back with words and hit the mark. She'd driven him away.

Then why did she feel so wretched?

Frustrated, she slammed down the brush and ran her fingers through her hair to dry it. The coal fire in the brazier spread a gentle warmth, and the thick carpet provided a comfortable seat.

She considered the reasons behind her attraction to Lord Edward. He was more handsome by far than other men of her acquaintance, and his winning ways could detract a nun from her vocation. Beyond the obvious, only sensible answers came to mind: for the first time in her quest to protect the innocent, Agnes had pledged her special gifts to a man. The danger that stalked him drew her like a magnet. Thwarting it offered temporary redemption from her great sin. Blind to all but that, she'd confused the man with the mission.

Therein lay her mistake.

Children were her cause. Better she had traveled that familiar ground. Adults could fend for themselves. Except, she thought morosely, when it came to removing stitches.

She'd tried to take out the worrisome thread and had stabbed herself twice in the doing. On orders from his lordship, Auntie Loo had refused to help.

108

Oh, she could have disobeyed his edict but chose not to. The privilege of a princess, she'd said.

"Fither her fate!" Agnes cursed.

An apology to his lordship was unthinkable. The alternative held less appeal. If she wanted relief, she must let him touch her with hands as icy as his look.

That decided, she resumed brushing her hair.

During the last three days, she'd busied herself as best she could, interviewing those who had commerce with the earl of Cathcart and his children. Arranging what appeared to be an accidental meeting with his mistress at the dressmaker's shop had involved inventiveness on Agnes's part, but the results had been disappointing. Of an age with Lord Edward, the well-kept widow MacLane supported herself on a generous pension from her late husband's tobacco concern. A second marriage would steal the woman's freedom, so her heart was not engaged in the affair.

Agnes had felt a moment's relief but convinced herself that respect for another independent woman was the cause.

The dancing master, the music instructor, and the young scholar who tutored Christopher were guileless. The vanishing nanny was another matter. According to information gathered by the agent, Mr. Trimble, the woman had not existed prior to taking the post in Napier House. She had left no belongings here. None of the people Agnes had spoken to knew more than her name. Small wonder Mrs. Borrowfield had fled Saint Margaret's Church moments before the attempt on Lord Edward's life.

She was a key piece to the puzzle of the assassin's plot. Agnes would find her. The long search for Virginia had taught Agnes which avenues were profitable to explore and what people were worthy to engage. Mr. Trimble managed an organization of discreet messengers and able "truth seekers," as he referred to his associates. With his help, she would find the nanny and the assassin in either order.

But first, the stitches must come out.

As she rose to dress, the door opened. Auntie Loo stepped inside, a tray in her hands, which she set before Agnes.

Agnes stared, struck dumb at the sorry fare. "A bowl of dried thistles? How very clever."

"I'd love to lay claim to it, but Lord Edward deserves the credit."

"You're only the messenger of this madness, I suppose. I hope both of you trip on a bed of jagged stones and share your dying breath with hungry carnivores."

"Now who's being clever, my lady?"

"Did you refuse to deliver his taste of sarcasm?"

"No."

If deceit had ever visited Auntie Loo, she'd cast it out early in life. Speaking the truth shared an equal post with family honor. None of her Manchurian kin possessed more.

"You like Edward Napier?" Agnes asked her.

"Yes. He's turned fierce, though, since we arrived here."

Auntie Loo hadn't seen him dictating to Agnes in the stables in Whitburn, else she wouldn't be so generous. "He's a beast prowling his den."

"You mean he's been beastly to you."

"At every turn."

Auntie Loo took a pale green day dress from one of Agnes's trunks, which had been delivered the day before. "This dress? The daring neckline should work to your advantage."

The implacable earl of Cathcart probably wouldn't notice. The upcoming meeting didn't require formal attire, and the gown was the latest fashion. "'Twill do."

Shaking out the wrinkles, Auntie Loo said, "Will you make amends with him?"

"I have. Dozens of times without speaking the words."

With an insight that seldom proved wrong, her friend said, "He is a man who must hear them."

"He'll probably gloat, too, or strut like the cock o' the walk."

"So?" She took the brush and motioned for Agnes to take the stool. "I have never known you to shy from an interesting and attractive man."

Agnes plopped down on the stool, the weight of dread dragging at her determination. She must relent or continue to suffer his detachment.

Under the circumstances, withdrawal from him was surely the better way. Nothing could sway her, no one could prevent her from finding Virginia. Word would come. On a fine blue day or winter's bleakest night, a messenger would knock on Agnes's door and say the magic words.

With a valise of only essentials, she'd hurry to snatch Virginia from the hand of fate.

Then she could wade neck-deep in romantic intrigues. She'd flirt with any gentleman she fancied. She'd sleep without nightmares. She'd turn her attentions to having a family of her own.

But she'd waded too deeply with Edward Napier.

Auntie Loo gave her hair a final inspection. "He's very handsome, for a red-haired Lowlander."

Agnes had cursed him in that fashion and twelve others in the last few days. But to set things aright between them, she must start now. She donned her petticoats. "Actually his hair is auburn, same as Papa's."

Holding the dress, Auntie Loo casually said, "Did you know that he helped the workmen build the partition between the children's beds in the tower, as well as our beds?"

As grouchy as ever, Agnes stepped into the gown. "Probably because the hammering prevented him from doing his great work in his laboratory. I've most likely set back the progress of man, you know."

Auntie Loo tugged the waist of the dress, then began fastening the buttons. "Why are you so cross? Have you forsaken the quest for inner peace?"

Facing the standing mirror, Agnes fluffed her sleeves. Part of her training in weaponless fighting involved the search for harmony within one's self. While physical, the exercises also sharpened her mind. "My stitches itch, and I cannot bear the strain between his lordship and me."

"Neither can the rest of us who reside under this roof. He's as cross as you are, but he masks it better with the children."

"I know what you are thinking, Auntie, but Edward Napier is not for me."

"How can you be so sure about him? He's like no other man you've ever met. Only yesterday you said as much yourself."

"Because I will it to be so. What if I do act on the feelings I have for him? News of Virginia could come on my wedding night."

"Should that come to pass, you will find a way. You are the Golden One. The doors of life fly open before you. The high holy man proclaimed it."

In China Agnes had visited the temple of an extraordinary monk. Without knowledge of Agnes or her language, and never having traveled more than a mile from his home, the priest had known Virginia's name and the events leading to her disappearance. "He said I would find her, and one prophecy at a time is enough for me."

"He said you would find love first."

Agnes could and would control that particular event in her destiny. "'Twas not a moment-by-moment chronicle of my life he foresaw."

Picking up Agnes's discarded robe, Auntie Loo took great care in folding it. "I will not argue with you when you are so vexed."

Agnes slipped the sling over her neck and rested her arm in the fold. The movement aggravated the itch. "Then wish me luck in braving the lion in his den."

"He's in the courtyard."

Agnes found him squatting beside the sundial. Her shadow fell over him, but he did not acknowledge her presence. Across the courtyard the glazier and his helper worked at replacing the glass in the newer wing with mullions. In tandem, the older fellow labored outside while the younger man stood in Lord Edward's study. Near the path that led around to the stables, one of the magistrate's men conversed casually with her father's messenger. The Highlander, distinguished only by his MacKenzie tartan, waved to Agnes. She returned the greeting, but she didn't know his name. He was one of many men her father employed for the purpose of communicating with his family.

The hedges at either end of the spacious rectangle had been neatly trimmed in conical shapes, and the herb garden in the center sported no weeds. The fountain gurgled softly, enhancing the peaceful ambience of the surroundings and belying the uncomfortable mood.

As had become his preference of late, Lord Edward wore his tartan plaid belted and a stylishly cut waistcoat. Today he'd chosen a pale gray silk shirt, but no neckcloth. Rows of tiny pleats circling the sleeves at the elbow gave the shirt a distinctive flare. It was also a practical touch, for it would prolong the life of the garment.

Patience waning, she stepped closer. "Am I disturbing you, my lord?"

He continued with his task. "You are disturbing *to* me." At the first of the twelve meridian bells, he began shifting the dial to align the shadow of the gnomon. Before the third pealing, he stepped back, wiped his hands, and faced her. "But there's little I can do to change that."

Drat his honesty and his appealing smile. Not to mention his penchant for quarreling. "Must you always draw a line in the conversation and bade me step over it?"

His interest engaged, he tipped his head to the side and studied her. "We could exchange a few niceties. My view of the weather for the next day or so. Your skill with a needle."

"My part in the discussion would be brief. I do not sew." Nor could she unsew; the bothersome stitches were proof of that.

A pair of butterflies danced on air, fluttering among the flowering hawthorns. The drone of a passing bee sounded extaordinarily loud to Agnes.

"Do I understand that my lady has something on her mind?"

She expected aloofness, but this cool tone put her

on edge. "You know very well these stitches are driving me to madness."

Feigning indulgence, he tisked. "Scratching only makes it worse."

"Then please take them out."

With the heel of his hand, he tapped his ear, then shook his head. "My hearing must be failing, or was that an apology?"

The beast. If she did not swallow her pride, the itching would go on and on. "I'm sorry for comparing you to a toad."

He fairly oozed satisfaction. "Do you promise never to do it again?"

Watching him and knowing he could put an end to the itching moved her to sarcasm. "Never will I repeat that you are a toad. I'll be much more creative when next you put me in a compromising position."

"That sounds interesting. What will you do?"

Reminding him of the risks she'd taken seemed unsporting, and she couldn't bring herself to stoop so low. "I'll stay out of the way of deadly missiles and falling objects."

"Oh, Agnes," he lamented. "I cannot stay angry with you." He laughed, but she could tell that he didn't want to.

She offered her hand. "A truce then?"

His grip was stronger than it had to be. "With conditions."

Wary anew, she watched him closely, but couldn't see past the alluring blue-gray of his eyes. "What conditions?"

He rubbed his chin, which bore no trace of a stubble. "I want to know everything you've learned about the assassin, no matter how inconsequential to you. If you leave this house again, I want to know where you are going."

Answering for her every action rankled, but his stern tone brooked no argument. Logic forced her to say, "I'm in no danger."

He stared at the tower, his profile limned in sunlight, his hair glistening like dark embers. "The bowman may have taken a liking to shooting you, and the next time, he may soak his quarrels in a stronger poison. You'd be dead before I could stem the flow of your blood."

She shivered at the notion, but common sense ruled. "He would not hurt me except to hurt you. Were that his motive, Mrs. MacLane would be dead."

His gaze riveted to hers.

She'd invaded his privacy for very good reasons. "She remains unharmed?" Agnes asked, undaunted at broaching the delicate subject.

Chagrined, he cleared his throat. "'Twould seem you've seen her since I have. Shall we move on to the second and more comfortable of my conditions?"

It was a minor point to yield, and they were finally conversing easily. "By all means."

"'Tis actually a request. Will you try to teach Hannah to read? I know she's young for it, but she has an aversion to the alphabet. I'm troubled by that."

Agnes glanced across the courtyard. Through the windows in the music room she saw Hannah, Christopher, and Auntie Loo huddled on the floor and examining something she could not make out. "I've noticed, and I think it has to do with the letters themselves."

Hesitantly, he said, "For any help you can give, I'd be grateful."

"Oh, I like the sound of that. Being indebted to me makes you much more agreeable."

In rueful mirth, he closed his eyes, and lines of laughter lent him a youthful air. "Do not teach her your saucy ways. I hope to find her a good husband someday."

Agnes abhorred arranged marriages, Lottie's notwithstanding. A woman should be free to mingle in society, to travel, to make a friend of a man before pledging her troth and giving him leave to rule her life.

"You seem far away," he said.

"Do I?"

"Yes." Honesty wreathed his handsome features. "Do you miss your family?"

Among the MacKenzies the bond went too deep, and neither time nor distance could break it. "Not to distraction. I've often been away from home for long periods of time."

She watched the occupants of the music room. As one, Auntie and the children rose and disappeared into the hall. Agnes realized what they'd been doing on the floor. "Oh, no," she said. "Auntie Loo's made the children a kite."

He followed the line of her vision. "You sound troubled by that. What's the harm?"

"'Tis a bad sign. Kite-making is the last of her ideas for occupying children. Something will have to be done."

The doors flew open and the children burst into the courtyard. Both were dressed in ordinary, serviceable clothing rather than smaller versions of adult apparel. Hannah wore a pink cotton smock, Christopher, a jacket and knee breeches of sturdier cloth. The girl's black ringlets had been tamed, braided, and wound into coils over her ears, same as Auntie Loo's.

Skipping over the paving stones, they chatted excitedly, too involved in their own fun to do more than wave to Agnes and Edward.

He said, "If Auntie's patience is gone, we'll postpone our visit to the mill until later tomorrow. Mrs. Johnson goes to market in the morning, but she and Bossy can watch the children in the afternoon."

Without thinking, Agnes said, "Why not take them with us? Except for an hour or two in the courtyard each day, they've been cooped up inside."

He plucked an errant piece of dried grass from the walkway, and using only one hand, tied the stem into knots. "I'd forgotten about your father's unusual way of raising children."

Most parents shunned the job of rearing children, but Edward Napier didn't strike her as that sort of guardian. "They'll be safe with us."

"Very well. They're usually on their best behavior at the mill."

Agnes scratched her wound. "I propose we leave them to their kiting."

"So this toady doctor can relieve you of those stitches?"

If she weren't careful, Edward Napier would relieve her of more than a few knots of silken thread. "If you play the toad again, I'll croak."

Laughing, he rested his arm at the small of her back and ushered her inside. Too involved in their kite, the children didn't notice them leave, but Auntie Loo did, for she winked at Agnes.

His study had been cleaned, the torn furniture replaced, and his desk chair repaired. Only the quarrel in the firescreen, draped with MacKenzie colors, remained as proof of the assassin's presence.

"Sit there on the window seat." He rummaged through his medical bag. "The light's better."

The glaziers had moved to the music room, but the faint smell of damp sealing paste lingered in the air.

Edward looked so comfortable in his role as doctor, she couldn't help saying, "I hope you will not rip up another of my gowns."

He stopped, instruments in hand, and glared at her. "Now who's drawing lines in the conversation and begging me to step over them?"

"'Twas a jest." But she couldn't look him in the eye.

"I see. I'd offer to send you to the modiste for a new frock, but I understand you've already been there. Take off the sling so I can get at your shoulder."

She did look at him then, and the effect was immediate but subtle. His gaze fell on her breasts, which were fashionably displayed.

"That's a Paris gown."

"Do you like it?"

The gentle shift of his focus told her he was considering several answers. Completely engaged, she was surprised when he said, "Yes, I do like it, especially in spring." He sat before her on a stool. "Do you like Paris in the spring?"

The sly creature. "I prefer Athens."

All interested companion, he smiled and reached for the bandage but stopped. The square of cotton was held in place over the wound by a narrow strip of cloth that passed between her breasts, around her side, and up her back.

"Would you rather dispose of that yourself?" he said, pointing at the spot where the strip disappeared into the bodice of her gown.

The catch in his voice gave him away. "You decide," she said.

With one hand, he worked at the bandage, untying the knot. When it was free, he said, "Take a deep breath."

She did, and her breasts came dangerously close to

spilling from the gown. He tugged on the end of the tie in front, and she felt the other end of the cloth crawl down her back and slide under her arm. Hand over hand, he pulled slowly on the strip, and the come-hither gesture, combined with the creeping of that cloth across her rib cage, sent shivers of longing to her toes. The dragging continued at an agonizing pace, leaving gooseflesh in its wake.

The tail end of the cloth met a snag. He glanced up, and his eyes were dreamy with distraction. "Exhale."

She'd probably stand on her head, had he instructed her to. Her breath rushed out, and time slowed, her senses fixed on the exciting journey of that strip of cloth crawling up her cleavage.

With a flick of his wrist, he pulled the fabric free and pitched it aside. Then he grasped her, his fingers snug beneath her breasts. As if she were a delicate vase on a shelf, he shifted her. "You'll need to sit upright."

Words of agreement lodged in her throat. He was too close, and she still tingled from his touch. But when he leaned back and began rolling up his sleeves, she acutely felt his loss. He had the most agile hands, she thought, as she watched him turn up the silk in cuff after cuff. His forearms were beautifully shaped with ropes of muscles and a light dusting of hair.

"You have an interesting glimmer in your eyes," he said.

Had her expression mirrored her thoughts? Probably. "I'm not the only one wearing a remarkable look."

"Your sister Sarah told me that you were always the first into the pond and the last to enjoy it." His voice dropped. "If you jump into a pond with me, I'll make certain you enjoy it."

There it was, seduction in its purest form. Only the boldest of rogues spoke so plainly. She said the only thing she could; she must stay on her side of the line. "Thank you, no. But I'm flattered all the same."

"You considered it?"

A reply was unnecessary; she knew he could read her thoughts.

"We'll see about that," he said absently.

Then he scooted the stool closer and examined the wound. "You tried to take the stitches out yourself."

The uneasy moment had passed. "Whatever you used for thread defies a Toledo blade."

"Even a very sharp one, 'twould seem. The thread is silk," he said in his doctorly voice. "Hence, the punctures are smaller and the scarring much less obvious than with cotton thread."

"I hope the smaller ones are less painful coming out."

"Somewhat."

He uncapped a vial of thick amber liquid, and the odor of spices drifted to her nose. With his index finger, he rubbed the oil over the stitches.

Agnes sighed with relief. "That feels wonderful. What's it made of?"

"The tongues and brains of toads."

She stiffened. "Never will I find humor in that!" But even as she said it, laughter captured her. She heard the snip of the clippers, but the sting had gone out of his treatment.

He must have again read her thoughts, for he raised his brows as if to say, "See, my dear?"

He'd distracted her from the pain. "Are all of the doctors in Glasgow so aware of the comfort of their patients?"

"The best ones are."

"Who is the very best?"

"I am." He smiled and patted her arm.

She believed him. Boasting was not his way, for he was comfortable with himself, and his medical procedures couldn't be faulted. Or could they? "I should think the very best of the doctors would have given me a vial of that magic potion days ago."

He rested his left hand on the side of her neck. In his right hand he held the tiny scissors. "Only a poor physician would prolong this treatment. Too much of the mixture is dangerous."

She couldn't be sure that he was truly talking about inept doctors or subtley warning her about the awareness that ebbed and flowed between them. When he lifted his brows in query, she knew.

Fither his fate. "You can challenge me until the Stewarts come home to rule, but I'll not cross over that line, Edward Napier. Not today."

The cool metal touched her skin. His attention wavered. "I haven't seen you wear the jade necklace. Was it damaged?"

Jewelry was the last thing on her mind. "Not the stones, but the thread is stained."

"Give it to me, and I'll restring it." He snipped a stitch.

Agnes winced, but the discomfort was minor. "You'd do that for me?"

"Of course." He clipped another.

"The thread will have to be strong."

"A double strength of this?" He held up a piece of the thread with which he'd stitched her.

"You could moor ships in a gale with that."

"'Tis the perfect material for stitching up beautiful skin."

Agnes sensed the movement of his hand before she

felt the smart of thread being jerked through skin. At the touch of the oil, she sucked in a breath.

"You're not paying attention," he chided. "Shall I restring your necklace?"

Thinking past the relief proved too difficult, and she nodded.

"What did Christopher's dancing teacher say to you?"

She wasn't fooled by the conversational detour, but she appreciated his effort. "The dancing master was most distressed over the beetles your son put in his lunch pail."

Edward grinned. "Tragic, that. He's newly wed and still enamored over every aspect of housewifery— even the packing of his lunch."

Above conversing with the steward, most noblemen didn't trouble themselves with servants, and certainly not the private details of their lives. "Will you punish Christopher?"

"Aye, I'll insist that he receive lessons in the 'heel and toe,' which he swears is a dance meant only for strutting cocks and silly females."

"He'll reconsider the advantages of dancing when he's older." She felt movement against her skin.

"Do you remember your first dancing teacher?"

"Aye, 'twas my father." Another prick. "Ouch!"

"Easy now." He dipped his finger into the oil again and massaged it into the wound. They were nose to nose. The sting vanished and the itch eased.

"I could purr," she said.

His hand stilled. Agnes held her breath. The mood changed, and she felt pulled toward him, yearned to arch her back and nuzzle his neck. The look in his eyes beckoned her to do just that, and it took a mighty effort on her part to quell the urge.

He grew pensive, and Agnes feared he'd cross the line again. But he didn't, and she relaxed when he resumed his ministrations.

"What else have you learned?" he asked.

She told him about the nanny.

"You verified the signature on her letter of reference? It wasn't Sir Throckmorton's?"

"Trimble says no, according to the banker, Robert Carrick, who is familiar with Throckmorton's signature. The reference indicated that Mrs. Borrowfield left Throckmorton's employ before coming to you. Did you never discuss the woman with him?"

"He's not the sort of fellow to know his servants," he said, an apology in his voice. "He lives in London and has yet to visit Glasgow."

According to Trimble, the Napiers had done business with Throckmorton's firm for over twenty years.

"Anything more?" Lord Edward asked.

"Trimble swears the forger was accomplished and possibly a Londoner, same as your Sir Throckmorton."

Lord Edward nodded and sat back on the stool. "Your Mr. Trimble found no trace of her? Not even at her church?"

Agnes hadn't thought of that avenue of investigation; most criminals did not bother with worship. "Which church?"

"Saint Vincent's in Trongate. We often left her off there on our way to services at Saint Stephen's."

"The cleric may know something more, and if we're fortunate, he'll lead us to her. Shall we stop in Trongate on our way to the mill, or will your pastor take offense?"

"I shouldn't think so." With a dip of his head, he indicated her shoulder. "You'll have a scar, but not a bad one."

Agnes strained to look, but couldn't see the wound. "I'll accept your word on it that my husband won't be repulsed."

His voice dropped. "If he does, have him visit me."

"What will you say to him?"

"That he should not complain, because I'm very practiced in medicinal stitchery."

"On whom did you practice?"

"Whom?" As if she were completely daft, he said, "On an orange."

Taken aback, she drilled him with a cold stare. "Are you suggesting that my skin is like that of an orange, and before you answer, I remind you that we are under truce."

He blew out his breath and studied the ceiling. "Shall I explain to you the scientific reasons why your skin is similar to the peel of an orange?"

Fighting the urge to huff in disdain, she said, "Only if I shan't be offended by it."

He rolled his eyes. "Pardon me, but I cannot predict *all* of your sensibilities. No mortal man could."

She did sound missish. "In that case, I do not think I wish to know how you mastered a needle and thread."

"Good," he said with finality. "I believe we can dispense with the sling when you are here, but for the next week or so, I'd like for you to wear it when you leave the house. You're healing remarkably well."

She almost said that it was because she had a remarkable doctor, but the tension between them had momentarily abated. Better she broached an innocent topic. "Auntie Loo said you helped the carpenters working in the tower. Does that mean you've forsaken your laboratory?"

He raked his sleeves down and fastened the shell

buttons at his wrists. "I've made some progress, but my theory is flawed, and I haven't the time now to find out where and why."

A scientist. He didn't look like any of the professors and inventors she'd ever seen. "Tell me more about your engine. What is it designed to do?"

"I'll show you tomorrow at the mill. Now tell me how you came to know this Mr. Trimble."

She pictured the efficient Haskit Trimble. "He was an officer in Her Majesty's Fourth of Foot. He received honors for his service during the battle for the American colonies. Something there changed him, but he would not say what or how. After the surrender, he cashiered himself out and ventured upon a career of information gathering."

"Never have I heard of such an occupation."

"All of his work is not intrigue such as we face. To hear him tell it, he's often mired in the mundane. A vicar with an eligible daughter might engage Trimble to verify the reputation of an interested suitor. That, I believe, is the crux of his work."

"When next I engage a nanny, I'll be sure to visit Trimble first." He stood and offered a hand. "Shall we see if my children have perfected kite flying?"

"Oh, aye. Let's do." Agnes preceded him through the door. As they walked, she said, "Does Christopher have a fencing master?"

"Yes, I'm teaching him myself."

That caught her attention. "I know something about the sport. Perhaps we could practice."

"Not until you are completely well. I will not be accused of taking unfair advantage of you."

She almost argued that she could better wield a foil using her left hand but decided against it. Teasing him was more fun. "You've done very well at taking unfair advantage of me, if my memory serves."

"Oh? Refresh my recollection."

"Absolutely not, and there's no reason to broach the subject again."

"But I've only begun, and I like having the advantage over you."

7

THAT NIGHT, AFTER A NEAR FEAST OF FRESH MUTTON shank spitted over the hearth, crusty scones, and potatoes roasted in ashes, Edward stretched as he led Agnes to the chessboard. He'd moved the gaming table into the tower earlier in the day. Everyone had dressed in medieval attire, and coupled with the close quarters of the common room, the evening had taken on a friendly intimacy. Thank the saints, Agnes hadn't worn that fetching green gown tonight, for certain defeat at any game awaited Edward if he were subjected to another lengthy display of her womanly charms.

Auntie Loo sat with Christopher and Hannah near the hearth, teaching them to weave cricket baskets. The staff had retired. Guards patrolled the estate.

After defeating Agnes twice at chess, Edward refilled their mugs with cider and relaxed on the bench. He thought his wins had been too easy;

he'd had the impression that she'd lost to him apurpose.

The cloying odor of roses filled the circular room, fouling the exotic fragrance of her hair and reminding Edward that a certain viscount had, according to his messenger, picked the bouquet of flowers from his garden himself for Lady Agnes.

"You've had gifts and well wishes from every eligible nobleman from here to Inverness in the north, Dumfries in the south, and Perwickshire in the east. No suitors in the west?"

A teasing light twinkled in her eyes. "Have the fishes begun to court?"

He had meant the Western Isles, but she knew that. Drawing her out posed a challenge Edward relished. "'Twill take some maneuvering on my part to keep the swains from rioting outside Napier House."

"I'm sure it's Lottie's doing. I was abroad for almost a year the last time." Agnes swept off the garland of heather and rubbed her temples. "She must have located a new crop of eligibles—a litter of fresh pups, as Mary says. Lottie will have told them the particulars about my dowries."

"You have more than one?"

"Aye, the duchess of Enderley endowed me with lands in France."

She looked damsel-like in the simple clothing of medieval times, the fitted surcoat, her hair hanging to her hips, and a long, golden cord tied around her waist. But the mischief she'd worked on him with that green gown begged for retribution.

He propped an elbow on the table and rested his chin in his palm. "Sounds as if you'll be popular."

"I've acknowledged their gifts and politely discouraged their pursuit."

He couldn't recall the moment earlier today, but at

some point during the removal of those stitches, he'd ceased thinking of her as his patient. It was just as well, considering both the ease with which she lifted the mug and the decidedly intimate turn his thoughts had taken. "If your suitors persist, I'll be tempted to ask his grace of Ross for advice."

"Do and he will descend on Glasgow to convey his advice personally."

Edward had only wanted to tease her. The last complication he needed now was a visit from the most reformed rogue in the Highlands.

Agnes eased her legs over the bench. "I yield, my lord. You've tromped me roundly."

Auntie Loo and Christopher still sat near the hearth. Slumping in the master's chair and clutching her new whistle, Hannah valiantly fought sleep.

Edward began repositioning the pieces. "You're a sporting loser."

Bracing her arm on the table, she stood. "I learned that necessity early in life."

Her golden hair fell around her in a gilded curtain, and the cord draping her hips dangled at an alluring spot. Edward wasn't ready to end the evening; too many questions about her remained unanswered. "Did your father teach you?"

"'Twas my sister Sarah. She has lost only once in her life."

He wanted to ask what scent she'd worn tonight. Instead, he indicated the chessmen. "I think you lost apurpose to me."

Over her shoulder, she said, "Tell him, Auntie Loo. I'm dreadful at board games."

The Oriental woman rose and put away her unfinished basket. She wore a sunny yellow overdress, and her thick black hair was plaited in a single braid that hung to her knees. "Lady Lottie proclaims her older sister an embarrassment in the parlor."

"Didn't I say so?" Agnes threaded the garland over her wrist and twirled it. "I'm also a sour note in the music room."

Edward noticed that she used her right wrist with no small amount of dexterity. Her swift recovery baffled him. "Your arm doesn't hurt?"

Quietly, she said, "Not enough to require doctoring again."

It was a sly reference to the intimate moments between them earlier in the day. "I heard no complaints from you at the time. Rather you confessed the need to purr."

"I'm not purring now. I've recovered from that ailment, too." Before he could comment, she said, "Good night, Auntie. I'll take the children up to bed."

The Oriental woman moved toward the stairs.

Hannah straightened in the chair. "No."

Edward braced himself for the battle to come. Hannah should have been asleep an hour ago, but the meal had been slow to cook and the cook slower to serve. A formal tour of the tower had taken more time.

In complete disobedience, his daughter banged her heels on the chair and shook her head. Christopher, bless him, put away his unfinished basket and headed up the new wooden stairs. He hadn't even balked at sharing the upper floor with his sister.

"May I help Hannah with her decision, my lord?" Agnes said.

He felt a prick of conscience but ignored it. Hannah knew few adults, and nannies had dried too many of her tears. Attention from Agnes MacKenzie could only help the lass.

"Hannah." He stared at his daughter until her eyes met his. "Do you promise to behave?"

Pouting like the last of the forlorn, she gripped the chair arms and stared at her toes. Lady Agnes knelt before her and whispered something to the girl. Even from across the room, he could smell that enticing fragrance.

"Truly?" Hannah's eyes grew large, and a smile blossomed on her face.

The change was pure magic to Edward.

Patting the girl's leg, Agnes rose and returned to the chessboard. "Good night, my lord."

"What did you tell her?" Edward asked.

Smiling, she toyed with the rope at her waist. "That you would buy her a pony."

"A pony!" piped Hannah, bucking in the chair.

He almost choked on the wine. The great pony debate had been raging since the day Hannah learned to say the word. "You didn't promise her that?" he whispered harshly. "She cannot even play hopping stones without losing her balance."

"Oh, ye of little faith," Agnes chided. "There are conditions. She must continue to go to bed without a fret, or she cannot select the pony herself. I explained that we couldn't ask the stableman to bring a herd of animals here."

If she couldn't pick it out, the pony wouldn't get bought. "That's devious."

"Remember, there were four of us, each trying to outdo the others. Be it making mischief or hugging Papa good night, we all wanted to be first."

The amber light from the old lamps bathed her in a golden glow. His fingers tingled with the need to explore the texture of her hair, to bury his face in it and languish in that heavenly smell. But there was more to discover about this Highland lass than the extent of her feelings for him. "Where were you in the MacKenzie pack?"

She tried for modesty and succeeded in radiance. "At the vanguard."

The air between them grew heavy with apprehension, and he felt as if she were on the verge of leaning toward him. But she had not moved.

Hoping to change that, he said, "The same way you plunge into a pond?"

She had a clever sally for him, he knew; the excitement of it glittered in her eyes. An instant later the look was gone. With the garland draping her wrist, she walked her fingers across the chessboard. "Most often, Papa was a step ahead of us."

He wanted to see that expression again and hear what she'd truly wanted to say. "At what age were you when you chose your first pony?"

She glanced at Hannah. "Five, but I earned the money to buy it for myself. Good night—"

"How?"

She hesitated but didn't look at him. "By standing guard over the stable lantern."

What was her hurry? "Your father let you sleep in the stable?"

"Nay, I watched the lamp for two hours every afternoon. Twasn't even aflame at the time, but I was too short to see that high."

An excellent way to teach a child discipline and responsibility and give a parent a reprieve. Edward couldn't imagine life in the MacKenzie family; Hannah and Christopher were challenge enough for him. "The more I know about your father, the more I like him."

"Should you truly wish to see him at his best, ask him how Mary fares. Good night again, my lord."

Edward knew finality when he heard it. "I'll bank

the fire." He put his tankard on the table, extinguished the lamp, and went to the hearth.

She glided away, her slippers swish-swishing on the new stairs. Overhead the old chandelier cast a wavering circle of shadows on the stone ceiling. Earlier, while awaiting the meal, Edward had allowed Christopher and Hannah to light one taper each before the wheel was again hoisted into the air. The candles were spent. The tower quiet.

The kite, fashioned from the pages of yesterday's *Glasgow Courant,* rested on the cabinet below one of the four arrow slits in the outer wall of the tower. Sharpened axes and a broadsword were mounted high on the wall, out of the reach of the children, same as the new crossbows perched above the low door.

His children were safe in this old fortress. The magistrate offered small hope of locating the bowman, but with the help of his beguiling houseguest and her man Trimble, Edward would find the assassin.

Edward gave the coals a final tamp, replaced the fire iron, then moved to the door. Even as he grasped the handle, he changed his mind. Work waited in his laboratory, but he hadn't the attention for it tonight. He knew he couldn't sleep; so he sat in the chair that Hannah had vacated. Silence descended, save the faint ticking of a clock from the chamber upstairs. Seated comfortably outside the pool of firelight, Edward let his thoughts wander.

Tomorrow they'd visit Saint Vincent's Church and hopefully glean the whereabouts of the mysterious Mrs. Borrowfield. After a visit to the mill, Edward and Agnes would take a late supper with William Arkwright, the mayor of Glasgow. Edward smiled, thinking of the lively conversation he'd shared with Agnes earlier in the day. As her host and a man of lesser rank than her father, he was obligated to escort her. Convention aside, he'd make certain that her hand rested on his arm when they were called into dinner.

A shape passed before the hearth. Edward froze. He recognized the slender figure wearing breeches, her hair hastily gathered at the nape of her neck, a weapon in her hand. In her passage down the stairs she hadn't made a sound. During an earlier climb to visit the upper levels, the new wood had creaked and groaned beneath Edward's weight.

How could anyone be so light on their feet?

She stopped, stepped back, and faced him. "I thought you had retired, my lord."

He sat in the shadows. She stood between him and the light. She couldn't have seen him, and he'd made no sound, but she'd known he was here.

Necessity played no part in her excursion; the upstairs garderobe functioned efficiently, there was food aplenty in the larder behind him. A barrel of water stood near the door. She certainly didn't need a sword.

"Where are you going?"

She moved toward him. Light glinted on steel as she tried to hide the weapon behind her. "The guard is absent from his post atop the new wing."

Edward went to the nearest arrow slit and looked across the courtyard. The sentry was drinking from the fountain. The arrow slits in the walls of the chamber above faced east, offering a view of the river Clyde. She couldn't see the courtyard from her vantage point.

Edward wanted to rail at her, but he'd done so before with disastrous results. But when he thought about the weapon she carried, gentle words failed him. "So you were going in search of the guard? And if you say you intended to walk about anyway, because you are stiff from sitting at the gaming table, I will take great umbrage at it."

"Shush! You'll wake the household. Do you wish to accompany me?"

In two strides he stood beside her. "What if the assassin did get past the guards and you had come upon him? Do you think your foreign fighting skills would have prevailed?"

"I thought to hold him off until help arrived, which I would be screaming for."

The attempt at humor was too weak. She was hiding something. "That blade is useless against a crossbow, Agnes."

"I also have a dagger, *my lord,* and my aim is excellent."

She wouldn't distract him with false formality. "The guard stands his post."

As quickly as it had come, the fight left her. "Humor me, Lord Edward?"

Something in her tone made him agree. Motioning toward the door, he followed her into the hall and closed the door behind him. Absolute darkness and silence surrounded them. Even without light, he could find his way in Napier House. To the left lay the entrance of the passage to his laboratory. Straight ahead, with a brief veer to the right, was the corridor to the new wing.

He touched her shoulder. "I'll lead the way."

She slipped her hand under his and drew his arm down. "How did you find me in this pitch?"

Had twenty proper excuses come to mind, he couldn't have voiced one. "'Tis the fragrance in your hair."

"Truly?" She sniffed. "I cannot smell it over those cloying roses."

What made him think and say such bold things to

her? He didn't know. Her hand felt perfect nestled in his. He gave a little squeeze, which she returned. It was then he realized that he held her right hand, and her grip proved that she was past being on the mend.

The tinny sound of a bell pierced the silence.

"That's the alarm in your study!" she said.

Edward moved and almost sent her careening into one of the suits of armor. Steadying her, he put her behind him and ran down the hall. She kept pace, and when they reached the juncture in the formal parlor, she darted left and tried to move ahead. Now in a race, they sped through the corridor. Edward glanced out the glass doors leading to the courtyard. He was moving too fast to see if the windows in his study were open. Moments ago in the tower, he'd looked through an arrow slit and spied the guard at the fountain. Nothing had seemed amiss in the new wing.

Something was amiss now.

They hurried past the music room and the library. Slowing enough to clutch the door handle, Edward burst into the room, Agnes fast on his heels. As if they'd made a plan of action, Edward moved to the left and dropped down; she moved to the right.

The newly mullioned windows stood open, the draperies gently billowing into the room. A patch of wavering moonlight spilled onto the floor.

His chest heaving, Edward strained to see into the shadowy corners of the room.

"He's gone," she said on a ragged breath.

"You cannot know that."

Shouts came from the roof. She sprang to her feet. Edward hurried to the window and called to the guard, "Is anyone about?"

The sentry moved to the edge of the roof and scanned the courtyard.

"Stand away from the window, Edward," Lady Agnes said. "You're an easy target."

Again Edward dropped down. He hadn't thought to bring a weapon but the woman behind him had.

Flint struck steel. Turning he saw her lifting a lighted taper. She stood before the firescreen. She wasn't in the least winded, and her hand was incredibly steady on the candlestick.

"Sweet Saint Ninian," she murmured.

When Edward realized what she was looking at, he understood why she'd cursed. Rolled inside the small MacKenzie plaid was a dove, another of the wicked quarrels skewering the bird to the Napier shield.

"There!" came a shout from outside. "He goes by the stables!"

Outrage boiled inside Edward. "Give me that sword, and find a way back to the tower," he said.

"Nay." Agnes could feel his anger, and it fed the fire that smoldered inside her.

"The sword!" In stance and determination he radiated fury.

The weapon grew heavy in her hand. His eyes widened, and she could feel him willing her to yield.

She tossed him the blade. "Find him!"

In a swipe of his hand, he snatched the sword from the air. "Stay out of harm's way, Agnes MacKenzie."

Mired in feelings she could not explain, she drew the dagger from her boot. "I'll be with the children." More needed to be said, but there was so little time. "If you get yourself killed, Edward Napier, I will take great umbrage at it."

With a quick nod, he gathered up his long tunic and bounded into the courtyard.

A drum of apprehension beat in her breast. "Fortune and God go with you," she whispered.

The candle flame wavered, then winked out. Smoke

from the smoldering wick worried her nose. She pinched the tiny ember and dropped the candlestick. Blinking back fear, she hurried from the room and moved down the dark corridor. Almost on her tiptoes, she ran, her passage a silent movement of the night air. The slender steel felt warm and deadly in her hand. The children were only moments away, and Auntie Loo was between them and the only entrance to the tower. If the assassin had so much as touched a hair on their heads, Agnes would give him a death that would make a Shansi warrior beg for mercy.

Come out, she silently begged. Show your blackened soul so I can send it to hell.

Blinded by the thought, she raced around a turn, the first in the square horseshoe shape of the corridor. As an image of the route formed in her mind, she ignored the possibility that the bowman could be behind her.

The parlor lay ahead, and to the right, the old wing. She slowed, then stopped to peer into the moonlit room. No evil presence lurked here. The dread she'd felt earlier, at the end of the last chess game, was gone. But at what cost to the occupants of this house? Did the earl of Cathcart now lie dying in the courtyard?

The children.

She moved into the old wing, picking her way through a legion of armor. At last she felt the curvature of the tower wall. Her fingers touched the handle. Gripping it, she flung open the door.

An eerie sound alerted her. "Auntie!" she cried and crumpled to the floor. In a whoosh, movement rent the air above her. When death did not come, Agnes looked behind the door. There stood her friend, an arm's length away, her face pure white, her hands gripping a Pe-tung backsword, its blade sharper than a razor.

Auntie Loo closed her eyes and let the priceless weapon fall. White copper clattered to the stone floor.

Agnes went weak with relief. Had she not recognized the sound and ducked, her head would be rolling across the floor. A chill swept through her, and dampness flooded her brow.

Auntie Loo murmured, "Oh, Father of Time, I heard no warning."

The blame lay squarely with Agnes. She'd been distracted by thoughts of Edward Napier. Concern for the children had fallen behind her feelings for him. Even her awareness of Auntie Loo had fled.

Her attraction to a man had caused her to fail a second time. She fought the urge to cry. "I gave you no signal, Loo."

As if she had not murmured the prayer, Auntie Loo calmly picked up the ancient weapon. "Death's door is closed to you, Golden One."

Still reeling, Agnes shook her head to drive out the ringing of fear. "Lay the cause to fate, if you will. I say 'twas put in motion by my own foolishness." She reached for the exquisite scabbard and passed it to her friend. "The children?"

"Sleeping through it all." With hands that could as easily crack bones as set them, Auntie Loo sheathed the weapon. "What happened?"

Agnes wanted to embrace her friend, but a display of affection would embarrass Auntie Loo. So Agnes bolted the door, poured herself a glass of brandy, and told Auntie what had occurred.

"This assassin is patient."

Agnes agreed. "Lord Edward's study was undisturbed, except for the dove, which was hastily placed."

"You came upon him too fast. He heard the ringing of the alarm bell and left hurriedly."

Praise the saints, she and Edward had moved quickly. "What else does the assassin want?"

Agnes was still pondering the question sometime later when Edward knocked on the door. Auntie Loo had retired. Agnes was alone. She capped the ink pot and threw the bolt.

His shoulders were drawn with fatigue, and her short sword dangled from his hand, but his gaze was sharp and apprehensive. "My children."

She grasped his arm and drew him inside. "Safe and asleep."

"I want to see them." Pulling her along, he moved to the stairs. Manners appropriately forgotten, he took the steps two at a time. Agnes had to work to keep up with him.

At the first landing, the glow of a lantern illuminated the chamber she shared with Auntie, who lay on her bed facing away from them. The new wooden steps contrasted sharply to the ancient stone walls. Without pausing, he climbed the second staircase. Agnes grasped the lantern and followed him.

He stopped beside the sleeping Christopher. With a shaking hand, he reached out and touched the boy's head.

Mumbling, Christopher opened his eyes long enough to say, "Night, Papa."

Sighing loudly, Edward walked around the partition. Close on his heels, Agnes watched him gaze at his slumbering daughter. Tears sparkled in his eyes. Seeing his tender expression, she thought of her own father. Lachlan MacKenzie had worn a similar look on the night dear Virginia had been born.

Agnes had seen that expression many times since and knew the sentiment behind it. Without conscious thought, she moved closer and rubbed his back. Lifting his arm, he drew her to his side and rested his cheek against her head. Heat poured from his body, purging the fear, and his chest heaved with every breath.

"My sweet, innocent Button," he whispered.

Hannah stirred. Edward stilled. Agnes eased the lantern behind her and moved to leave. He followed. She waited at the landing while he took the light and examined the other exit to the tower—the bolted hatch in the ceiling that led to the battlement. A new hand ladder rested on the floor a safe distance away. If the assassin managed to climb the tower and to pry open the door, he'd face a drop of twenty feet to the stone floor. The small door in the common room downstairs offered the only entry to the tower.

The children were safe.

Agnes preceded him down the steps. In the common room she poured him a heavy measure of brandy. "Will you trade?" she asked, offering him a drink and indicating the short sword in his hand.

He yielded the weapon, accepted the tankard, and took a mighty swallow. The fabric of his long tunic hosted an array of twigs and stains.

"You've ruined your new clothing."

"Man was not made to run in a dress." With a scratched hand, he kneaded his neck and rolled his head.

Agnes felt an outpouring of affection for him. She pointed to a nearby bench. "Sit and let me help."

He ripped off the tunic. Beneath it he wore only linen trews. Firelight glistened on his bare chest and arms, and she marveled at the true strength of him. He was a scientist and scholar, not a warrior shedding the garments of a civilized man. But the proof was there, displayed vividly before her. His hips were narrow, his belly nicely rippled.

"Agnes? What's amiss? Have you opened that wound?"

Again she'd fallen prey to softer feelings. The earlier lapse had almost cost her her life. No more, she promised herself. "Nay, my lord. I haven't a scratch or a bruise."

"My lord?" He stared at her blankly. "We're beyond formalities, Agnes."

"Then I wish to go back to them." She tapped the bench with the tip of her sword. "Sit and argue the issue no more."

"As you wish." He dropped to the bench. "But you cannot always carry a sword."

She put the weapon beside him on the bench and began kneading his shoulders and neck. At his first groan of relief, she worked harder, releasing the tension, relieving the strain.

"You did not find him?" she asked.

"Not a trace, above that bitter message. But why would a Scot choose a dove?"

"He's no Scot. He's a mercenary and loyal only to his own causes."

"Then why would he defile your plaid with the blood of a dove?"

"Is that a blight in the Lowlands?"

Tried patience softened his features. "Nay. But surely it is to those of you above the line?"

He spoke of the Highland Line, an ambiguous boundary from near Aberdeen in the northeast to the lands near Loch Lomond in the southwest. Glaswegians had seen their share of war, but the city lay south of the infamous demarcation.

"You speak of us as if we are another nation, separate and apart from you. Have you never been to Tain?"

"Nay."

"'Tis as fertile and free a place as God ever made. We haven't your shipbuilding or tobacco and textiles, but our air is not fouled with coal dust, and fish thrive in our harbor."

"What has the beauty of the land to do with Scottish differences?"

"You think we are savages, occupied only in petty clan wars. You disparage us."

"'Tis safe to say, Agnes, that you are anything but a savage."

She huffed in disdain. "How can both my father and Michael Elliot agree that you will be the man to lead us into the next century, Edward Napier?"

He turned his attention to the weave of his trews.

"'Tis misbegotten praise. Machines will lead us there, not I."

The acclaim discomfited him. In a different way, Agnes, too, was troubled. In the span of the evening he'd progressed from the charming host to the valiant defender to the loving father. Now he revealed a gentle heart, and it frightened her to her soul. Tonight she had faced accidental death at the hands of a friend, and she couldn't shake the terrifying memory. But she could not seek comfort in the arms of Edward Napier; thoughts of him had driven her to blunder.

For lack of a better excuse to retreat, she walked to the basin and washed her hands. "Was anyone hurt?"

"Nay, except your father's messenger; he skinned a knee."

She strove for lightness. "Impossible. Haven't you heard? The skin of a Highlander is tougher than a ship's keel."

His gaze snapped to hers, and he studied her for so long a time, she grew uneasy.

Quietly, he said, "You've ducked into your shell again, and I've driven you to it."

Desperation urged her on. "You talk nonsense."

A sly smile banished the last of his worry over the evening past. He snatched up his tunic. "We will stay within the walls of this house until he is found," he said.

She fought the urge to follow him. "As prisoners? Then you aid him, for he wants no witnesses to his deadly mission."

Unconvinced, Lord Edward waved her off. "He did not fear a crowd in Edinburgh."

Fact defeated that theory. "He met with failure there," Agnes said. "We've succeeded tonight, Edward. Henceforth he must depend on stealth, a weakness to him. We have him at the disadvantage. I say we flush him out."

Bracing the flat of his palm against the wall, he propped the other hand on his hip. "I say you are now in danger."

The old excitement was slow in coming, but she knew better than to explore her feelings now. In less than three days her father would know that the assassin had included the MacKenzies by defaming their plaid. "I've written to my father. He must know."

"You can tell him yourself. I'm sending you home to him."

She retreated. "I will not go. You cannot force me."

Her words hung like a specter between them. He sighed loudly and sat on the bench. Little light fell on his features, but she needed no illumination to see his resolve.

Desperate to change his mind, she addressed his weakness. "You need me here with the children."

"I will not have the duke of Ross wreaking havoc in Glasgow o'er an insult to his Highland pride."

He'd gotten it wrong. "Listen well, Edward Napier. If Lachlan MacKenzie comes here, he will not come for his own sake." Righteous anger kindled to life inside her, tempering soft thoughts about a man she could not have. "Lest you think you are the only father who cares for a child, Lachlan MacKenzie will prove you wrong."

In the blink of an eye, his demeanor changed. "I take it back, then. His devotion to his children is well known."

"Papa will not leave London. Mary needs him more. He knows I am capable of dealing with the assassin."

Edward tipped his head toward the letter she'd left on the desk. "Then you must have colored up the truth."

"Nay. Nothing comes here that we cannot defeat. Tonight he was fortunate. The glazier's paste had not yet set; the assassin easily lifted out the windows in your study. Tomorrow you will remedy that."

Summoning the glazier again was a simple matter; Edward intended to see to it first thing in the morning. His other problems would not be so easily resolved. Foremost in his mind were his strong feelings for Agnes MacKenzie and the dilemma they posed.

He thought of Elise, the wife he'd cherished and lost. He did not worry about loving Agnes as much; he worried over loving her more.

8

Standing in the courtyard, Edward examined the new mortar around the windows in his study. The assassin had been careful and silent; not a single pane of glass bore the slightest crack, and the pebbles in the walkway appeared smoothly raked. The man had crouched here, between the low boxwoods and the building.

Turning, Edward studied the distance to the foun tain where the sentry had come to take a drink last night. He judged it twenty-five feet of unobscured view in a direct line to the target. The bowman could have made that shot on the run. In the crowded church in Edinburgh he'd had only one chance and a narrow line of vision. His aim had been true.

Why hadn't he killed the guard last night?

When Agnes had come downstairs, she'd said the sentry was not atop the new wing. A moment later, Edward had spied the man at his post. A moment after that, the bell had sounded. They'd run through the corridors like deer before a pack of hungry wolves.

The bell had saved their lives. The guard had been spared. The incongruity of both confounded Edward. Knowing he could not leave the inconsistency alone, he went in search of his beguiling houseguest. He didn't have to go far; he found her alone in the music room.

She faced the windows. He stopped in the open doorway and, unnoticed, observed her. Barefoot and dressed in loose-legged breeches and a jacket of coarsely spun and tightly woven cotton, she stood in the center of the spacious room. A strip of undyed flax, embroidered with black diamond shapes, belted her waist. A bright red ribbon secured her golden hair at the nape of her neck. Sweet-smelling smoke streamed from a brass pomander sitting on the floor nearby.

Pressing her palms to her thighs, she lowered her head and bowed. Her left arm was stick straight, but her right elbow was cocked, a lingering effect of her injury. Soundlessly, she dropped to her knees and thrust her hands, palms up, into the smoke. As if anointing herself, she scooped up handfuls of the scented air and smoothed it over her head and shoulders. He'd know that fragrance anywhere, but he'd mistakenly thought it came from soap.

That part of her ritual done, she rose on tiptoe and began a series of movements that resembled a dance with a spirit. As graceful as a bird in flight, she stretched and swayed, always with her right arm bent, like a wounded wing. Her balance never wavered until she stood on one foot, folded herself over, and touched her nose to her ankle. That's when she saw him.

Upside down, she teetered briefly before righting herself. Staring blankly, expectantly, she waited.

Feeling the need to explain himself, Edward tapped the lintel. "The door was open."

The glow of exertion flushed her cheeks, and she tugged at the knot securing the unusual belt. "How long have you been watching me?"

"For a short time," he lied. "That's a remarkable dance."

"I was not dancing."

"No? Then what were you doing."

"Seeking harmony with myself."

"Have you found it, then?"

With the end of the stiff belt, she blotted her forehead. "Nay. I am a seeker still."

"Where did you learn this art?"

His choice of words pleased her, for she moved toward him, and her gaze was direct and open. "In China, from a relative of Auntie Loo's."

"She also knows foreign fighting skills?"

"They are not foreign to her."

Abashed, Edward chuckled at himself. "I stand corrected."

"Auntie's knowledge is a hundred times greater than mine."

"Gentle Auntie Loo is skilled with a knife and sword? You're having me on."

She swallowed nervously and stared at her hands. "Nay, 'tis true. She is highly skilled with a sword."

"Then I cannot come upon her unawares?"

"It has been done, but I do not recommend it."

Something about the subject affected her strongly, but he doubted she'd share the details with him. "Auntie Loo also learned them from the relative you spoke of?"

"Aye. From her mother's father, Chang Ling. He is the greatest living master of weaponless fighting."

"Forgive my lack of knowledge, but it did not seem to me that you were aggressive in your movements."

"Those were not, but others are. Most were perfected centuries ago by holy men."

"Will you show me?"

"When I know you better."

A state they were rapidly approaching, Edward hoped. "I await that day, my lady."

She again tugged on that belt, as if it were vital to have the knot in the right place. "Were you looking for me?"

Until now he'd forgotten the reason for seeking her out. "Aye. Something about the bowman is troubling me." He told her his theory about the assassin and the guard being in the courtyard at the same time.

Her interest engaged, she stared at his chin and considered what he'd said. At length, she nodded. "Yes. The timing cannot have been happenstance. The assassin waited until the guard had turned his back to climb down from his post to get a drink at the fountain."

"So . . . why did the bowman spare the guard?"

Her gaze sharpened. "A valid detail, Edward. As we know them, his actions make no sense. He left an armed man at his unguarded back."

Two possibilities came to mind, but Edward thought them weak.

"What are you thinking?" she said.

"'Tis improbable."

"Perhaps. Perhaps not, but if you keep it to yourself . . ."

Looking past her, Edward saw a wayward gull fly into the courtyard. Pigeons flocked to protect their domain, and with a piercing cry, the seabird moved on. Protecting one's home had taken on new meaning to Edward.

"You were saying . . . ?" she prompted.

"Either he carried only one quarrel, or he knew he hadn't the time to cock the weapon again. Or he does not work alone."

With a slight shake of her head, she disagreed. "He has no accomplice. What if he purchased the guard's loyalty?"

"Absolutely not. The man is Hazel's nephew."

"That's unfortunate for us. I believe our man is the worst kind of foe . . . an honorable assassin."

"A decent mercenary? What logic is that?"

"Do not scoff at the theory," she said. "I grant you, it sounds contradictory, but there is considerable truth to it. He's been paid, and paid well, to kill you. A substantial part of his worth lies in his anonymity."

"But why try to kill me in Edinburgh and then ransack my papers here?"

"I do not think he is foremost a thief. He traffics in murder. It is his livelihood, his commerce. Should his face become known, his value lessens."

"Then whatever item he seeks is second in importance to—" Edward couldn't voice the possibility.

Her hand touched his. "What he seeks will fall short of our ability to prevail against him. He will not succeed. Trimble is very resourceful. We should hear from him soon. Worry not."

The gentle comfort wasn't enough for Edward. He twisted his wrist until their palms met and their fingers entwined.

She gave him a tight, sweet smile. "Have you lost faith in me so soon, my lord?" Tugging, she tried to withdraw her hand.

He was stronger than she and more determined to have his way. "Nay, Agnes. I've lost patience with formalities between us. I should like for you to call me Edward."

Regret shone in her eyes and in the sad pursing of her lips. "I should like for you to let go of my hand."

"Coward."

She shrugged, but the gesture lacked conviction. "Perhaps I do not want your attentions."

"And I'm a merchant without a rag of business or a penny of reward."

Her gaze was level, her tone sincere. "A poor jest, my lord. All of Scotland and beyond know your worth to mankind."

Her flattery soothed, but Edward wanted more from her. "Has it crossed your mind that one or both of us could have died last night?"

"Aye." She sighed, as forlorn as Hannah at bedtime. "One of us came very close to death last night."

In the course of the discussion, they had traded roles. Now it was Edward's turn to bolster her confidence. Her statement about one of them almost dying surely applied to him, for she'd returned to the tower and stayed there, safe with his children and Auntie Loo.

"I feel very much alive today, Agnes, and you are the reason."

The tether of passion grew taut between them, and with slight effort, he pulled her against his chest. Her lashes were long and golden brown, a perfect contrast to the darker hue of her eyes. But within their depths he saw a battle raging, an all-out war between denial and desire.

She did not pull away, and with a look, he dared her to.

Quietly, she said, "'Tis natural to feel confident after an escape with death."

Entranced and determined to see passion prevail,

he leaned down until they were nose to nose. "If this is confidence, the world has gone flat." Licking his lips, he added, "I feel at harmony." Then he touched his mouth to hers.

She resisted valiantly until he eased his tongue between her lips and traced the sweet slickness there. Breathing faster, she opened for him, and when he deepened the kiss, her body stiffened with a last attempt to refuse him. But his need for her was greater than her will to resist him, and one blessed moment later, she gave him her slight weight and sent her hands on a mission of their own.

"More," he whispered.

In a featherlight stroke, she dragged her palms up his arms, only to pause to caress his neck and thread her fingers through his hair; then she splayed her hands and began a slow journey down his chest. Even with a barrier of clothing in the way, her touch started his skin to tingling. Other regions of his body reacted more urgently to her tender touch. A fire raged in his loins, and to cool the heat, he cupped her shapely bottom and undulated against her.

"More, still," he encouraged her.

Her purring surrender harmonized with his growl of victory. She did want him; her body sang to him in a tone only he could hear. Aching to get closer, he lifted her and wound her legs around his hips. At the first brush of their bodies, his knees grew weak and his head spun with lust.

He must find a place, carry her there, strip off her clothing and his, and drive their demons away. But he couldn't get enough of kissing and exploring her. He cupped a breast, and the pillowy softness swelled in his palm, the sensitive nipple pebbling at his touch. Wild cravings surged inside him, and she felt those yearnings, too, for she darted her tongue into his mouth and began a seduction that he was tempted to finish here and now.

Breaking the kiss, he peered into her passion-flushed face and thought he might drown in the depths of her need.

Suddenly alert, she tipped her head. "Someone comes."

"Who?"

"Mrs. Johnson."

Edward hadn't expected an answer; he'd asked the question impulsively. He tried to hear the sound of approaching footfalls; only hunger buzzed in his ears.

"Take your hand off my breast and let me go." Her ragged breathing belied the soft command.

To prove she wanted him still, he lightly rolled her nipple between his thumb and forefinger. Her teeth closed over her bottom lip, and her head lolled to her shoulder.

He heard sounds in the hall. Cursing to himself, he moved his hand to her throat. A pretty groan of complaint vibrated against his fingers, and he entertained the idea of bolting the door and tasting Agnes MacKenzie's every delight.

But she had mastered herself. As agile as a yearling doe, she eased her legs to the floor, righted her clothing, and gave the belt a hard tug. "Wretch."

"You are not angry at me. You want me, and your belly aches with it." He reached to touch her there.

"Nay." She darted back, glanced past him, and smiled. "Mrs. Johnson. Good morning to you."

Hazel entered the room, a small covered basket in her hands. "'Tis the surprise you asked for, my lord. It took a little longer than I thought."

Thank the saints, she hadn't come upon them sooner. Taking the basket, he held it above Agnes's head. "Can you guess what it is?"

She closed her eyes and inhaled deeply. "Oatcakes?"

Edward gave her high marks, for she'd recovered her composure quicker than he expected. Certainly quicker than he had.

"You win the prize." He lowered his arm.

She peeked under the cloth. "Hoots! The farrier and his wife have arrived from Whitburn. You remembered."

Her joy was contagious, and Edward couldn't keep himself from smiling. The tightness in his groin eased to a manageable ache. "Yes. He came highly recommended, as did his wife."

"I'm flattered, my—" She hesitated and reached into the basket. "Thank you, my lord."

Damn her for a strong-willed wench, and pity him for wanting her so.

Hazel gave a diplomatic cough. "I'll be off to the market forbye, my lord." She was dressed for the outing, wearing her best shoes, her frilly bonnet, and the new umbrella hooked over her arm. "The farrier's wife offered to watch the children this morning. She wasn't blessed with wee ones of her own."

Lady Agnes bent to retrieve her pomander from the floor. "I'll watch them." In as smooth a retreat as he'd ever seen, she took the basket and eased around him. "I'm certain you have other things to do."

"Aye," he grumbled, watching her leave. "'Tis a passion of mine, finishing every task I begin."

"Task?" She stopped and turned. He knew he'd misspoken.

Innocence wreathed her exquisite features. "Task," she repeated. "Sounds loathsome. I much prefer—"

"My choice of words was poor."

Unmoved, she went on as if he hadn't interrupted her. "I much prefer to admit when I've overreached myself and try my fortunes elsewhere. Taskmasters can be so tiresome."

The cryptic words inflamed him. Hazel was absorbed in Lady Agnes's unusual attire. With more force than was necessary and less than he wanted, Edward said, "Be dressed and ready to leave for the mill at one o'clock."

She waved with her fingertips. "I wouldn't dream of keeping you waiting." Louder, she said, "Thank you again, Mrs. Johnson."

Hazel chuckled. "Didn't take her ladyship long to know that you put a high price on punctuality. The MacKenzies are also known for their love of a good jest. Fine family, the MacKenzies of Ross."

His cook had fallen victim to the charming Agnes MacKenzie, a simple task and a bleaker thought.

"I hope you will find that Mrs. Borrowfield," Hazel said. "She ought to be made to pay for foisting herself off as quality service."

Edward put aside troublesome thoughts about his houseguest. "We'll find her."

Hugging an arm to her waist, she straightened. "Aye, sir."

He showed her to the door and ushered her out first. "Ask one of the guards to go with you. I'll entertain no discussion to the contrary."

As they walked toward the door leading to the carriage house, she shook her head. "Wretched times when a noble gentleman and his house ain't safe. What's it come to, my lord?"

"Nothing for you to worry about. 'Tis a puzzle that we'll solve. Then everything will return to normal, and we'll lament our ordinary lives."

She lifted her gaze to the ceiling. "Praise it be so."

His household had seen their share and more of upheaval since the day Elise had sailed to Boston.

Until now, the mourning had been the worst. After that, a string of unacceptable housekeepers and nannies had disrupted the household. But Hazel and Bossy had made every adjustment.

For Edward, Agnes MacKenzie had chased the loneliness from Napier House. Keeping her here was fast becoming a course to consider. He thought of the afternoon to come, and wondered if she would dare to be late.

Holding Hannah's hand and hiding a smile of satisfaction, Agnes took her time descending the stairs. Fashions of the day were unsuited to the narrow doorways in the tower, so she kept her gowns in the room in the new wing that she had first occupied at Napier House. "I hope we haven't kept you gentlemen waiting?"

Lord Edward reached for the door. "Not at all."

"But, Father, you said they'd fuss—"

"Not now, Christopher."

Agnes wanted to laugh, but Hannah, entranced with the new carpet, jumped down the stairs with both feet, one step at a time. "Stop that, Hannah," she said. "Watch where you're going or you'll hurt yourself."

She stopped but tried to pull her hand away. When Agnes resisted, the girl tugged hard. Agnes winced.

"Hannah!" her father shouted. Dashing up the stairs, he scooped the girl into his arms. "You know that Lady Agnes has a hurt, and you mustn't pull her arm."

"I was hurting your arm?" Hannah asked, her eyes round with worry.

Lord Edward hefted the girl to his hip.

"Nay." Agnes straightened the girl's dress so it covered her knees. At Hannah's age, Agnes had had three siblings. As a consequence she'd seldom enjoyed her father's undivided attention. But she had three wonderful sisters, and her life was rich with love and friendship. "I'm fine, truly."

Lord Edward didn't look convinced. "I thought we agreed that you would keep your arm in the sling."

She'd forgotten it, but wasn't about to tell him that. If kissing her was a task, she'd make sure he didn't get close enough to do it again. "None of them matched my dress."

"I see."

Had he asked, she would gladly have told him that he couldn't see past his own nose. "Are we off then?"

He leaned back and gave her a thorough examination. "Your gown, my lady. Would you proclaim that color blue or green?"

Wary of his sly tone, she chose a neutral answer. "Both, my lord. Or either."

"Her petticoat's blue," piped Hannah.

Christopher made a bitter face and huffed in embarrassment. Lord Edward lifted his brows, but the gleam in his eyes boded ill. "Then we can assume that is what took you so long."

"So long?"

The focus of his attention moved to her breasts, which were only modestly displayed. His smile was pure devilry. "You're seven minutes tardy, but 'twas certainly worth the wait."

"We watched the clock," Christopher said proudly.

Uncomfortable beneath Lord Edward's scrutiny, she gave him a fake smile. "Then perhaps you should turn your attention to opening the door."

"How kind of you to remind me."

He opened the door and waved them out. The guard helped her and Hannah into the carriage; Lord

Edward spoke briefly to the driver, then sat with Christopher on the facing seat.

Judging from the high quality of the Napiers' clothing, Agnes thought Lord Edward must keep the best fabric from the looms for his own family. He wore a jacket and breeches of dove gray linen and black knee boots. His shirt and fancy neckcloth were of white silk. The subdued colors suited perfectly his reputation as a scholar and a statesman; but the bright yellow waistcoat gave him a dashing air. He carried his high-crowned hat, and his hair was unpowdered and clubbed at his nape with a black ribbon.

During that last explosive kiss, Agnes had plunged her hands into his hair and crushed the wavy strands between her fingers. Her stomach still floated at the memory.

To banish the feeling, she smoothed her gloves and broached a congenial subject. "How many people do you employ at the mill?"

"I know," piped Christopher.

Splendid. She preferred the lad to his despicable father.

"May I tell her, Father?"

"Of course."

Behaving very much like Agnes's sister Sarah had as a child, Christopher cleared his throat and lifted his chin. "On any given day, we employ one thousand people." He spoke with pride and confidence. "And that doesn't count the carters and the cooks and the chimney sweeps."

Agnes fought the urge to peek at Lord Edward. The attention belonged to Christopher. "You serve your workers a meal?" she asked.

"Aye." His voice broke. "We try our utmost to engage the labor of families."

She did look at Lord Edward. "The children work?"

"Nay," he said with no small measure of sarcasm. "They go to school."

"I forgot to say that we employ a teacher."

Agnes felt a grudging respect for Edward Napier, but textile mills were notorious for exploiting laborers and enriching the purses of the owners. However, Lord Edward was held in high regard by academics and nobility alike. She hoped to find proof of his humanity in the mill that bore the family name.

"Christopher," she said. "Are there modern machines in the mill?"

The boy fairly beamed. "Oh, aye. Mr. Watt visited himself. But soon Papa's machine will make the Newcomen steam engine look like a plow horse standing beside a racing steed."

Watt's invention had revolutionized every industry from coal to textiles. "Will it, my lord?" she asked.

"Those are Mayor Arkwright's words, not mine."

"Then how would you phrase it?"

"In less than entertaining terms, to be sure. The new engine is far from perfection."

He was resisting the subject, which was odd to Agnes. Lord Edward wasn't shy in the least. "I cannot be sure until I hear the words."

He stared out the window and nodded to a passerby. "The engine will allow us to spin thread from raw cotton, rather than import ready-wound spools from India."

Christopher added, "At a substantial savings all the way 'round."

Agnes had her answer. "So, my lord, greater profit is at the heart of your modernization."

He didn't like her conclusion, for his mouth tightened with anger. "'Tis better said that independence is the genesis of my efforts. No longer will the Napier mill be dependent on foreign sources. But also my conscience wants to aid the poor Indians who labor under unspeakable conditions to spin the thread."

The carriage rolled to a stop, and when Agnes realized their destination, she thought Edward Napier a scoundrel. "Oh, the modiste." She plucked at the lace on her bodice. "Settling a friend's account?"

"I'll only be moment," he murmured ruefully, donning his hat.

Christopher gaped. "A ladies shop? Must I go in there, Father?"

"And leave Lady Agnes unattended? Not the gentlemanly thing to do."

The boy pressed against the carriage seat and folded his arms over his chest. "I'll stay and attend Lady Agnes."

"Will you, lad?"

The boy kept his composure, but his eyes shone with relief. "Aye, Father. I insist on doing the proper thing."

Lord Edward stepped out and motioned for Hannah to follow him. "Will you come with me, Button?"

Squealing, she nearly flew from the carriage and lunged into his arms. Her whistle clipped his chin.

What mischief was he about? Agnes learned the answer a short time later, when he strolled from the establishment with Hannah perched on his hip. The girl clutched a package in her hands.

Christopher was just finishing his explanation of how his mother had died at sea.

Opening the door, Edward whispered something to Hannah.

"'Twill?" she piped.

He put her on the seat beside Agnes. "I'm completely certain of it, Button."

The girl looked at Agnes, smiled, and handed her the package. "'S'for you."

He was lower than a badger's belly to use these children to his own selfish ends. But they were innocent and deserved the best that Agnes had to give. She untied the string and opened the package. Folded neatly inside were two lengths of blue silk in a shade suspiciously close to that of her petticoat.

As if it were a revelation, Hannah turned up her hands and lifted her shoulders. "'S'one for you. One for me."

His lordship was obviously trying to make amends for his boldness in the music room. It was beautiful cloth, and she had played a role in letting the kiss get out of control. But the feelings he inspired went beyond her experience, and their situation defied convention.

Hannah leaned over and put her face very close to Agnes's. "'S'pretty?"

"Aye, and 'tis very thoughtful of you both." As she kissed Hannah's forehead, she stole a glance at Lord Edward. Giving her a challenging look, he touched his finger to his cheek.

Ignoring him, she gave Hannah the smaller length of cloth. "What shall we make of these, bows for our hair?"

"A sling for both of you," said Lord Edward, taking the smaller of the cloths from Hannah. To Agnes, he said, "You forgot yours."

Keeping her temper in check, Agnes watched him deftly tie a knot to fashion the sling, then slip it over Hannah's head. The girl cooed and squirmed with pleasure, which his lordship encouraged with quips about how well the girl behaved and how pretty she was.

"Button," he said, tucking Hannah's whistle into

the sling. "Tell Lady Agnes what the shopkeeper said to you."

Hannah concentrated so hard, she grimaced. "I remember! Romance's afoot at our house."

Now that he'd finished pretending to minister to his daughter, he turned to Agnes. "Allow me."

Giving him a fake smile, she stayed where she was. When he'd knotted the cloth, Hannah put another good spell on Agnes's injury. Agnes returned the favor.

Christopher leaned forward. "My lady, you could carry one of your knives in that sling."

"Knives will cut me," Hannah said, admiring her own sling.

Agnes did carry a weapon, a deadly stiletto she'd found in Spain. But that was her secret. "Enough about knives." Leaning forward, she curled her finger, and Lord Edward moved close. "You're shameless," she said.

In a deep and sensual murmur, he said, "Wrapping your legs around me and kissing me hungrily with your tongue was not?"

She gasped, and heat rushed up her face.

Hannah grumbled, "Whispering's polite."

"*Im*polite," her brother corrected, but he'd turned his attention to the passing scenery.

Agnes marshaled herself. "What if we were planning a surprise for you, Button?"

As perky as could be, Hannah squealed. "Like Papa 'n' me did for you?"

The promise of retribution inspired Agnes. "Oh, my surprise for your father will be very different."

Christopher joined in. "Can we guess what 'twill be?"

"Guess! Guess! Guess!"

A game ensued, occupying the children during the

ride across Glasgow. The visit to Saint Vincent's Church proved a waste of time, except to hear a confirmation from Bishop Brimston that no Mrs. Borrowfield attended services there.

"But we drove her here in our carriage every Sunday morning," Lord Edward said.

The bishop, a fellow as old as the tales of Toom Tabbard, squinted up at his noble visitor. "What time did she arrive at service, my lord?"

"Our services at Saint Stephen's Church begin at ten o'clock, so we would have left her here at half past nine."

"Odd, my lord." The bishop scratched his head. "I begin promptly at nine, and my congregation's not so large as my brethren at Saint Stephen's. I would have noticed her coming in so late."

There must be more, Agnes thought. "How did Mrs. Borrowfield get home to Napier House after the service? Did you fetch her?"

"Nay. She said she enjoyed the walk."

"What did she look like?" the bishop asked.

Lord Edward described an older woman with graying hair and a healthy frame. But his description was too general and mannerly to suit Agnes.

She searched her memory for the image of the woman who'd held Hannah in Saint Margaret's Church in Edinburgh. She said, "Mrs. Borrowfield's chin was weak and dimpled, and her lips very thin. My lord, what color was her cloak?"

His gaze went out of focus. "Very dark brown, as I recall, with a black ribbon tie at the hood. 'Twas lined with . . ."

"With what color?" She willed him to see it.

"I have it!" he exclaimed. "'Twas yellow."

Shaking his head in apology, the bishop said, "Yellow or black, I cannot help you, my lord. No woman of that likeness attends my service. But should *you* ever wish to join us, I'd consider it an honor."

As they returned to the carriage, Agnes thought of other ways to locate the elusive Mrs. Borrowfield. She was still considering the possibilities when they arrived at the mill and Lord Edward handed her down from the carriage.

His hands lingered far too long at her waist. When Agnes protested, he whispered, "I heard no cry of foul play when you were panting in my arms this morning."

"No, 'tis only the lingering effects that are foul."

9

FUMING, AGNES STARED AT THE PASSING TRAFFIC WHILE Lord Edward helped the children from the carriage. A wagon stocked with barrels rumbled past and veered onto a side road that led to the larger buildings in the rear.

Hannah complained that her sling needed attention, which her father patiently gave. Christopher grumbled.

According to the lad, the mill occupied three square furlongs of land, and Agnes believed him. The structures stood at the crossroads of Cathcart Avenue and the west wagonway, the best route to the Port of Glasgow. At Napier House the oldest structure, the tower, was shielded by the newer buildings. Here at the mill, the opposite was true. The first building, a stone rectangle built in the thirteenth century, fronted the massive structures housing the looms and spinners.

Lord Edward motioned to the driver. "Take the carriage 'round to the side, Jamie. Wait for us there."

Inside the old structure the walls served as a chronicle of the Napiers' contributions to the design and manufacture of cloth. Centuries' worth of progress marched along the walls, beginning with the seal of office of the Napier first charged with the care of the royal napery. With surprise, Agnes noted that the family had not kept the most valuable remembrances for the gallery at Napier House; rather they displayed them here.

In the far corner of the room an iron gate barred entrance to a downward spiraling staircase. The grill-work depicted the Napier shield, a hand holding a crescent.

Lord Edward joined her. "Did I lie, my lady?"

His seduction was getting out of hand. Ignoring him posed her best option. "No. The mill prospers, and you're from a very illustrious family."

A knowing grin gave him a rakish air, which was perfectly fitting. But how could she have known that the scholarly earl possessed the heart of a rogue? She couldn't have.

Christopher stepped to the fore. "The Napiers are weavers, inventors, and mathematicians. One of our ancestors invented the logarithm." He pointed to a state portrait of Queen Charlotte holding one of her many children. "We made the christening gown."

"Are you eager to carry on the family tradition?"

"Aye." With more enthusiasm, he said, "But I'd also like to build a ship that will sail to India in a week."

"A week's time?" said his father. "That's very ambitious."

Stubbornly, the boy held his ground. "I'll try all the same, if you'll let me."

The earl of Cathcart grew pensive, and Agnes wondered if he was thinking about the assassin. The mood fled as quickly as it had come. He ruffled his son's hair. "I predict a lively discussion or two on the subject."

Footfalls sounded in the circular staircase. Agnes tensed. Lord Edward had turned his attention to Hannah, who had reverted to gibberish. Keeping her touch casual, Agnes rested her hand on Christopher's shoulder. If trouble were coming up those stairs, she'd push the lad to the floor and reach for her dagger.

She was certain that the approaching man was not the assassin; he moved quietly, but she'd take nothing for granted.

Through the iron grillwork she saw a portly man emerge. Dressed in the clothing of a gentleman, he wore a ready smile. He carried a heavy ring of keys. As he moved into the room, the iron hinges on the gate squealed like a frightened gull.

"Mr. Peel!" shouted Christopher.

Singling out an iron key that bore a Celtic knot, the man locked the gate. Over his shoulder, he said, "Good afternoon, my lord." He nodded to the children. "Christopher, and Miss Hannah."

Edward extended his hand. "Afternoon, Peel. Lady Agnes MacKenzie, may I present the fine superintendent of this mill, Avery Peel."

"Good afternoon, Mr. Peel."

His gaze strayed to the sling on her arm. "My lady, welcome to the mills of Napier. I had heard that you were in Glasgow. May I say that I had the pleasure of meeting your father once." To Edward, he said, "Best man o' the Highlands, 'tis said of the duke of Ross."

Rather than offer her left hand, Agnes acknowledged Peel with a friendly smile. "He is indeed, Mr. Peel. And he speaks fondly of your city until the conversation comes 'round to the time he brought my sisters and me here about a decade ago."

"You would have been in Boston at the time, my lord," Peel said to Edward, but his attention wandered to the matching sling that Hannah wore. "To this day, the ladies of town go on about that Harvest Ball."

Interest sparkled in Edward's eyes. "Did the MacKenzie lassies behave dreadfully, Peel?"

The superintendent moved closer to Hannah. "I wouldn't be knowing the gospel truth of it, my lord. Gossips have their own way of stitching up the event." Peel squatted before Hannah. "Have you hurt yourself, lassie?"

Swaying from side to side, she held up her arm. "'S'fashion."

"And quite well done, young lady," he said with enthusiasm.

Edward rested his hand on her head. "Lady Agnes met with an accident, and Button couldn't let her suffer alone."

"Of course she couldn't, my lord. Hannah's got a big heart." Peel stood and addressed both children. "There's sweet buns left in the kitchen, and luncheon aplenty."

Christopher discarded his heir-to-the-family-business demeanor and chuckled with glee. "May we, Papa?"

Turning to Agnes, Edward tucked his hat under his arm. "You were rather hungry earlier, were you not, my lady?"

The innocuous remark, delivered in an overly concerned tone, held a world of meaning to Agnes. He was thinking of the intimacies they'd shared in the music room, the hunger that had raged between them.

The charlatan. "I've had my fill and more, Lord Edward. Are you still hungry?"

She watched him deliberate over how to reply. At length he said, "For some delicacies, I am always hungry."

He deserved a slap in the face, but she would not lower herself.

Into the stilted silence Mr. Peel said, "My lord, you might want to visit Dunbar. I believe he has made some progress. Rather boisterous about it, he was."

At the mention of the name, Edward grew attentive. "Splendid."

Hannah and Christopher led the way down a corridor of rooms where hundreds of swatches of cloth and samples of thread were displayed. The hum of machines grew louder with every step. Agnes wondered why Edward had stopped at the dressmaker's shop when there was cloth aplenty here. She asked him.

The question caught him unprepared, for he stared at her in surprise. "The children need warmer sleeping gowns. The tower rooms hold a chill, even in summer. The modiste was convenient, and you had forgotten your sling."

Consideration for others had been his motive, and Agnes felt a twinge of shame. She touched his arm. "Have you told anyone here about . . . ?"

"Nay, and the constable will not have spread the tale, since he cannot solve anything above common thievery or a romance gone bad."

"Then you're left with me."

"A very interesting alternative, I must say."

"You needn't say anything about that."

"About how you whimpered—"

She pressed her gloved hand to his mouth. *"Haud yer wheesht!"* she hissed.

170

When the scoundrel winked at her, she stepped in front of him and continued down the hallway.

In a larger chamber, a bevy of clerks and accountants worked at desks made in the distinctive style made popular at the turn of the century by Queen Anne. As they traveled farther into the buildings, the sound increased to a muffled roar. Christopher opened another door, and the noise grew so loud it seemed to move the air.

Leaning close and speaking behind his hand, Edward said, "'Twill lessen when we're out of these stone rooms. The shed itself is made partially of wood."

Agnes followed the children into a cavernous room built of stone and wood. The earthen floor was covered in sailcloth. Oddly the sound quieted.

Taking her arm, Edward guided her toward the center aisle.

"A shed?" she asked, taken aback by the size of the place. "That being the scale, Westminster is a chapel."

He chuckled.

The busy atmosphere held none of the gloom she'd seen in similar textile concerns in China. At either end of this building, huge steam-driven fans, that had the appearance of great iron flowers, kept the air fresh but not drafty. Spaced ten across in long rows, hundreds of looms, with giant spools of thread in an array of colors, filled the room.

The workers looked sober and clean, their clothing worn but cared for. They appeared as Christopher had described them: family men. But women were also a part of this work force, some operated looms, others pushed wheeled carts with fuel to replenish the many lamps.

The workers paused to acknowledge the presence of

the earl. He returned their greetings, addressing them by name. Agnes was reminded of her father, who could be counted upon to roll up his sleeves and labor alongside the farmers at harvest time. Agnes and her sisters had been allowed to ride in the wagons. Later she had driven a wagon herself.

In a corner of the mill, near a bank of windows, fabric was stretched on frames. Women, old and young, worked side by side, embroidering designs on the cloth. One loom, different from others, sat off to itself. Of iron, the machine rested on great blocks of wood. The loom produced a long roll of heavy white fabric. "What is that, my lord?"

"A canvas loom. 'Tis the only one of its size and kind in Scotland."

For years Agnes had helped her sister Mary stretch canvases, but she hadn't considered where and how the cloth was made. "For artists who employ larger canvas."

"Much larger." The loom itself was at least ten feet across, and its spools as tall as she.

"The greater part of this will be shipped abroad to Dutch painters. 'Tis fitting for their grander style."

"Is it profitable?"

"Surprisingly so. Every year the profit from that loom pays for itself, for Riley, who is the operator, and for Dunbar's workshop."

"Then why not have more of the machines and hire more Rileys."

"'Tis a peculiar trade. The younger weavers have no liking for working with flax." In the clickety-clack dialect of Glaswegians, he said, "The warp and the woof of silk 'twill give us tomorrow's wages." In his own voice, he added, "Sailmakers will have to take over the craft when Riley's had a belly of it."

Looking to the left, she saw a sea of white spools of thread. "Or is the profit too paltry for your tastes?"

"My dear, you cannot wound me with a wee prick of your tongue, and do not expect me to apologize because my business prospers."

Agnes knew her remark was unfair, but the earl of Cathcart didn't bother to follow the rules of decorum. "I will wound you as you embarrass me. I've heard no apologies from you."

His chuckle turned cunning. "I apologized once to you. I've learned my lesson since."

He referred to that first kiss they'd shared at the inn in Whitburn. *Desire, base and raw.* The truth behind his seduction saddened her.

"Banish that dire notion that spins in your head, Agnes," he insisted, moving close. "For it does not aid our cause."

"We have no cause."

"Another truce, then. Have you other questions about the operation of the mill?"

She thought of the colorful thread in the looms and the white thread against the wall. "Where do you dye the thread?"

"At the rear of the property. 'Tis a distance away, and the road is muddy."

Christopher dashed in front of them. "May we go to the kitchen, Papa?"

"Aye, but you're to have only one bun each." He spoke pointedly to both of them. "Hazel's making partridge."

"One for you," Christopher said to Hannah, "and one for me."

Moving between the children, Agnes said, "I'll accompany them." She had no intention of leaving them alone.

He paused, uncertain. "I should like to consult with Dunbar."

"Go on with you, then," she encouraged. "We'll entertain ourselves."

Indicating a windowed room beyond the great canvas loom, he said, "There's Dunbar's workroom. I shan't be long."

Progress to the kitchen was slow. The children were hailed by one person after another, all of them solicitous of Hannah's fashionable sling. Agnes felt a warmth about the people, certainly no artifice. But what about the clerks? And what had sent Peel down into that room with the locked entry?

Looking across the building, Agnes saw Edward enter the workroom he'd spoken of. He spoke briefly to the man who must be Dunbar, then followed him to a bench. As one, they examined a bulbous glass containing an amber liquid. After another lengthy discussion, Edward removed his jacket and waistcoat and rolled up his sleeves. Even from this distance, she couldn't mistake his enthusiasm or avoid comparing him to her father.

Wondering what had captured his interest, Agnes followed the children to the kitchen. But when next she saw the earl of Cathcart, his first words shocked her.

"The bloody bastard's been in the carriage. I found this in the seat." He held out the smaller golden version of the MacKenzie badge, the one she'd attached to the tartan and placed over the damaged Napier crest in his study. She'd been so shocked at seeing the dead dove wrapped in the plaid, she'd forgotten the brooch.

They stood in the side yard of the mill, outside the

kitchen and near the building housing the school. Hannah and Christopher were saying their farewells to the other children in the yard. Jamie, the driver, was examining the harnesses.

The wide road leading from the front of the building was rutted and worn from the constant stream of wagons. Beyond it lay a pasture with a few fat cattle and a small herd of recently sheared sheep. The area between the school and the mill proper served as storage for a mountain of cone-shaped spools, now empty of thread.

Baffled, Agnes said, "How could he have come onto the property unnoticed? When could he have gotten inside the carriage?"

"Jamie didn't leave it unattended for long, just for necessity. But surely someone would have noticed a stranger."

Agnes remembered seeing the cooper's wagon enter the yard earlier. "Perhaps he stowed away on one of the delivery wagons."

Distraught, Edward surveyed their surroundings. "I'm at a loss, Agnes."

Frustration laced the informality. She asked him about the stairwell behind the iron grate.

"'Tis the old dungeon. We keep the treasury there, and our charter."

"A dungeon?"

"Aye, complete with manacles and an iron maiden."

This was not the first time trouble had visited the mill. She remembered their conversation at the Dragoon Inn in Edinburgh. "You said there had been a fire here. When did it occur?"

He pointed to a scorched brick building on a patch of blackened ground beyond the schoolhouse. The roof, doors, and windows were gone, leaving only the charred masonry. "'Twas there. It occurred last March."

"The same time as the arrival of Mrs. Borrowfield?"

"Yes, by God. I did not link the two."

That was her expertise, but she wouldn't remind him of it. "What was in the building at the time of the fire? Was anyone hurt?"

Lines of worry creased his forehead. "'Twas Dunbar's workshop, and the fire was set at night. Only progress was hurt."

"Progress," she repeated, and felt a spark of intuition. The assassin had rummaged through the papers in his study. The workroom had been destroyed. Progress. She'd learn the reasons behind it, but now he needed reassurance. "Worry not, my lord."

With a wave of his hand, he indicated the whole of the property. "How can I not?"

Gazing at the huge wooden structure and imagining how rapidly the contents would ignite, Agnes felt a shiver of apprehension. "You should put a cistern here and a supply of buckets beside it. Build another atop the stone building to catch rainwater and pipe it along the support columns. You must increase the night watch. Men should patrol the yard during the day. Begin a log of every delivery wagon, its origin, and the name of its driver."

"Have you any other orders for me?"

"Yes. Can you think of any tie he might have to this mill?"

"A well-paid assassin? Nay." Absolute denial harshened his tone. "This is a community of people. They stage a harvest fair on this land, have for decades. On wages day the family members congregate here. I will not believe one of them has betrayed me."

"None of your employees could afford the assassin's fee."

"None of them would, I tell you!"

His vehemence was rapidly turning to anger. Agnes knew she must calm him down before the children joined them. She chose an easy path. She gave his arm a smart pat. "Careful, Edward Napier, one might mistake you for a Highlander, so patriarchal do you seem."

Quickly, boldly, did he react. "At least I do not stoop to flinging your words in your face." In carefully precise motions, using only his fingertips, he pulled paper and pencil from his waistcoat. One side of the paper contained a drawing with symbols, notes, and measurements. Turning it over, he began writing on the clean surface. As he wrote, he recited her suggestions, but his voice was high-pitched and cocky.

She recalled his saying that he couldn't stay angry with her for long. Adding that memory to his actions now, she decided that he possessed a mild temperament. She wondered what he'd been like before the attempts on his life. Last night in the tower he'd donned a long tunic and pretended to be a medieval lord as he presided over the meal and the evening.

He'd cleverly convinced his children that the whistles they wore around their necks were special toys. He'd invented a game he called Castle Keep, wherein he'd dubbed the children vital sentries. He'd charged them to blow their whistles to sound an alarm should a stranger enter Napier House.

"Agnes?"

At the gentle insistence in his voice, she pulled

herself to the present. Her gaze went immediately to the children. Seeing that they were safe, she studied their father.

Sunlight turned his gray eyes to sparkling silver. "What were you thinking?" he asked.

Only in exchange for knowledge of Virginia's whereabouts would Agnes have revealed her tender thoughts of him. She took the golden brooch from his hand. "I was wondering how I will clean the blood off this."

"That wasn't what you were thinking. But I'm a patient man." He took the brooch. "Allow me. I've a solvent in my laboratory that will do the trick."

He didn't need a solvent to perform trickery; he could captivate her at will, a situation that both surprised and frightened her. She said, "Thank you," when she wanted to ask why he continued his seduction game. She'd made her position clear on the subject of romance, and even if she did fall in love with Edward Napier, she would not forsake her search for Virginia.

The wind changed directions, and the smell of the sea filled the air. She thought of her home in Tain, of the docks in Cromarty, of an older sister and her younger charge, of a tryst the former had arranged with a dashing young beau. Agnes saw herself give Virginia a penny for a pie and another for her silence. The image blurred.

With an effort, she put away the past. "I think you should send our apologies to the mayor tonight."

"Oh, nay." He opened the carriage door and called for the children. "This villain will not make a coward or a prisoner of me."

The children would be safe in the tower with Auntie Loo. The assassin had braved a crowd in Edinburgh, but would he show himself in Glasgow? Agnes hoped so. "Pray he crawls from his hole, for I long to meet him face-to-face," she said.

He snapped his fingers. "We will draw him out and away from my children."

"Not apurpose. He's too clever for that," she warned. "We must be careful, and stop shouting orders at me."

Having a plan inspired confidence in him, for his mood brightened, and he winked at her. "Of course. I wouldn't want to sound patriarchal."

He'd also tossed her words in her face, and for that act of deviousness, he would pay. "Aye, you take every opportunity to lord yourself over me."

"Since you've found me out, I may as well confess."

Busying herself with the fit of her gloves, she feigned disinterest. "You may, but please be expeditious about it."

He put his face very close to hers. "Do not wear that green dress tonight."

Of all the gall. "Is that a warning?"

"Aye. That gown draws my eyes to your breasts and turns my thoughts to earthy impulses."

He was too close, and the promise in his eyes set her heart to racing. "Then you must learn to contain yourself."

"As must you. Unless—" With the toe of his boot, he drew a mark in the ground between them. "You'd care to don that dangerous frock and figuratively step over this line."

Roguish didn't begin to describe him. "You're an admitted ravisher."

"Only when taunted beyond restraint." He took her arm. "Wear that green dress or its like, and we'll have a long and memorable carriage ride to the Arkwrights."

He was promising to seduce her over the cut of her clothing. Pity that he didn't want her for herself, not that anything would come of an affair with him. She wouldn't be intimidated by him, but she wouldn't act recklessly either.

Later that night, when she joined him in the foyer, Agnes wore her best gown, a gift from her father on her last birthday.

"I stand corrected," he drawled. "The green gown is a rag." Dressed in his own evening finery, he walked in a circle around her. "What friend of man made this gown for you?"

Bristling with excitement, Agnes let her spirit fly. "My sister Lottie designed it."

"Off with her head. You look dazzling."

She struggled against a blush and won. "Thank you, my lord."

Edward whistled. "Men will have to sign treaties in advance to get near you in that gown."

Dressed as he was in steel gray velvet, a white shirt, and hose, he'd attract attention of his own tonight. "Does that mean I have your promise of good behavior?"

Never had Edward seen a finer blending of light and dark fabrics. A full bolt of white velvet made the skirt and sleeves, but the long black cape and floppy hood were cut of shimmering black satin. Five thin strips of the ebony cloth, sewn an inch apart, marched up the center front of the skirt. Beginning at the waist, the black piping fanned out over the bodice. The design was repeated on the back of the black cape, with white piping soaring up the back and fanning out at the hood.

"Define good behavior."

"An absence of seduction."

BEGUILED

She'd foregone the sling, and he couldn't bring himself to suggest it. The gown was too beautiful. "Rest assured, no one will ravish you while I'm nearby."

Upon arrival at the mayor's home, Edward had second thoughts. The swains were out in force.

10

Viscount Lindsay droned on about his great-grandmother's love of roses. Agnes had listened to four generations of the saga and thought it sweet that the young noble who'd sent her roses carried on the family gardening tradition. But the longer he spoke, the more tiresome he became. Her opinion did not matter, for he did not ask questions or invite comments.

She searched for an escape.

Her gaze moved to the earl of Cathcart, who stood with a group of men near the potted palms across the ballroom. The evening with Mayor Arkwright was not the quiet dinner Agnes had expected. At least fifty people milled about the brightly lighted room.

Observing Edward Napier, she decided that in public he possessed an overabundance of reserve. An image she couldn't quite square with the aggressive rogue who made her feel and act the wanton. More puzzling was why someone had ordered his death. Taller than the other men around him, he shared rather than dominated the conversation. Scanning the others in the room, she saw no one sending him vengeful stares. Passing among the guests, she'd heard no disparaging words, not even a slight spoken in jest.

Their eyes met. In a glance he bathed her in admiration. His subtle and effective seduction went straight to her heart. Cast off propriety, he seemed to say, and play a trysting game with me.

He looked pointedly at the side exit, and with a subtle expression, he invited her to join him there.

Agnes couldn't stand still. The legacy of the Lindsay roses had regressed to the Reformation Age, when a kinswoman had stolen holy water to nourish the last Lindsay rose. When the viscount stopped to draw a breath, Agnes took her leave and moved toward Edward.

He tipped his head to the side to hear the conversation of the constable, but his eyes and his interest followed her every step.

He's trouble, her better judgment warned.

Have a go, her heart replied.

Halfway to her destination, she felt his warmth and his anticipation. His eyes gleamed a welcome, and when she reached him, he grasped her arm and drew her in.

"Gentlemen," he began in his scholarly voice. "Let us not bore Lady Agnes with our ruminations over the loss of the American colonies. If we do, she'll elude us again."

Agnes had stood among these same gentlemen shortly after arriving at Mayor Arkwright's residence. She'd been captivated by Edward Napier, by his fair assessment of history, by his enthusiastic outlook for the future. The very real possibility that his future could be in peril had driven her to mingle among his acquaintances. That was when Viscount Lindsay had caught her unawares, and with his penchant for hearing himself talk, he had given her the opportunity to observe the others in the room. If any of the people here wanted the earl of Cathcart dead, Agnes saw no sign of it.

All of the men in the group except the mayor excused themselves. Agnes said, "What societal revelations did I miss?"

The mayor stumbled for words. Their conversation had either been vulgar or had concerned her. Agnes looked up at Edward. "Tell me what was said."

"You will not like it."

"I insist."

"Uh, may I fetch you a glass of punch, my lady?" The mayor moved to leave.

"Water, please, Mayor Arkwright."

Murmuring, "My pleasure," he ambled toward the door.

"Out with it, my lord," Agnes said.

He sighed. "I'll probably regret this."

"But you'll tell me anyway."

"The constable believes that the duke of Ross keeps you too long in the nest."

If he sought to shock her, he'd find disappointment. A bastard child knew scorn at an early age. But Agnes was a daughter of the Highland rogue. The blame for her illegitimacy was his, and a lifetime of love was his restitution. "Because I have not wed?"

Edward didn't bat an eyelash at her bluntness. But he moved close and whispered, "Yes. But before you tell me why, know that the telling itself is a gift to me."

Her head went light. In Edinburgh he'd witnessed the battle she waged with her father, but he had not pried into the reasons behind it. Early on in their association, Edward had tried to dominate her. But that was in the past. In matters pertaining to his safety and that of his children, he treated her as a respected equal.

Her most heartfelt reason rushed to be said. "When I find a man as honorable and as loving as my father, I will leap into his arms."

Pleasure glowed in his gray eyes. "His grace of Ross sets a lofty standard for the rest of us mortals to follow. But this very mortal man thinks 'tis a task worth the undertaking."

Flattered to her toes, Agnes fought the urge to simper.

Fifty people mingled around them. If Agnes disgraced herself in public, she'd regret it tomorrow. But Edward was nothing if not compelling. As she normally did when faced with a difficult decision, Agnes thought of her family. If she made a scandal in Glasgow, the MacKenzies would suffer disappointment. She thought of Lottie, the great traditionalist. For one who asked so little for herself, Lottie deserved Agnes's consideration.

"What are you thinking?" Edward asked.

"I was recalling something Lottie often says."

"Remember, I found the countess of Tain a charming woman. What does she often say?"

"That love awaits in the marriage bed, but good character must bring you to it."

"I find it contemplative that you coupled me and the marriage bed in the same thought."

She had, but she wouldn't own up to it. "I cannot imagine why, unless I've gone daft or have been thinking about Lottie overmuch."

The mayor returned, and Agnes sipped the tepid water.

Edward watched her. "Lottie told me your dowries were considerable."

Ruefully, Agnes said, "A veritable bounty waiting to be bestowed."

Toasting her, Edward said under his breath, "To say nothing of your more bountiful charms."

Excitement rippled through her.

Into the tumult, she heard the mayor say, "Or lands in Burgundy from her mother."

Edward's mouth twitched with humor. "Do you favor the duchess of Enderley?"

"Aye. In appearance I resemble her people, Clan Campbell. But in temperament, I am more like my father and the MacKenzies of Ross."

"A devil of a rogue, too, is that MacKenzie," barked the mayor. "Gossip out of London credits your father with calling the earl of Wiltshire to answer for making fast with the Lady Mary."

Poor Papa, Agnes thought. First the trouble in Edinburgh with Sarah, and now worse circumstances for Mary. Her father's messenger had left this morning for London. The trip took sixty hours each way. Unless another carrier was already on his way to Glasgow, news was almost a week away.

Edward said, "Young Wiltshire's reputed to be a master with a blade."

In spite of the fact that Lord Robert Spencer, Mary's love interest, was a lamentable subject, Agnes chuckled. "Wager a purse against an angry Lachlan MacKenzie, and you'll see paltry returns on your coin—especially if he is defending one of his daughters."

Keen interest glimmered in Edward's eyes. "What do you think his grace will do?"

The motive behind the question was curious to Agnes. "I think that he will listen to both sides. He will understand Wiltshire's motives. But he will take his daughter's part. Unless Mary gave her word. If she made a promise to the earl, Papa will see that she honors it."

"Other guests have arrived. If you will excuse me." The mayor headed for the door.

Edward wasn't done with the subject. Moving even closer, he said, "Mary is with child. If the greatest of intimacies cannot be deemed a promise, what can?"

To her dismay, Agnes had to confess, "I do not know. I didn't see much of Mary in Edinburgh." But if Mary were in trouble, she'd come to Agnes for help.

"Then your knowledge of certain intimacies and their repercussions is limited?"

"Are you asking if I am a virgin?"

Caught off guard, he stumbled for words and settled for, "Of course not. I was merely soliciting your opinion on the matter of promises made in passion."

"Our father warned us of those. Did yours?"

Edward was staring beyond her, and he'd stopped listening.

Agnes scanned the room, searching for what or who had distracted him. She saw nothing untoward, no bowman lurking in the shadows. She felt no trouble in the air. "Is something amiss?" she asked.

"Only that I'm surprised." He nodded to the mayor's wife, who hurried after her husband. "I didn't expect to see Sir Throckmorton here."

Relieved, Agnes tried to place the name. "Who is he?"

"Sir William Throckmorton. I'm certain I mentioned him. He is part of a consortium that owns a spinning concern in India."

Agnes remembered. "You buy those spools of thread from him."

"Aye, my family has done business with his company for a very long time. The partners in the firm have changed over the years, but our dealings with them have not."

Bewigged in the grand style, the object of their conversation had even dusted his thick brown eyebrows with powder. Sir Throckmorton was fashionably decked out in a clashing ensemble of orange, lime, and yellow satin. His black cane seemed a sober accessory to an otherwise parti-colored attire. Six fashionably dressed females trailed behind like goslings after the gander.

"How long have you known him?"

"Many years."

Among the reasons that inspired villainy, profit seemed the most logical. Unusual occurrences could not be overlooked. If this visit by Throckmorton was an uncommon event, it warranted investigation. Trimble could easily arrange a search of the Throckmorton rooms. Or Agnes might conduct it herself.

"Agnes . . ." Edward's gaze sharpened. "Do you think he is behind . . . ?"

She could not mistake the distress in his voice. "I do not know." To ease his troubled mind, she added, "Probably not. But we could discuss it later if you like."

"I'd prefer to use our 'laters' for more pleasurable activities."

An uncontrollable blush was her reply.

Leaning heavily on his walking stick, Throckmorton approached them. "Nice to see you, my lord. May I present my wife and my daughters."

Agnes listened with half an ear as he drew each of the Throckmorton flock before Edward. Under the gander's watchful eye, they performed as if at court, a sure sign they were English. The mother goose even deferred attention to her offspring, no doubt anticipating the day they would leave the nest.

Ever the gentleman, Edward bowed over every proffered hand and murmured a pleasantry to each of the girls.

The eldest of the daughters gave him a sultry smile and squared her shoulders, which lifted her nipples into plain view. Agnes almost choked with laughter. Were Lottie here, she'd have taken the girl aside and ridiculed her to tears.

"Lady Agnes MacKenzie." Edward's eyes danced with black humor. "May I present . . ."

Stifling the need to repay him in kind, she assumed her proper place in the scheme of social standing and accepted their greetings.

Until the last and the youngest girl stepped forward.

Garbed in a smaller version of the current styles, she wore a dusted wig with pink bows to match her panniered skirt. A folded fan dangled from her wrist, and her nose was splashed with freckles.

"I'm Penelope, and that's the most beautiful gown ever."

"Be gone, tadpole." The elder sister tried to push her away.

Agnes smiled and touched the distinctive black piping on the gown. "Thank you, Penelope. One of my sisters designed it."

As if it were an impossibility, Penelope said, "Your sister is pleasant to you, and you like her?"

"Aye, but I do not live with her now." The girl's gaze grew keen, and Agnes added, "Do you understand?"

Proudly, she said, "Aye."

The niceties exchanged and his duty discharged,

Throckmorton dismissed all but the eldest of his daughters. To Edward he said, "I called to see you at the mill, my lord."

"There was no need for you to go to that trouble. Had you sent word, I would have come to your lodgings."

Rather than be flattered by the generous gesture, or at least acknowledge it, Throckmorton did neither. With too much enthusiasm, he said, "I had hoped to see you demonstrating that new engine."

Edward smiled blandly. "What time were you there?"

"About sunset. Should have arrived sooner, but who could, I ask you. I've seen better cart paths in a Madras monsoon than the rutted beasts you Scots call roads." His gaze swung to Agnes. "Not that you are at fault, my lady."

"How can I be when the king's exchequer allocates our taxes?"

He looked as if he'd swallowed a midge and it buzzed in his gullet. At length he said, "The king's exchequer did not rut the roads."

She wanted to tell him to take his superior British attitude and boil it with his dreadful beef. She settled for a mild insult. "How regrettable, Sir Throckmorton. But since you find travel in the north a bother, the MacKenzies will be forced to strike your name from the guest list."

That got the attention of his remaining flock. As spokesman, he said, "But we've never been on your invitation lists."

Before she could deliver a stinging retort, Edward said, "William, I'm surprised to see you in Glasgow." To Agnes, he said, "This is Throckmorton's first visit to our city."

Agnes fumed at his interruption. "Pray our king finds it in his Hanoverian heart to follow your lead."

As jovial as a diplomat at court, Throckmorton laughed in a self-effacing way. "My wife and daughters insisted that we come. The gels are of an age that requires travel to round them out at the edges, you know."

Agnes thought a liking for food had rounded out the entire family, especially the five daughters, who stair-stepped in age from Penelope, who had yet to get breasts, to Mary, who displayed hers at will.

A butler carrying a huge platter glided up to them. "Would you care for angels on horseback, my lady?"

Agnes's stomach protested at the thought of eating oysters with anything, least of all bacon. "Thank you, nay."

"Are you well?" Edward asked.

"Bonny as a London summer," she said between her teeth.

Sir Throckmorton waved the servant over and downed three of the delicacies.

His eldest daughter flipped open her painted ivory fan and wielded it with an originality even Lottie would envy. "We've just come out of India."

Waving the butler off, Sir Throckmorton said, "Nothing in that place for a well-bred gel, except second sons trying to make an easy catch."

If living in India didn't qualify as traveling, Agnes couldn't imagine what did. The offensive remark about second sons begged for a reply; her sister Sarah had recently married a second son. But Edward was giving Agnes pointed stares.

"Did you like India?" she asked.

For answer, she received a chorus of negatives. Mrs. Throckmorton's shiver of revulsion sent a cloud of wig dust raining onto her shoulders.

"I liked it there," chirped the youngest girl.

The eldest, who kept sneaking glances at Agnes's dress, lifted her chin in disdain. "That's because you are as rude and uncivilized as the natives there."

Sending her eldest sibling a glare that promised retribution, the youngest moved to the punch bowl.

Edward leaned close and whispered, "Please be civil."

Agnes relented. She'd been introduced to all of them, but she only remembered the names of the eldest and youngest. "Mary," she said to the busty one. "That's a pretty name. I have a sister named Mary."

"The painter." Mary Throckmorton cocked an eyebrow in disapproval. "Contrary Mary, they have named her. She really has broken her reputation now, but I doubt you've heard, being trapped up here in the wilds."

Agnes grew chilled inside. An insult to Mary was an insult to every MacKenzie. An insult to Scotland went beyond forgiveness. If this spoiled Englishwoman wanted to make a fool of herself in Scottish society, who was Agnes to stop her? Better she should give the girl a verbal push.

"Are you bursting at the bosoms to tell us, Mary?"

Edward coughed to disguise a burst of laughter.

Challenged, the viper revealed her fangs. "Imagine, being presented to the king and having the gall to speak Scottish to him." In delicate outrage, she fluttered her eyelashes and jiggled her head. "I cannot believe your sister is allowed in society. Bad for all of us."

Agnes thought it fortunate that the English snake did not know about Mary's delicate condition. She'd spread that news like the plague.

Edward gripped Agnes's arm above the elbow. "I'm sure you exaggerate, Miss Throckmorton."

"No. 'Twill be in the papers in a day or so. Do you have printing presses here? Well, never you mind. We've brought the news straight up from London with us." She stepped closer to Agnes. "What do you think of that behavior?"

Agnes felt gentle pressure on her arm. This needle-minded English twit could do with a blackened eye and a toothless grin. But Agnes didn't follow her instincts. She drew upon the lessons she'd learned from her sister Sarah. She gave the poor English cow a piteous smile. "I think a king should learn the language and respect the customs of all of his subjects."

Matched, Miss Throckmorton stiffened her spine. "I think a king should speak whichever tongue he chooses. I don't suppose a Scot would know about the divine right of kings."

Agnes chortled and lost the grip on her composure. "You silly, uneducated girl."

"Yes, she is," her father prudently said. "Mary, a Stewart king was the first to make such a proclamation."

Undaunted, his daughter snapped her fan shut. "So? Next you'll have our genteel Hanoverian kings wearing Scottish tartan plaids. Imagine that, Papa, our monarch showing his knees and paying respects to the Scotch."

Which, Agnes thought, was the root of the differences between her people and the human rubbish that occupied the southern part of the isle. Scotch, indeed.

The youngest of the girls stepped into the fray. "You're a snake, Mary. A wicked snake, and I hope you marry an old vicar who gives you the pox." The girl looked at Agnes with unabashed kindness. "Mary's a horrid sister."

Agnes almost reached for the young girl. "My sister Mary is not."

"She's the painter who says Parliament cheats the people."

"Papa!" exclaimed the eldest. "Send her home. She's starting to whine like a monkey."

Penelope wasn't done. "You're miffed because the men here are more interested in Lady Agnes than you. She's prettier and she's nice."

Throckmorton leaned on his cane. "Do you wish to retire, Penelope, dear? We have gone beyond the pale of polite conversation. I can have the driver return you to the inn."

"No, Papa. I'd like to stay. You promised that I could sing tonight."

Her sister said, "Then find someone else to bore until after dinner."

"Penelope," said her father. "Should you misbehave once more, you will be excused immediately. Do you understand?"

"Yes, Papa."

Agnes watched the young girl make her exit. She walked casually until she reached the stairs; then she lifted her skirts and ran. At the first landing, the staircase split, one flight heading left, the other right. After a brief hesitation, the girl raced up the left side.

Agnes was thinking of herself at that age and remembering similar exits she'd made, when she heard Edward say, "William, I didn't know you were friends with Mayor Arkwright."

"A rather new acquaintance." As if it were a secret, he lowered his voice and said, "Unless you insist on having the consortium's business to yourself, I thought to meet the other textile concerns here and see if they are in the market for our products."

The answer confused Edward, for he said, "But I've always been in favor of the free market. Had you sent word, I would have arranged the introductions for you."

"That's our Lord Edward," the mayor said expansively, now that the conversation had reverted to pleasantries. "A most equitable man."

"When did you arrive in Glasgow?" Edward asked Throckmorton.

"Just today. The mayor offered us his hospitality, but we could not impose."

The house was spacious, but from personal experience, Agnes doubted the logistics of supporting so large a family of guests. None of the Throckmorton women wore wrinkled gowns, and their wigs were perfectly dressed. Had they each traveled with a maid, or did they harry the servants at their lodgings? Probably the latter, Agnes decided.

"I'm delighted you've come to Scotland at last."

Like young Penelope, Agnes had had a bellyful of Throckmorton and his flock of vile females. If Edward and the mayor wanted to hoist the welcome banner, let them. Excusing herself, she unfortunately made eye contact with the persistent Viscount Lindsay.

Pretending she had not seen him, she wended her way through the crowd and eased through the side door. Expecting Edward to follow, she strolled down the steps and admired the moonlit garden.

The door opened behind her, and her heart tripped fast. But judging from the footfalls, she knew that disappointment was on its way. The viscount had followed her.

After listening to two more stories about the Lindsay roses, she complained of a parched throat and sent him after punch. When he was gone, she searched for another exit from the garden. She discovered a locked gate and several bolted doors.

"I could show you the way out."

"Penelope!" Whirling, Agnes spied the girl on the balcony. She'd shed her wig; without it, she looked too small for the full-sleeved dress. "Have you been listening up there?"

She giggled. "You called him a toad, and he didn't even suspect. You're very clever."

"I'm very desperate. Where is the way out?"

"What will you give me?"

This girl had the upper hand, which Agnes suspected was a rarity, considering Penelope's position in the Throckmorton pecking order.

She must think of something to please a young girl who stood awkwardly between childhood and maturity. That or befriend the girl. "I'll give you a book of sonnets," Agnes teased.

"Do and I'll pitch them into the privy."

"A jar of Jerusalem sand?"

"I can buy that in Bartholomew Fair on any Saturday."

This girl knew how to drive a bargain. "A pair of Moroccan dice."

Hesitating, she said, "What else?"

The offering was generous by far. "A good spanking if you do not take your spoils and be done with it, Penelope Throckmorton."

"'Tis there." Her arm shot out, and she pointed to a fat urn overflowing with China roses. "Behind that pot of flowers lies the stairs."

"Where do they lead?"

"Up here."

"Must I also buy your company?"

Suddenly shy, she murmured, "No. Please come up."

Carefully Agnes maneuvered her white skirt around the urn and into an alcove. The stairs were dark, but she climbed them without mishap.

She was met with, "When do I get the dice?"

Agnes also got down to business. The character reference presented by Mrs. Borrowfield had contained the forged signature of Sir Throckmorton. That linked him to the assassin, albeit an accidental pairing. Through Penelope, Agnes could put to rest any suspicion that Throckmorton was a part of the conspiracy. "Tomorrow, but our meeting must be a secret."

Warming to the plan, the girl whispered, "There's a mercantile across the street from the Culross Inn. That's where we've taken rooms. What time can you be there?"

Agnes intended to visit Trimble tomorrow, but she could see him afterwards. Yes, that might be better. She lowered her voice and played along with the intrigue. "At the meridian."

"I'll be there. Someone's coming!"

The doors opened again; noise from the crowd drifted into the peaceful garden.

"Agnes? If you are here—"

"I am." At the concern in Edward's voice, she shot to her feet. "Up here." Without question, he was thinking about the assassin and fearing for her life.

His smile was pure relief. "Good. Who have you there?"

"Penelope. We've become very fast friends, haven't we?"

She giggled.

He moved to stand beneath them. "'Tis better

197

company to be had out here all the way 'round, wouldn't you agree, Miss Penelope?"

Her giggles turned to chortles.

"You mustn't embarrass her, my lord," Agnes chided.

"He's very handsome," said Penelope in an awed whisper.

When he chuckled, Agnes couldn't resist saying, "Aye, and well he knows it. Dub him comely again, Penelope, and he'll preen like a peacock."

The girl said, "I saw a white peacock once in the royal menagerie."

Bless her, she still knew the art of honest conversation. Pray she did not let her siblings drum it from her. "Truly?"

"By my oath," the girl swore. "The next time I visit, I shall bring it a crust of bread. That's what peacocks like to eat."

"How exciting. Do you promise to tell me about it at *another* time?"

"Must I go?"

"Aye, Penelope." Agnes extended her hand. "With friends, there is always tomorrow."

The girl shook hands as if she were priming a pump. "Until tomorrow." Then she dashed down the stairs.

"Wait! You've forgotten your wig." Agnes tossed it over the rail to Edward.

"May I?" he asked, holding the mass of white curls.

"Why must I wear it? You and Lady Agnes don't."

As he replaced the wig and adjusted it, he said, "'Tis another of those adult choices that await you."

"I will not be like Mary when I'm grown. I'll be a good person, like Lady Agnes."

"You are a delight, Penelope. Now hurry inside before you get into trouble."

Waving to them both, the girl rushed to the doors,

then slowed and made a graceful entrance into the ballroom.

Edward joined Agnes.

"You were looking for me?"

"Aye. Young Lindsay convinced you to try the punch."

The casual remark was too leading; Agnes knew he was headed somewhere, but she intended to make his journey as difficult as possible. *"Young* Lindsay? How old are you?"

"Nine and thirty."

"So old as that?"

Ignoring the jibe, he moved beside her at the railing. "Young enough to harry a Highland lass until her hair turns gray."

The words were too romantic. If she did not challenge him now, he'd forget where they were. Agnes strove for boldness. "You're desperate enough to boast of your prowess to a virgin."

He moved so close she could smell his minty breath. "I am experienced enough to know her worth."

Agnes had used those words in praise of him. "But my innocence or lack of it is not why you came searching for me."

"Nay." He reached for her hand. "What other things did Lindsay convince you to try other than the punch, which you claim you do not like?"

The cool night air turned warm. He wanted to kiss her, of that Agnes was sure. She could not allow it, not here, not when the evening was so young. But she had considered it, and that realization gave her pause. She must manage this man. She must protect his life and those of his children. Boldness had not worked. She moved on to brazen. "Are you jealous?"

Pursing his lips, he nodded, slowly and deliberately.

"'Twould seem I am, Agnes MacKenzie. What do you think I should do about it?"

"Put into my hands, the choice is a foregone conclusion. You will behave as your station dictates."

The bell rang, indicating dinner would be served in half an hour. Agnes couldn't have eaten a bite even from God's own table.

"Agreed. Shall we stroll in the gardens and hold hands?"

A perfectly acceptable activity, and considering the passionate encounters they had already shared, Agnes liked the idea of reverting to the old-fashioned ways of courting.

"I'd like that." She descended the stairs before him and waited. When he again stood beside her, she extended her hand.

Threading his fingers through hers, he tucked her arm against his waist. "Tell me about Vicktor Lucerne."

"What brings the great composer to your mind? Are you a patron of music?"

"'Twas something the Throckmorton girl said after you left. According to her, you're the reason Lucerne will not perform in England."

At the thought of her former charge, Agnes laughed. "Vicktor performs where he will and when he will. Even at the age of two and ten, he is a true genius of music."

"You'll get no argument from me on that count. How did you meet him?"

"You have something on your nose." She touched him there and frowned. "Must be a bruise from putting it where it doesn't belong."

"Clever. Now tell me how you came to travel as Vicktor Lucerne's bodyguard."

Some people referred to Agnes in that fashion; others styled her a companion. "After a near-successful kidnapping of their son, the Lucernes contacted me. For almost a year I traveled with Vicktor."

Edward stopped before a thriving rosebush and picked a bloom. Taking a whiff, he closed his eyes. "Were you ever injured in defense of him?"

"Aye. I tore a nail off my thumb. It bled profusely."

With a flourish, he presented the flower to her. "The truth, please."

She'd been bedridden and in agony for two days, but an understatement seemed best. "I suffered a bruise."

His gaze slid over her in a proprietary way. "Where were you bruised?"

"My ribs."

"Were they cracked or broken?"

To conceal her discomfiture, Agnes laughed. "A stranger would think we were discussing china plates."

He did not laugh. "'Twas no accident, was it?"

The mating calls of insects buzzed in her ears. "Nay."

"Were you attacked?"

"Yes. By two ruffians and a club."

"Your foreign fighting skills prevailed?"

The event was in the past; she could jest about it now. "After a taste of that club, aye."

"Where was Lucerne?"

"Where any lad in the circumstances should have been—crouching in fear behind a rain barrel outside the Burgtheatre in Vienna."

"The ruffians left you alone after that?"

"Not exactly. Their employer was persistent."

"Oh? Who was he?"

"A wealthy Turkish prince. He invited Lucerne to Constantinople. Vicktor declined. The Turk took offense and used force."

"Only once?"

"Yes. I advised His Highness to be more creative in his inducements to a lad of two and ten."

"Was he?"

"Very much so. He lured young Vicktor with the promise of his very own caravan."

"A much more enticing bribe to a lad. What happened then?"

"I learned to ride a camel and wear a veil."

He slid an arm around her. "What a wonderful adventure."

She had the advantage of limited time, for they'd be going in to dinner soon, but in her heart, she didn't want to move away from him. "'Twas actually, and I'm pleased that you asked."

"There is much more that I would know about you."

But rather than ask another question, he turned her to face him. Moonlight bathed his features in a soft glow. Just as he bent to kiss her, the door opened and the butler announced dinner.

Agnes almost wilted in relief.

Edward cursed but said, "The night is young, Agnes MacKenzie, and good food makes me more determined to get what I want."

As it happened, the meal was an inventive collection of veal florry, ham with chestnut sauce, and an assortment of soused fish roes. Seated between Edward and the mayor, Agnes declined a glass of red wine, fearing that she might stain her dress.

Silver clanged against crystal, and the parson, who was seated on the other side of Edward, rose. When last Agnes had seen the man, she'd been scandalously cradled in the earl's arms. The mayor's wife and Commodore Hume had been there, too.

In his overlong blessing, the cleric made reference to friends and loyalty and staying true both to one's faith and to the messenger who delivered it. Agnes thought the topics unusual until the cleric sat down and brought up the subject of Edward's visit to Saint Vincent's Church.

Edward put down his fork and addressed the cleric. "With all due respect, John, this is hardly the place for such a discussion."

The ensuing conversation so angered Agnes that she excused herself before the dessert was served. Edward caught up with her in the music room, where she'd taken a chair in the back row.

11

AGNES STARED AT THE SILVER BUCKLES ON HIS SHOES. "You did nothing to change the cleric's mind, you wretched Lowlander."

Edward sat in the chair beside her. "Change it from what?"

"Wipe that innocent grin off your face," she spat. "You could have contrived a reason for our presence at another church. But did you? Nay. You allowed that cleric to think that we are contemplating marriage."

"How can that be?" He could have been discussing the arrangement of the chairs, so casual was his tone and manner. "I do not recall ever hearing you say that you like me."

Now he was being obtuse. "I do like you, but do not ask me why, for at the moment a reason escapes me."

"Very well. I'll rely on those occasions when you are the most friendly to me. Truly, though, the cleric's mistaken assumption does have a beneficial aspect." Crossing one knee over the other, he picked at the velvet of his breeches. "If he tells Mary Throckmorton, she may become discouraged and treat some other fellow to that game of peekaboo with her breasts."

The image tickled Agnes. "You did not look away."

"'Twas an interesting observation in some respects. You see, one of her breasts is quite larger than the other."

"What!"

"A commonplace occurrence, and one that is well documented in anatomy texts."

To keep from slapping his face, Agnes folded her arms.

"Yours are perfect."

He thought she was covering herself. She dropped her hands to her lap. "You are outrageous."

"But to return to your original complaint," he went on. "Had you not hurried from the table, you would have heard me ask the good cleric to keep his assumptions to himself or risk losing my patronage."

She'd spoken too quickly. "No one will think we are getting married?"

"Short of your leaping into my arms forthwith? Nay."

The door opened, and the other guests streamed in. Agnes had taken a seat at the back of the room near the exit on purpose; if the music was boring, as was often the case at these affairs, she could slip out unnoticed. Others among the guests had planned to do the same, for they glared at her as they were forced to take chairs in front of her.

For entertainment, four of the Throckmorton sisters performed using spinet, fife, and mandolin. Poor Penelope must have been sent back to the inn, for she was not among the performers. The quartet began with several selections from Mozart. Next came an unusual rendition of a Vicktor Lucerne sonata. Unfortunately for the music, the women had switched to three-string lutes and a drum. The *Butterfly* Sonata sounded more like a cricket fest.

Agnes winced at the travesty.

Beside her, Edward nodded to sleep. In repose he looked like the scholar and loving father and younger than his age. She understood completely why Mary Throckmorton had flirted shamelessly with him tonight. Thinking of the many evenings he must have spent at similar affairs, Agnes wondered why he had not married a second time. Finding no plausible answer, she decided he was happy in the bachelor's life.

She didn't for a moment believe his doctorly story about unusual female anatomy; he'd said it to provoke her. But if she chose to verify his appalling claim, she could easily find the answers in the medical texts in his study or in the library. Every day women died in childbirth, and doctors spent time worrying over differences in breast sizes? No. He was having her on.

With that particular embarrassment in mind, she couldn't resist retaliating. Leaning close, she opened her fan and spoke behind it. "Wrecked ships and forever cabbages."

He started, then tried to collect himself.

Moving back, she stared at the musicians but watched him out of the corner of her eye. "Were you napping, my lord?"

"Nay." He yawned but didn't have the decency to look guilty for it.

"Then what did I say?"

He blinked and looked around the room, as if seeking his bearings.

"You were napping," she said.

He moved so close, she could feel his breath on her face. "Sleep with me tonight, and you'll find out for yourself what I truly look like upon awakening."

He uttered scandal with reckless abandon. She should rap him atop his head with her fan and storm from the room. But her heart was racing with that peculiar excitement only he could inspire. "What were you dreaming about?"

"If I were, which is not to say that I was, but merely for the sake of this discussion. If I *were* dreaming, 'twould take more than gibberish from you to wake me up. Several enchanting ways come to mind. Shall I tell you—"

"Go back to sleep. At least then you cannot embarrass me without shaming yourself in the doing."

"Consider this, my philosopher." His shoulder bumped hers. "I could have pretended to sleep to get you to talk to me, which you've not done enough of tonight."

"Incorrect. After the misconception you perpetrated on the cleric, I spoke to you. I distinctly remember saying that I hoped you grew an ear in the middle of your forehead."

"Ghastly image that." He cringed. "I'd as soon sleep through my next wedding night as hear with the flat of my face."

She tried not to laugh but failed.

"See?" he crowed. "You do like me."

His immodest reaction reeked of swelled male pride. Eager to put him in his place, she said, "May I offer my felicitations now on your anticipated wedding night?"

"Anticipated being the important word." His eyes gleamed with wicked light. "Aye, you may, and be sure to mention the part about being fruitful."

Desire, base and raw. That's what he wanted from her. "The conjugal aspects of marriage interest you the most."

"Nay." Turning, he mapped her face with an intense gaze. "A bright mind behind enchanting brown eyes will catch my interest first."

Smooth didn't begin to describe his methods. "I'm sorry I awakened you."

"Did I mention a mouth and a tongue that fit perfectly with mine?"

Mortified, she glanced at the people around them. To her relief, half of them were either snoozing or fighting off sleep, and the other half were bemoaning the poor entertainment. Agnes thought it best to whisper. "You're a rogue and much too familiar."

"Because I find pleasure in telling you that your hands have magic in them?"

"Aye."

He patted his knee. "We are agreed then. I am familiar with the way your hands feel, and they inspire magic."

"Your roundabout logic will fail with me. Go back to sleep."

"You will awaken me if I snore."

It wasn't a question. She sighed loudly. "Of course."

His smile was sinful, wicked. "I knew you would."

Agnes thought he smelled like linen dried in the summer sun. Why hadn't she noticed that before? "How can you be sure that I will awaken you again?"

"Your stepmother told me that you are loyal to a fault and considerate of others. I've been in your company long enough to agree." He closed his eyes and squirmed until he found a comfortable position. "Unless you'd like to return to the subject of what I look like upon awakening . . ."

"I'm certain you resemble a troll."

He grinned but didn't open his eyes. "You could put it to the test tomorrow morning."

But the next morning Agnes learned that Edward had left orders that he was not to be disturbed. Upon their arrival home the evening before, he'd gone into his laboratory.

"He'll come out for meals and to tuck the children in, but little else," said Mrs. Johnson. "'Tis his way when an idea is upon him."

That was Agnes's first disappointment of the day.

She filled her pomander and went to the music room. After a fitful night filled with disturbing dreams of Edward, she desperately needed inner harmony. An hour later, she conceded defeat. Soon she must face her growing feelings for him. The coward in her hoped they found the assassin first.

Riddled with worry for both her family and his, Agnes went in search of Hannah. She found her sitting on the carpet in the Elizabethan wing. Chattering a steady stream of gibberish, the girl spoke to her menagerie of carved animals, which she'd herded into groups on the floor. As usual, she avoided books, drawing paper, and writing utensils.

Edward had not exaggerated the girl's aversion to letters. Agnes thought Hannah believed there was a finite number of letters, and that Christopher possessed them all.

Agnes spent a fruitless morning trying to teach the girl the alphabet. Sarah had the skill of teaching. At the thought of her sister, Agnes felt loneliness settle over her. She glanced at the tapestry covering the alcove. Behind it lay the locked door that led down to Edward's dungeon laboratory.

Fighting melancholy, she got to her feet and extended a hand to Hannah. "Would you like a slice of c-a-k-e?"

Trancelike at the notion of letters, the girl stared at nothing. "Want Papa."

Tears choked Agnes, and she pulled Hannah against her, swaying from side to side. "I know, and he misses you, too. But he's making important things."

Her sweet face puckered with sweet concern. "'S'progress."

"Yes, it's very great progress." Agnes's father had seldom locked himself away. At five years old, she and her sisters had mounted their ponies and ridden with him into the fields at harvest time. They'd slept in haystacks and sung songs around the fire.

But the MacKenzies of Ross had never been plagued by an assassin.

Agnes's second disappointment of the day came when she learned that no messenger had arrived for her from London. What had arrived at Napier House was another bouquet of Lindsay roses.

She plucked at the petals. After that dreadful gossip from Mary Throckmorton, Agnes longed to know what was occurring in her sister Mary's life. Passion ran high between Mary and Robert Spencer, the earl of Wiltshire. But was passion enough? Mary didn't think so. Edward believed that physical intimacy constituted a promise, and Mary and Robert had undeniably become intimate. Would Papa see it the same way?

Agnes didn't know, but instinctively she thought the choice should be Mary's. Had Papa been forced to wed any of the women who'd conceived Agnes, Mary, and Lottie, he would not have married Juliet White. That would have been a tragedy, for Juliet was the mortar that held the MacKenzies together.

Agnes felt apart from them now. Even in Canton, she had not felt so isolated. The reason for her loneliness frightened her. She was falling in love with Edward Napier, and she couldn't find the will to prevent it. Her life's course had been charted years ago on a dockside quay. Family came before romantic entanglements, and Agnes needed her family now.

Word would come soon. Papa wrote to his children on Saturday. Sixty hours later, she'd have the news.

With Auntie Loo and the others to watch Hannah and Christopher, and Edward barricaded in his dungeon, Agnes put the Moroccan dice in her bag and left for her appointments. Her first stop was Saint Nicholas Hospital, where she left half of Lindsay's flowers and twenty pounds. To deliver the other half of the roses, she traveled by barge for the second time across the river to the orphanage. She'd visited the home before and hired some of the girls to clean the tower. Today she left a purse of twenty-five pounds and references for the maids.

After an informative meeting with Penelope Throckmorton, Agnes staved off a wave of guilt. She had used the girl, coaxed her into disloyalty, drained her of information, and received a gift in return. Through teary eyes Agnes stared at the small book in her hands. A book of sonnets. A memory of the night before.

Penelope had been sent back to the inn early for the crime of putting a lizard in Mary's lute. "Made her screech like the monkey she accused me of being," Penelope had bragged.

In parting, Agnes committed a further act of betrayal against her new young friend; she'd convinced an unsuspecting Penelope to leave the mercantile first. Only the shopkeeper knew of the meeting, and her silence was easily bought for the purchase of a butter-colored apron for Mrs. Johnson and nightcaps for the children.

The carriage rumbled down the unpaved streets. Surrounded by fields and hills, Glasgow was a city of merchants and tradesmen. Only London boasted more wealth and commerce than Glasgow. Every year tons of American tobacco found its way here. Ship-building thrived. The textile industry flourished.

The driver shouted. The carriage lurched. Agnes braced herself, but not before she was thrown against the side. Pain shot through her shoulder, and she gritted her teeth to keep from crying out. She should have worn the sling last night, but vanity had defeated good sense. Edward hadn't protested.

What fiend of man made that dress?

A cocky compliment, and the most original she'd ever received. What was he thinking now? She pictured him poring over drawings, blunting quills, crumbling paper and tossing it into the hearth.

Rancid smells assaulted her nose, and she covered her face with her gloved hands. Shouting people and braying animals announced that the market lay ahead. A tripe shop and a peruke maker shared a storefront. In the next block a plumber and a sign painter stood cheek by jowl.

Trimble kept his office in the top floor of the Anchor and Wheel Tavern, a respectable establishment near the brewer's guild.

He opened the door, yanked a napkin from around his neck, and waved her in.

She stopped. "I've interrupted your meal."

He wiped his thick mustache and tossed the napkin onto a table. The remains of his lunch, a pile of quail carcasses and a hunk of bread, littered a platter. The sweet odor of cabbages hung in the air.

Patting his flat stomach, he said, "I've had my fill. Come in and sit down. I'll put these dishes in the hall."

Past fifty by a year or two and gray from forehead to nape, Trimble had a youthful air about him. He could be stern and harsh when circumstances dictated, but when he met with success, he rejoiced like a lad who'd collected his first wages.

Agnes removed her cloak and hung it on a rack with an array of similar garments. Then she took the chair nearest the window.

Trimble set out the rubbish and began tidying the table. Across the room, boxes were piled to the ceiling. Packed inside were garments of every kind, from lepers' rags to princely robes, disguises used when necessary by those in his employ. Agnes had worn a costume or two in the course of her search for Virginia.

Trimble had established a web of knowledge gatherers that stretched from the Baltic to Canton. Some of his associates were retired soldiers, same as he; others were ship's captains, nannies, and roomsetters.

He made a fist and pounded the desk. "Congratulate me. I've found your bowman."

Agnes slumped in the chair. "Good work, Trimble."

He laughed and poured her a glass of ale. "It's not the item of information we long for, but it will save Napier's life."

The item he spoke of was Virginia's whereabouts. For five years, he'd been in Agnes's employ, but from the start, he'd adopted her cause. In private they dropped formalities. He was practical about the search and mindful of the odds; Agnes was neither.

The differences between them formed the basis of their unusual friendship. He'd traveled with her to Canton and enlisted the harbormaster into his web.

Agnes touched her glass to his. "Tell me about him."

Trimble whistled. "Name's Van Rooks, and we've not seen his like before."

"A Dutchman?"

"Yes." From a niche in his desk he produced the quarrel she'd given him. "A queer one the Rook is. That's what the fletchers in London call him. The Rook. How many of these"—he brandished the arrow—"do you have?"

She recalled each of them. One in her shoulder. The second in Edward's chair. A third in the Napier crest. The fourth skewering the dove in the MacKenzie plaid. "Four, why?"

He chewed his lip, a sure sign that the subject troubled him. "He commissions only five for each job."

Odder still, this assassin. "What if he doesn't succeed in five tries?"

"Hasn't happened. That's why no one questions his price."

"Which is?"

"Five thousand pounds. One for each arrow."

It was Agnes's turn to whistle. "He must be good."

"They say the word hasn't been uttered yet to equal the Rook's skill."

Agnes gazed out the window. A group of seamen swaggered down the lane; a pack of scrawny children followed. Sunlight turned the panes of glass to mirrors. Did the bowman stand behind one of those windows?

Agnes scooted her chair back. "I was bothered

when he did not kill the guard. Now I know why and it frightens me. He is an honorable assassin."

"There's worse news, so I won't argue the point."

Impossible, she thought. "If you tell me he is a ghost, I will tell your wife that you gifted your mistress with a new carriage."

In mock misery, he wrung his hands. "Crafty women, you Highlanders."

He'd always teased her about her heritage. Agnes took no offense. "Give me the ill tidings and end my misery."

"He's skilled with a blade."

Bitterness filled her. "Does he poison them as well?"

Trimble shook his head in shame. "No honor in that."

Agnes didn't necessarily agree, but she wouldn't broach the argument either. "The fletcher who makes the quarrels. I don't suppose he can be bought."

"Everyone can be bought."

"Well then?"

"Not every price can be met."

"Oh, now *that's* symmetry of thought, Trimble. I'll pay dearly to learn the Rook's location and a description of his face."

Trimble sipped the ale. "The fletcher has a brother in the workhouse of Saint Andrews, Holborn. Gain his release and you'll get the location of the Rook and a likeness of his face."

Holborn was a district of London. "But that will take a fortnight at the least. I'll have to hire a barrister in London. Take it to Sessions." She stopped. She understood. "'Tis a price we cannot meet."

"Exactly. The Rook will have finished the job by then."

"Or the job will have finished him." Agnes didn't wince at the prospect of taking the man's life. The world would be better off without the Rook.

Trimble leaned forward, resting his elbows on his knees and clutching the glass with both hands. "He's very dangerous. His peers and those who know him say the first scruple has yet to find him."

She straightened her fingers and made a slicing motion. "But can he bring a man down with the edge of his hand?"

"No." He sat back. "But you'll have to get within arm's length of him first, and I tell you, Agnes, it will not be easy. Those ruffians in Burgundy? That childmonger in London? Those were amateurs. I'll wager my firstborn son that the Rook knows all about you. He'll be prepared to deal with your unusual abilities."

Some people did not speak kindly of Agnes's skills. Other people did not believe in weaponless fighting, but she no longer took offense at their disparaging words. "Perhaps I'll brew up a little Chinaman's poison."

He scoffed. "You never would stoop to that. 'Tis a coward's weapon, and you're no coward. That brawl in Canton convinced me." His voice dropped. "The Rook will not stay long in Scotland. Word from the fletchers' guild says he'll come and go within a fortnight."

"That doesn't give me much time."

He turned his attention to her sling. "Are you healing well?"

"Aye, I have an excellent doctor."

"Cathcart's a ruddy good man. In the event you are interested, he hasn't visited his mistress lately."

Feigning boredom, Agnes examined her fingernails.

Trimble wasn't done. "Every Wednesday and Saturday, regular as England will war with France, she entertains him. Stays over, they say, but only on Wednesday."

"Then we can assume that the widow MacLane does not snore."

Trimble howled with laughter. "Dismiss those deadly hands and feet, Agnes MacKenzie. A solid prick of your tongue, and a man'll bleed to death."

"I learned it from Lottie."

"So you've said." Wiping his eyes, he sniffed. "One of my sources saw you in the carriage with the Napiers."

She told him about visiting Saint Vincent's Church in search of Mrs. Borrowfield. "Have someone question the sedanchairmen and the runners in the area. See if Mrs. Borrowfield, or however she styles herself, hired a ride on Sunday mornings between nine-thirty and ten o'clock. She did not attend services. Learn where she went, whom she met."

He jotted down the information in a small book. "I should have thought to check with the churches. Anything else?"

Agnes felt another twinge of guilt over her treatment of Penelope, but tucked it away and explained her suspicions about Sir Throckmorton.

Nodding in agreement, Trimble made another notation. "If he brought that many women with him, the laundry maids at the inn will probably aid us out of spite."

"Nay. Pay them." Agnes withdrew a sack of coins from her bag and handed it to him.

He gave it back. "The duchess of Ross sent me fifty pounds. Lady Lottie sent ten." In reproach, he said, "But you did not hear that from me."

Her family might swear that Virginia was dead, but some of them helped Agnes finance the search for her. She thought of her father and Mary. "Did your man in London have any news of Papa or Mary?"

"Glad you reminded me." He went to his desk and fished out a newspaper clipping. It was dated a week ago. In a cartoon Mary had sketched Lord Robert Spencer, the earl of Wiltshire, standing in the winner's box at Longacre Downs, his steed dead at his feet. Written across the horse's body were the words, "Common Man."

"Saint Ninian help her," Agnes murmured. "Now she's ridiculing him for his stable of horses and his fondness for the races."

"You'll be off to London to lend a hand after you've cleaned up this nasty business here."

"Of course, if she needs me."

"You never did like Glasgow. Never stayed more than a night, even if your friend Captain Cunningham was at dock."

She hadn't had good reason to linger in this part of Scotland. She and Trimble corresponded through the web of messengers and truth seekers. In her vocation she couldn't travel to Glasgow at the drop of a hat. Unless he sent word about Virginia. "Where is Cameron?" she asked, speaking of Cameron Cunningham.

Trimble consulted a canvas-bound book. "On his way back from Penang. He's bringing back the first official shipment of pepper since Britain opened the port. He's a fortnight overdue. Did you know that he is also a friend of Lord Edward? Stays at Napier House when his ship docks in Port Glasgow."

Obviously Cameron hadn't mentioned Virginia to Edward, because Edward hadn't known about her, but that seemed strange, for Cameron was anything but shy.

Agnes pulled on her gloves and rose to leave.

"Give my best to Lord Napier," he said.

"If I see him." She related Mrs. Johnson's news about the earl's dedication to his work.

Trimble stared at the ceiling and scratched his cheek. "Didn't you tell me that you thought his work was involved and that Throckmorton's presence alerted you to it?"

"Yes. Everything in Lord Edward's life, except his newest invention, is ordinary. He doesn't own a prison as some nobles do. He hasn't vast lands in the Borders with tenants to ill-treat. I've seen his mill, and the people are happy and safe there. It must be that machine he's perfecting."

"No accidents at the mill?"

"Hoots. I'd forgotten. Yes, a fire in the workshop of a man named Dunbar. He helps Lord Edward with his inventions."

"I'll make the acquaintance of this Dunbar. He may know something of importance and not realize it."

"An excellent thought." She moved to the door.

"I'm surprised you haven't discovered what's in that dungeon laboratory at Napier House. You've been known to pick a lock with those deadly hands."

Agnes slowed her steps. She knew why she hadn't picked the lock; she'd waited for him to invite her down there. How foolish that she'd let pride get in the way of prudence. If burgling led to saving his life, that was what mattered. She'd examined the lock and could open it with ease.

"Have you fallen in love with him, Agnes?"

"Nay." To cover the lapse in good judgment she thought of an excuse and a lie. "'Tis an ancient lock. Have you a heavy pick?"

He pointed to a chest in the corner. "You know where the tools are kept."

Removing her gloves, she sifted through an array of keys and lockpicks, hasps and bolts, and even a chastity belt. She couldn't resist hefting it. If wearing such a device would protect her from her own weakness toward Edward Napier, she'd don the thing and throw away the key.

But that would be cowardly.

She chose a sturdy awl with a bent tip and decided it would work better than one of her knives to spring the old lock on the heavy oaken door to the laboratory.

"Thank you, Trimble."

He stopped her short of the door. "Agnes, listen to me. As soon as I find the Rook, I'll tell you where he is, but take Auntie Loo with you when you go after him."

"I'll consider it. You find him."

"Will you tell Napier about the Rook?"

A difficult decision; Edward was no match for the Rook; yet he'd go valiantly to his death. She could not let that happen. "I'll tell his lordship some of it."

Weary and frustrated, Edward pounded the surface of his work table and pushed to his feet. The air reeked of damp steel and oil. The pressure in the vessel was too high. He must find a way to regulate the temperature of the steam, thus controlling the power of the engine. It was as if he were trying to harness the power of the wheel without ever having seen a circle.

Clearing his mind, he walked around the engine. He rethought the design of each part, the manufacture, the assembly, the failure.

Twice more he tried. Twice more the solution eluded him.

He ripped the drawing of the last design from his tablet and wadded it in his fist. Sighting the glowing hearth, he cocked his arm, but stopped. When he found the answer, he'd want this page as a guidepost. Once the engine was perfected, he'd work backward to discover his mistakes and learn from them.

Frustration had blinded him to his own ways and means of invention. Knowing his children were safe had inspired him to selfishness. A part of him thrived in this dungeon, fed on the science of man building machines. It was why he could close his eyes and feel gravity work, or why he could see mathematics in a linear field. But he couldn't make this engine work.

He slid the page into a basket with its predecessors, then bathed and changed into clean clothes. Drying his hair with a towel, he banked the fire and turned down the lamps. Another unfinished enterprise of a less frustrating nature rested on a throw of black velvet at the end of the work bench. But he wouldn't complete that task now. He wanted to kiss Hannah goodnight and, in return, receive a messy smack of her lips against his cheek. Then she'd tell him her fondest wish, and he'd bite his tongue to keep from weeping with joy.

Christopher would talk to his mother, but what would he tell her tonight?

Buoyed by the moments to come, Edward tossed the towel at the crib that Hannah had often slept in as a babe. Then he left the dungeon and went to the tower to see his family.

Auntie Loo sat in a chair in the common room. "My lady is reading them a story." She lifted her eyes to the ceiling. "Are you well, my lord? You look tired."

He rubbed his neck and remembered sitting before this hearth, a pair of nimble fingers kneading his sore muscles and inspiring other earthier parts of him. "I haven't met with much success today."

As if it were a foregone conclusion, she said, "You will. Difficult times sharpen the mind."

He'd only chatted with Auntie Loo during meals or in passing in the halls. Now was a good time to get to know her and to learn a few things about Agnes MacKenzie. "Which of your ancient philosophers said that?"

She tucked her legs beneath her. "One who will surprise you." From the low table beside her she picked up a flat, palm-size star made of shiny metal. Absently, she twirled it between her fingers. "My mother said it, but she lets the emperor take the credit for her wisdom. Please sit. You have other questions in your eyes."

Taking the opposite chair, Edward couldn't help asking, "Do you miss your home?"

"Very much so." Dipping her head, she reverted to broken English, but the movement of the metal star in her hand stayed constant. "But Auntie's soul is now twined up tight with that MacKenzie woman's."

"Because she saved your father's life."

"Yes. All of my people owe her a gift. A lowly concubine's daughter is a small price to pay."

He could feel the strength of her conviction and warmed to the conversation. "May I ask you something personal?"

"Yes, so long as I may decline to answer."

He entertained a second thought about the question he wanted to ask but banished it. "I have read in medical texts that the females in your culture compress their feet to the point of deformation. Yours are normal. Is foot-binding a custom practiced only in the lower classes?"

She put down the star. "The power of fashion is great among the rich and poor alike in China. When I was six years of age, the time when binding begins, my mother forbade it."

"Were her feet bound?"

"Yes, and eventually she will lose most of her toes. I suffered much scorn."

"What did people say?"

"Referring to my large feet, they'd say, 'Just look at those two boats going by.' I tried to bind them myself, but the pain was too great."

He recalled what Agnes had said about Auntie Loo's skill. "Is it true that you are superior in skill to Lady Agnes?"

She paused for so long, he began to think she would not answer. When she did, her words surprised him. "I've had more schooling in the ancient arts. Chang Ling was my teacher from an early age. But I do not have Lady Agnes's heart for the kill."

Agnes had taken a life? The knowledge should have appalled him, but it did not. "How many people has she killed?"

"Three. In each instance she saved the life of a child."

She'd saved Edward's life, and had she killed the assassin in the process, he would have rewarded her. "What of conscience?"

"I also have more of that than the Golden One, as my people have named her. But her cause is greater."

"What is her cause?"

"In the church in Edinburgh, when you were tending her wound, the duke of Ross spoke about Virginia."

Edward knew the girl was missing and assumed dead by all of the MacKenzies except Agnes. *The ache*

in your heart will hurt you more than this latest wound.
Auntie Loo had said that of Agnes; she had been
referring to the loss of Virginia MacKenzie.

"Tell me about the lost girl," Edward asked. "What
happened to her?"

Auntie Loo folded her hands. "Do you believe she
is lost and not dead?"

"Yes."

"Why?"

"Because Lady Agnes believes it."

"That is the burden she must carry. I am at liberty
to say no more. Maybe she will confide in you
someday."

"I hope she does. You addressed her as Golden
One. Why?"

"Among my people, there is a very great holy man.
He has touched the spirit of Agnes MacKenzie. He
found it as pure and fine as gold. And so she is revered
as the Golden One."

More enchanted than ever, Edward rose. "I'll remember your advice."

As he climbed the stairs to the second level of the
tower, the new wood creaked and groaned beneath his
weight, announcing his presence to any within hearing distance. How had Agnes managed to walk down
these same steps and not make a sound?

He heard her voice before he mounted the second
flight of stairs. She was beginning a story about a
young girl who ran away from home by hiding in the
tinker's wagon.

"Why did she run away?" Christopher asked.

"Because her father spanked her."

"Spanking hurts my bottom," said Hannah.

Edward paused. He had never spanked the girl, and
he'd left strict orders to the servants that his children
were not to be whipped.

"Who spanked you?" Agnes asked.

Christopher said, "Mrs. Borrowfield did. She was knocking on the door to Father's laboratory and Hannah came upon her."

"'S'Bad."

"Why should Hannah get a whipping for that?"

"We are—were not allowed in the old wing."

"'S'old, and will break from wee hands."

"But now it's our home, Hannah. Leave my soldiers alone."

Something clattered against the wall.

"Now you've done it," Christopher spat. "You Hugotontheonbiquiffinarian. You've thrown the commodore."

"Draggle tail."

Edward paused on the threshold. Lady Agnes and the children sat on the bed. Christopher and Hannah wore new nightcaps and sleepy-eyed expressions.

"Papa, she threw Commodore Lord Chesterfield against the wall."

Hannah stuck out her bottom lip. "You took all the letters."

Agnes grasped Hannah's hand. "Why do you think Christopher has all of the letters?"

The girl pointed to the toy box. "'S'there."

Christopher pounded the bed. "You stay out of my toys, you Piscinarian."

"Dandy prat."

"Quiet." Edward scooped Hannah off the bed. "Find that commodore, Button."

"'S'there." She pointed to the spot where the chamber pot sat.

Praying Chesterfield hadn't fallen in, Edward put Hannah down. The toy lay on the floor. "Pick up the soldier and give it back to your brother. Then tell him you are sorry."

She squatted, retrieved the toy, and held it as if it were a slimy toad. Her new sleeping gown dragged the floor, and she almost tripped. Her eyes were wells of misery. "Sorry." She dropped the toy on the bed.

Lady Agnes excused herself saying, "I'll await you downstairs, my lord. I have news to share from Trimble."

Edward's heart raced. "Good news about our . . . *friend?"*

"Friend?" said Christopher. "Ha! You mean the man who's trying to kill you with a crossbow?"

A stillness settled over Edward, and he drilled Agnes with a cold stare. "Did you tell him?"

She looked beautifully baffled. "Nay."

"I'm not a lack-wit, Father. I see what goes on."

"Then you've seen enough. Where are the whistles Lady Agnes gave you? You promised to wear them."

He flapped his arms and sighed dramatically. "Not to bed, Father."

Shaken, Edward struggled to speak calmly. "Then keep them at hand, and do not f-r-i-g-h-t-e-n your sister."

Hannah wailed.

Half an hour later, when they'd fallen asleep, Edward extinguished the lamps. Anticipation clawing at his gut, he headed for the common room. How much had Lady Agnes learned about the assassin?

12

"I think you should buy Hannah a set of alphabet blocks of her own—pink ones with the letters styled differently from Christopher's." Agnes moved to the chessboard and absently touched the game pieces. "Or if you'd like, I'll get them for her."

Edward had expected her to rush into the subject of her visit with Trimble. "You're distant. Why? Is the news bad from Trimble?"

"Family should come first. You asked me to teach Hannah to read. I've made a small progress."

"What would that be?"

"Hannah thinks there is only one of the letter *A* and Christopher has it on a block, and the block belongs to him."

"That's inconceivable."

"I'm certain it seems that way to a man of your intellect. Lassies are different."

The air grew chilled. "Are you trying to insult me?"

"No." But she wouldn't take her eyes from the pink castle on the chessboard. "I was trying to explain what Hannah means when she says Christopher has all the letters."

She was also staying as far from Edward as she could. But the time for cat and mouse nonsense between them had passed. "I'll take her to the toy maker. Now, I'd like for you to come here and tell me what you learned from Trimble."

With the tip of her finger, she tipped the castle onto its side. Then she crossed the room and sat in the opposite chair, her gaze never meeting his.

His patience dwindling, Edward spied Auntie Loo's star. He reached for it.

"No." Agnes's hand shot out, but too late.

The metal sliced Edward's finger. Loosing his hold, the razor-sharp device clattered to the table. It hadn't appeared dangerous.

Agnes sprang to her feet and fetched a towel from a storage chest.

The cut was not deep and would heal quickly, but the foolishness Edward felt would linger. "Auntie Loo was twirling this."

Agnes put pressure on the cut and held it there. "Only one?"

Berating himself, he snapped, "I suppose you can twirl two."

She wiggled the fingers on the hand that rested in the sling. "Usually. But I'm better with a knife."

"It looks like a trinket."

She smiled for the first time. "In China's arsenal of weapons it is."

He could feel her facade of coolness melt a little. Seizing the moment, he said, "What do you do with it?"

She picked up the star, holding it like a skipping stone. With a flick of her wrist she sent it whirling in the direction of the door. It landed in the center stock of one of the crossbows on the wall. Edward thought of the skill involved in hitting a narrow wooden target from that distance.

Amazed, he tried to reconcile the contradictions about this woman. She looked like a Scottish princess. She'd sent three men to their deaths without damage to her conscience. She kissed him with the passion of a woman losing her heart. She had a devious mind for the most ordinary details. She'd discovered the reason his daughter could not learn to read. For all of those things and many more, he loved her.

He glanced again at the star in the crossbow. She'd declared she was better with knives. "Very impressive," he said honestly. "I approve completely of your target."

"He's a dead man."

Edward felt a thrill at gleaning information about the stranger who stalked him. "What did you learn about him? I was right about him being a Scot, wasn't I?"

"Yes," she said, but didn't sound convinced herself. "What clan?"

She shrugged and picked at the sling. "An outcast from the Borders, possibly a Kerr. He wears no tartan or badge."

"Where is he?"

"We do not yet know."

She was keeping something from him. "I don't believe you."

"'Tis true." She faced him, and her expression was guileless. "The fletcher in London revealed only the man's reputation and his penchant for the odd feathers. Make no mistake, Trimble will find our man."

The faceless assassin was taking shape. "What is his name?"

"The fletcher is an ordinary man, Edward, and he does not know you. From his stall in London he values his life more than he values your Scottish one."

She'd resorted to philosophy, an indication that she did not like the subject. Who could? "Surely you know something about him."

A sad smile curled her lips. Pensively, she said, "'Tis a luxury to know that what you seek is close at hand."

He knew what she sought. Now that they'd identified the assassin, Edward asked the question that had riddled him since the day he met her. "Tell me about Virginia. What happened to her?"

Her movements turned jerky, and she raked her teeth over her thumbnail. "I was foolish and irresponsible. I lost her."

"How long ago?"

She stared at the lamplight flickering on the ceiling. "Six years, three months, and twelve days."

He knew Agnes's age, three and twenty. She'd been only sixteen or seventeen at the time. His heart ached for her. "What occurred?"

"I . . . ah . . . I had met a beau at church," she said, her voice thick with apology. "Papa thought him fast, which he was. With Mary's help, I arranged an innocent tryst with him on a Monday afternoon."

"Virginia followed you?"

"Nay. I could not manage the outing alone. Mary offered to go with me, but Virginia begged. Cameron had left that morning for his manly tour of Europe. Virginia had an affection for him. She was upset over his leaving."

"What happened on that quay?"

"A great act of selfishness."

Small wonder she guarded her heart; she'd broken it and never allowed it to heal. "Then it follows that holding yourself apart from others is a greater selfishness."

"I gave Virginia a penny to leave us alone." She swallowed noisily. "I never saw her again."

Edward despaired of ever breaking through her wall of reserve. Her father maintained that she hadn't let herself grieve over the loss of Virginia. Edward thought she grieved every day. "How old was she?"

Her eyes drifted shut. "Just ten."

Edward had to touch her. Dropping the blood-stained cloth on the table, he knelt beside her chair, and held her hands in his. "You'll find her."

Her breathing turned choppy. "Aye."

"Can I help?"

"Believing is enough. Do you know, I cannot even recall that fellow's name." She gave his hand a squeeze and collected herself. When she opened her eyes, her gaze was clear and sharp. But she was as distant as the moon. "What progress have you made on your machine?" she asked.

"I've botched it today."

"But you haven't forsaken it completely?"

He strained to keep his hands still when he wanted to take her in his arms. "God has forsaken it, but not I. It will work, I know it will."

"Good. I'm sure you'd like to get back to it."

She moved to rise. Edward felt dismissed.

He stood and held out his hand. "It's early. Are you tired?"

Ignoring the offer of assistance, she got to her feet. "Rather I am, my lord."

No, his heart said. She'd given him a glimpse of what lay behind her defenses. He must build on that success. He checked the mantel clock—half past eight. "Agnes, this indifference of yours toward me is a lie."

She laughed, but the sound held no mirth. "Neither is it humorous, my lord. But there you have it."

He cursed his clumsiness, but if she could sling words, so could he. "I will not believe that you do not want me."

She gritted her teeth. "I want you . . . alive."

Edward knew she'd made light of the information from Trimble. She was trying to spare Edward. Anger roared to life inside him. He stepped away from her. "You think I'm some dandy, too weak in spirit to take the life of that bastard who's trying to kill me."

Plaintively, she said, "I think you will fail."

Fury rose up in him. "That's a wheen o' blathers."

Her expression went blank. "What did you say?"

"I said, I think you are full of your own Highland self."

She gave a little laugh, an honest one. "You spoke Scottish."

For now, the fight to win her heart went out of him. She'd closed herself off, was content to wallow in past guilt and ignore the pleasures of today. But she would not do it at his expense. "We speak Scottish here in the Lowlands now and then."

"I did not mean—"

"Aye, you did." He marched to the door and threw it open. Ducking beneath it, he said, "Take your Highland pride and put it to bed, Agnes MacKenzie."

"Where are you going?"

"That's none of your affair."

Agnes had to bite her tongue to keep from calling him back, but it was better this way. Word from Trimble of the assassin's whereabouts could come at any time. With Edward locked in his dungeon and unaware of the messenger, Agnes could slip from the house unnoticed and deal with the assassin on fair ground.

For tonight she'd made Edward forget about the assassin. His head was filled with disappointing thoughts about her, not about an enemy he could not defeat.

When she heard the muffled slamming of a door, she knew he'd entered his laboratory, and she said a silent prayer for forgiveness. Heavyhearted, she climbed the stairs and went to bed.

Sometime later she was awakened by shouts from the guards. One of the bells had rung. Instinct and training drove her from the bed. She thrust her feet into soft boots. Auntie Loo handed her a robe and a short sword. Sliding her favorite stiletto under her belt, she dashed for the steps. Backsword in hand, Auntie Loo ran upstairs to stay close to the children.

Agncs freed the bolt, and the door opened without a sound. Faint light poured into the gloomy stone corridor. To the left lay the tapestry covering the entrance to the dungeon. She knew that Edward had strung a bell down there, and it would alert him, but Agnes wanted the Dutchman to herself.

Pulling the door closed behind her, she crouched and dashed for the new wing. Up ahead, moonlight streamed into the formal parlor. Mrs. Johnson had left the drapes open. The hallway to the east wing gaped like a black maw. Intuition drove her there. Pausing, she flattened herself against the wall. To ready herself for the plunge into darkness, she closed her eyes.

A clock struck once. She cringed at the unexpected noise. Was it marking one o'clock or the half of some other hour? Outside, a shape ran past the windows, his shadow darting across the floor. She knew it was the guard, recognized his form. But her heart beat like a drum, and danger buzzed in her ears.

The Dutchman had come. She could feel his intrusion.

She freed her mind of everything, save her training and her purpose. One deep breath followed another. Harmony settled over her. Silently, she moved into the dark corridor.

The farther she traveled, the more her anxiety ebbed. But why? Unless the Rook was behind her. Suddenly fearful of that, she ran in a broken line. At the end of the hall she stopped.

Voices sounded outside. Two men stood between the house and the stables. She recognized the voices and yelled to the guards. They'd seen no one and heard only a bell. Which one, they could not say.

Agnes checked the bolt and found it thrown open. After locking it, she stopped to search each room as she retraced her path. In the parlor Boswell and Mrs. Johnson awaited her.

Roused suddenly, they both wore heavy robes and nightcaps and carried lanterns. Their eyes were wide with shock at the sight of Agnes, a noblewoman, dressed in black silk and carrying a sword. What must her expression look like to them?

"One of the front doors was ajar," Boswell said. "What's amiss, my lady?"

"A bell sounded." Agnes eased the sword behind her and moved to the front door. Closing it, she searched the foyer and the dining room. Knowing the assassin would not take the servants' lives, she raced up the stairs and searched every room in the new wing.

She found nothing amiss, felt no invasion. Hurrying down the stairs, she went outside and spoke to the guard. He had seen nothing amiss. Who had opened the front door?

In the parlor Boswell was still fuzzy from sleep. Mrs. Johnson elbowed him in the ribs, then whispered in his ear.

Agnes watched as they both flushed with embarrassment.

Boswell cleared his throat. "Being as how 'tis Saturday night, his lordship could have had an appointment elsewhere. He could have forgotten about the bell."

His mistress? No. The guard would have mentioned seeing him order his carriage and leave the property. Or had he been returning? Trimble had said that Edward stayed with his mistress on Wednesday nights, but not on Saturday. *Being as how 'tis Saturday.*

"Mr. Boswell, did you see Lord Edward leave or return?"

"Nay, my lady. But I've been abed since eight o' the clock."

Agnes could not stave off a feeling of impending doom. Was the Rook still here? "The guard would have told me if Lord Edward had passed this way."

"Perhaps he left out the front. You know he often walked to Mrs. MacLane's."

"Walk at night with a madman after him?" Mrs. Johnson shook her head and moved toward the old wing. "That guard came in the front door to raid my pantry again. His lordship's in his laboratory, I tell you."

Agnes and Boswell took off after her. As soon as she could, Agnes dashed in front of the cook. Scruples wouldn't keep the Rook from using Mrs. Johnson as a hostage. But he'd have to go through Agnes MacKenzie to do it.

Holding her sword at the ready, she stepped into the room. As the servants approached, light from their lanterns seeped into the room. Agnes gasped at what she saw.

A pair of dead doves littered the floor, their heads here, their bodies there, and blood spatters everywhere. The bowman had strewn it on the walls, the carpet, the precious illuminated manuscripts. But he had not spent that last arrow.

Mrs. Johnson wailed. Boswell comforted her with soothing words and a shoulder to cry on.

Unable to breathe, Agnes approached the door to the tower, which now stood open. The common room had been dark when she left it moments ago. Did someone await in there? How did the door get open?

As a precaution, she pitched the scabbard through the opening. It slid across the floor of the common room and caught on a rug. Then she listened.

The assassin would make a move. Auntie Loo would not. Agnes had learned that the hard way.

"All is well," Auntie Loo said and stepped into the light. Her arms were behind her, probably gripping the hilt of that deadly backsword.

Mrs. Johnson sniffed and examined the room. "All is well? 'Tis a wretched mess."

Scanning the destruction, Auntie Loo said, "I heard odd noises and came down here. Did you leave this door open?"

For the benefit of the servants, Agnes said, "Aye." But as she passed Auntie Loo, she sent her a look that said she wasn't sure.

Lighting a lamp, she surveyed the common room. The towel, stained from the cut on Edward's finger, rested on the low table. On the wall above the door the crossbows hung untouched, one wearing a star. Nothing was out of place, but Agnes could feel danger lingering in the air. The Rook had been in this room. She could have passed him in the corridors.

She walked around the room, taking in every detail. At the chessboard, she found proof of the intrusion.

The pink rook was gone.

He'd gotten too close this time. But if Agnes examined each of her movements since the alarm, she would not have acted differently. The children were safe. They were her primary concern. She joined the others.

"Where is Lord Edward?" Auntie asked.

Agnes stomped to the tapestry and threw it back. "'Tis something I'd trade my lands in Burgundy to know." Inside the square alcove she spied the niche to the left and the heavy door on the right. She grasped the handle, but the door was locked tight. With the hilt of her sword, she pounded on the ancient oaken surface.

"He's as deep a sleeper as there is," said Mrs. Johnson.

Boswell added, "Don't much sound make it down to the dungeon or through that old tapestry."

What if the bell in the dungeon had not rung? Or if it had, had Edward not been roused by the noise? The Rook could have picked the lock and come upon Edward unawares. What if the assassin, at this very moment, were waiting behind that door to make his escape? What if he'd already found his mark?

Agnes whirled. "Where's the key?"

"His lordship's got the only one. Don't take to visitors, except the children."

Boswell patted the cook's back. "Kept his wee Button down there with him, and her still in nappies. Do you recall that, Hazel?"

The cook gazed at the blood-spattered walls, but she'd gotten control of herself. "Aye, Bossy. An' didn't I show him the proper way to care for the wee lass?"

"That you did, Hazel."

Agnes looked at Auntie Loo. "Please get me the awl from my blue velvet bag."

She nodded and moved toward the new steps. Agnes faced the servants. "Go back to bed."

"But, my lady. What of this wretched business?" asked the cook. "It must be cleaned up proper."

If the Rook was still here, Agnes wanted no audience for the fight. "'Twill be here in the morning. Find your beds."

They left reluctantly. Auntie Loo returned with the tool, a lantern, and the scabbard for Agnes's blade. She sheathed it.

"What do you sense?" Auntie Loo asked.

"I do not know. If he got this far, he may have found his target."

"Or perhaps he saw that his cause was lost and fled."

Agnes again moved to the tapestry. "Return to the tower and bolt the door."

"Your arm is weak. Let me go after him."

"Nay. You must stay with the children, no matter what occurs."

Slipping behind the tapestry, Agnes put the lantern in the niche and squatted before the door. She tucked the sword under her right arm and worked the awl with her left. In two tries she sprung the lock.

But she faced poor choices. She did not know the configuration of the downward stairwell. She did not know the arrangement of the dungeon space. She stood in a pool of light. If the Rook lurked beyond that door, he would glimpse her before she spied him.

Choosing the only option that allowed a measure of

safety, she flattened herself against the wall to the right of the door. Unsheathing her sword, she used the tip of the scabbard to push open the door.

The loud screeching of the hinges hurt her ears. Why hadn't she heard that before? She'd heard Edward slam the door, but the sound had been muffled.

Senses alert, she held the sword in her left hand, ready to swing, and waited, praying that the Rook would rush out.

Stillness surrounded her. Quiet prevailed, save the metered cadence of soft snores from below. The wretched earl of Cathcart had slept through it all.

Agnes's mouth went dry, and she slumped with relief. Should she awaken him and tell him about the intrusion? It served him right to find out in the morning, but she couldn't do that; he should know what had transpired.

Taking the lamp, she started down the narrow steps. If she stood on tiptoe, her head would touch the ceiling. Edward must crouch to travel through this space.

She came to a landing of considerable size. Niches, larger than but like the one upstairs, were carved into two of the walls. In ancient times or times of war and siege, guards had likely been stationed here. To the right, the corridor led down another flight of steps. The snores were louder down there.

She ducked again and followed the corridor to its end. Once in the laboratory, she stopped and gaped like a child at the wonder of what she saw.

Odd lamps with strange metal roofs reflected the light throughout the chamber and illuminated the earl of Cathcart. He slept on his back on a tufted cot, one arm shielding his face, the other dangling to the floor.

Near his hand was a wicker baby crib that now served as a laundry basket. A faded pink ribbon graced the handle. Boswell had said that Edward kept Hannah here with him after her mother's death.

The notion was so sweet, Agnes's throat grew thick. Her father had also kept his children near him. This wasn't the first similarity she'd found between her father and Edward. Physically, however, they were as different as two men could be. Edward's hair was thickly waved and darker in its red hue. His features were not ruggedly handsome, but striking and expressive in an appealing way. Dressed in a casual tunic of faded black wool and marred leather breeches, he radiated nobility. Even that manly snore had a refined quality to it, and Agnes felt enchanted with him anew.

Moved, she turned and gawked at the contents of the room. The stone ceiling was blackened with age and lamp smoke. Brass braziers warmed the room. Wooden bookshelves stood against one wall, playing host to an assortment of what could only be called creations. On the top shelf rested the older, simpler gadgets: a spinning top with a removable crank on the side, and a two-headed hammer. The middle ground displayed archetypes of now popular tools: an adjustable flail, and clamps in dozens of shapes and sizes. The lower shelves contained his more sophisticated machines—metal shapes with pulleys and handles. Their purpose eluded her, but the story they told was clear—the legacy of Edward Napier.

A long, slate-topped workbench marched down the center of the room. An assortment of quills, pots of colored ink, drying sand, and lead pencils mingled on the table with jars and apothecary bottles. At the far end, on a square of black velvet, lay her jade necklace.

Beside it lay his open medical bag. He'd restrung the stones but had not attached the clasp. A spool of pink silk thread and an assortment of tweezers and scissors lay nearby. Upon inspecting the knots between the jade pieces, Agnes found them perfectly tied and spaced.

On a wooden pallet sat what must be his new machine. Pipes and a chimney jutted from what she recognized as a steam engine, but this device was smaller and more modern than any machine she'd ever observed. She tried to picture the scholarly earl moving from the difficult work of his complex engine to the simple task of restringing her jewelry.

She stumbled on the word *complex,* for it perfectly suited Edward Napier. She also examined her feelings for him and discovered emotions so strong they terrified her. Later, when the crimes against him were revealed and the men responsible were punished, she'd look into her heart. But not now; she hadn't the strength. In the meantime, she would learn as much about him as she could.

In a flat basket beside the machine lay a stack of drawings, weighted down with a larger version of his folding knife. The top page was crumpled, as if he had considered discarding it and changed his mind.

What did the assassin want in this room? What value could be placed on the first model of a spinning top that had become as common a toy as the hoop? Or the Napier flail, a tool as widely used as the plow? Whatever the assassin's employer wanted, it was something very valuable to him, else he wouldn't have spent five thousand pounds to get it.

She recalled Edward's explanation of what the new machine would do. The engine would enable him to spin raw cotton into thread here in Glasgow, thus eliminating the need to import expensive spools from India. He would no longer trade with Throckmorton, who just happened to have made his first visit to Glasgow at the same time that an assassin was stalking the inventor of the machine.

Throckmorton had to be behind it all. He could have faked his own signature on the letter of reference.

Edward's breathing changed. She knew he'd awakened.

Sleepily, he said, "Have you come to slay me with that blade?"

"Nay. The assassin was here."

Edward ran to the stairs.

She stopped him. "Nay. 'Tis too late. The danger has passed."

He shook his head, then rubbed his face in an effort to gather his wits. "What occurred?"

"The assassin slaughtered two more doves and painted the walls in the Elizabethan wing with the blood."

"Why?"

"He's taunting us."

"Was anyone hurt?"

"Nay. Auntie Loo is with the children. The door to the tower is bolted from the inside. Bossy and Mrs. Johnson have gone back to bed. You are safe down here."

"How did you know that our defenses had been breached?"

"A bell sounded, and the guards awakened me. We could not discover which bell. The east door was unbolted and the front door was open."

His gaze shot to the wicker crib and the niche in the wall above it. A carelessly tossed towel hung on the ledge. "Damn!" He yanked the cloth free, revealing the alarm bell. The towel had cloaked the sound. That explained why he hadn't come running; he hadn't heard the bell.

Agnes couldn't resist saying, "When you did not come upstairs, Bossy thought you were with your mistress."

"So you assumed I had returned and forgotten about the bell in the east wing. You thought I sounded it as I entered."

She had considered it, but now she knew the Rook had come in that way. What was Edward getting at? "Actually, I thought you had left to visit her, rather than returned. By the way, you snore."

Leaning against the table, he crossed his arms over his chest. "We had a wager on that very thing."

"On your snoring?"

He growled a warning. "For spoils you agreed to tell me about the MacKenzie way of scolding."

Agnes had forgotten the wager. And why not with an expert assassin after them? "I've had other things on my mind."

"You made a bargain, and at the moment, the subject of your father holds more appeal than anything else in this house."

Telling the tale offered a diversion from the harrowing events of the night. She rested the sword on the workbench. "When my sisters and I were very young—before Juliet White came into our lives, my father had been appropriately dubbed a rogue."

"Four illegitimate children, all of an age, born to different women?" He laughed so hard his shoulders shook. "Naming Lachlan MacKenzie a rogue is an understatement."

She bristled a little. "He was foremost a devoted

father, no matter on which side of the blanket his children were born. Do you wish to hear the story or not?"

Raising his hands in surrender, Edward murmured an apology, but he was smiling. "I meant no offense. The honest truth of it is every Scotsman admires your father's devotion to the fairer sex."

Agnes squared her shoulders. "Indeed. But from the time I learned to walk, the fairer sex was *devoted* to my father. They came in droves to conquer the infamous Highland rogue and wear his ducal coronet."

Edward slapped a hand over his heart. "Oh, to be vanquished so often and by so many beautiful foes."

Put that way, it was rather flattering. Unable to contain her mirth, Agnes laughed too.

"So how did scolding come into it?"

A thought of the carefree days of her youth brought peace to Agnes. She moved to a tall bench near the new engine and sat down. "You must know that privacy was impossible at Kinbairn Castle. My sisters and I were always underfoot. Juliet was our fifteenth governess."

"How old were you when she came?"

"About six."

He whistled. "Did the duke of Ross scold Juliet?"

"Nay. He married her."

"Then whom did he scold?"

"All of the maids, governesses, and nannies before her. But he didn't actually discipline any of them. He only told us he was going to scold them so we wouldn't interrupt him."

"I see. He took them to his chamber to make love to them."

"'Twas the scullery he used most often."

"So you grew up with a rather twisted understanding about getting a scolding."

"There was nothing twisted about the way my father looked when he emerged from an afternoon of scolding."

Edward laughed again, but as his humor abated, another much stronger emotion took its place. Familiarity filled the distance between them, and Agnes felt it in her soul. His probing gaze moved over her, lingering at her mouth and the satin belt at her waist.

Suddenly serious, his eyes met hers. "You should not have come down here in that robe."

13

APPREHENSION THRUMMED THROUGH AGNES, AND SHE
knew without a doubt, if he she didn't leave the room,
she'd surrender to him. Taking pleasure in his arms
was a sweet treason she could not commit. "Then I'll
leave now." She started forward, hoping to ease
around him and get to the stairs.

He did not move. "Were you bothered by the
possibility that I had gone to my mistress tonight?"

How dare he mention that woman now, when
Agnes struggled to hold on to her pride. "Go there to
live, for all I care."

"Liar."

His voice surrounded her, and the words echoed in
her ears. She paused before she reached him. "Good
night."

He stepped into her path. "You do care."

She could not look away from him. He towered over
her, a giant in his world of invention, but Agnes

MacKenzie was only a visitor in his life. She had promised to find his assassin, and she would. After that, she'd get on with her search for Virginia. But denying any feelings for him would be unfair.

She told him the truth. "Of course I care."

"Why, Agnes?"

"Because I cannot have you for myself." There, she'd said it.

He reached for her. "Oh, but you can."

The roguish remark buoyed her resolve. "You stormed from the tower."

"For good reasons. You were indifferent to me, and you lied."

The indifference had been an act, the lies a necessity. But she couldn't lie now, not when the promise of death hung in the air of Napier House. "You said your whereabouts were your own affair."

"Let me see if I understand." He raked a hand through his hair. "Your mind worked on the assumption that if I couldn't have you, any woman would do."

She edged closer, but the going was not easy. Her heart tripped fast, and her feet had turned to lead weights. "Aye, you said you wanted me. Then you ruined it by saying your desire for me was base and raw. But—"

"Physical desire is a hunger, no?" His gaze dropped. "Tell me your belly doesn't ache for intimacy between us. Swear you did not feel passion the very first time I kissed you."

Her stomach tightened. "Let me recall your words. You said that first kiss was born of lust and nothing more."

Challenged, he lifted his brows. "If that is so, then why do I recall each beat of your heart and every breath you took?"

"'Twas not a tender moment for you. You said any milkmaid could rouse you as well.'"

In mock bewilderment, he said, "And you believed me?"

"We were strangers at the time, and you were—"

"A stranger at being shot at!"

His fury fired her determination. "You turned from me in Whitburn when—"

"Because I was eager to get myself and my children home to Glasgow alive."

He had a valid point. "I allow you that one defense, but I will not believe that you wanted *me*. So we needn't—"

"Then listen, my delicious skeptic, and I shall remedy that. Our first kiss lasted the better part of four minutes, hardly milkmaid-and-master fare. Your pulse ran fast—above one hundred beats for each of those moments, and you breathed twenty-one times. On three occasions you tried to wrap your right arm around me, but the pain in your wound stopped you."

Agnes stared, struck dumb by his detailed recollection.

"Now that I have your attention," he went on, bolder than before. "Would you care to know how often you thrust your tongue into my mouth? Or how often you caressed me with that very agile left hand? 'Twas a memorable time for me, I assure you."

Beguiled by his seductive words, she dredged up the teachings of her youth. "What of honesty, then? What of belonging and of trusting? Are they not as important as physical desire? You cannot lessen the need for honesty."

Throwing back his head, he held out his arms in surrender. "How much more honest can I be? I did not think I had to color up the truth for the woman who saved my life." He sighed and looked at her again. "Sweet Saint Columba! I am a changed man since Edinburgh, and seeing that poisoned quarrel through my family crest solidified my determination. Life has greater importance to me now, and I am quicker to fight for what I want." Narrowing his eyes, he quietly added, "And I want you."

Being the object of his desire filled her with joy, but Edward Napier was not for her. Gathering her robe about her, she held his probing gaze. "We were and are still newly met."

"Perhaps in the number of days we have known each other, but under the circumstances, that can hardly be counted. Much has occurred between us, Agnes MacKenzie, and you harbor deep feelings for me." Gently, he touched her wound, and his voice dropped to an intimate whisper. "You spoke of trusting. I have and do trust you with my life and with the safety of my children. As for belonging—" His hand curled around her neck. "You belong to me, Agnes."

"No." She turned toward the door. "I cannot, Edward."

"Aye, you can." Grasping her waist, he lifted her onto the workbench.

Her long chemise and silken robe offered little protection from the cold slate, but she couldn't mount a protest.

The warmth of his lips on hers burned the last of her resolve to cinders, and hands that had tended her in doctorly fashion now stroked and comforted in a way that made her heart soar and her conscience protest. When he eased her legs apart and stepped closer, she embraced him freely.

His manly growl of approval spurred her on, and she kissed him with certainty, with freedom, and with gratitude. He had not meant those cruel words in Whitburn; he'd been preoccupied with the safety of his family.

"The truth, Agnes," he insisted.

Words begged to be said. She whispered, "I do want you."

As if she'd given him his heart's desire, he closed his eyes to savor the moment. Happiness wreathed his handsome features, and she couldn't resist kissing every one. She touched her lips to his chin, his nose, his eyes, and when his lashes fluttered, Agnes sighed with satisfaction. "I shall never be happier than at this instant," she pledged.

"Then let me see if I can improve upon that." He melded his mouth to hers, and she opened for him, welcomed him, savored the desire that raged between them. The kiss both drained and inspired at once, and she couldn't get close enough, couldn't feel enough of his skin beneath her fingers.

Tearing his mouth from hers, he kissed her cheek, then moved to her ear. Hovering there, he whispered, "I've dreamed of having you here, of feeling your hands touching me just so."

"I want to touch more of you."

He pulled back and gave her a boyish grin. "You do?"

"Aye." To prove the point, she splayed her fingers and slid her hands up his chest.

Boyishness fled. He removed her dagger and put it on the table. "You've given me an idea." As agile as ever, and without even glancing at his hands, he freed the knot in her belt, moved her robe aside, and revealed her long chemise. "What have we here?" He encircled her breasts. "Attributes draped in black silk. My very favorite kind."

Lightness bubbled inside her, and she couldn't

resist saying, "You're an expert on the subject of . . . breasts, as I recall."

"I'm not sure." With a sly grin, he moved down. "I'll need a closer look."

The instant his hot breath touched her nipple, Agnes gasped. When he licked her there, she shivered and clutched handfuls of his tunic. In a deliciously slow rhythm, he alternately stroked her with his tongue and bathed her in his warm breath, and as a swoon curled up her neck, he stopped. A protest died on her lips, for he moved to her other breast. Knowing what to expect made her hungry for more, and she fidgeted under the urge to twist her shoulders and shed the undergarment. She wanted no barrier between them, but he worked his magic again, and thoughts mingled with sensations.

She felt heavy and light at once, her head spinning with anticipation and her body yearning for a respite from desire. At their own direction, her hands pushed his tunic above his waist and her fingers mapped her tautly muscled belly. He sucked in a breath, and as if answering a call, she reached into his breeches. His manliness felt like velvet against her palm. With her other hand, she moved to free the buttons.

"Oh, no." He jerked away, threw off his tunic, and grasped her wrists. His eyes blazed with banked need, and perspiration glistened on his brow. He moved her arms back and placed her palms flat on the table. "If you'll stiffen your arms."

She locked her elbows, but her attention was fixed on the breadth of his chest and the strength of his arms. A doctor, she mused, and so much more. A teacher. A scholar. An inventor. A wonderful father. The man who owned her heart.

"Oh, yes," he said. "That's it exactly." Involved in his lusty task, he reached around her and scraped aside a stack of books. Then he pressed an index finger into her cleavage and drew a line to her navel.

"What are you about?" she asked.

"A poor idea." But the gleam in his eyes spoke of excitement.

"Tell me."

"I warn you. What I'm thinking is out of the main."

"A place to which I aspire. Tell me."

"I'd very much like to rip this garment off you."

Agnes looked pointedly at her stiletto. "Why not cut it?"

New interest sparkled in his eyes. "May I?"

He could have been asking her to dance, so cordial was his tone. "You think I am serious."

He licked his lips. "I am as serious as sin on Sunday."

It was completely unexpected, but so was the man himself. "Sounds thrilling."

"Doesn't it?"

She looked at the spot where he touched her, his skin a rich golden color against the black silk. Her gaze moved to him. To her fascination, the swollen tip of his manhood peeked from the open placket of his breeches.

Boldness invaded her. "Only if I may return the favor." When his brows shot up, she went on. "I'm very good with a knife myself, and if you have no objections, I could rid you of what is left of your clothing."

"I care nothing for them. Less than nothing. These breeches are completely dispensable. Do with them what you will."

"Truly?"

He realized she was teasing him. "This, my dear Agnes MacKenzie"—he kissed her nose—"is not the time to lie or tease. So I will say to you that if you use that knife to slice the breeches from my body, I will recall it fondly on the day I die."

A chill of pleasure rippled through her. "Cut away, my lord."

Unsheathing the knife, he held it gently, as if it were an instrument, rather than a weapon. Put to the sharp blade, the silk parted without a sound. He cut the cloth cleanly, precisely, in a line so straight it defied measure. A narrow gap opened between the two halves of the cut chemise. But the cloth didn't part completely; moisture from his suckling of her breasts made the silk cling to her nipples.

At her lap, he paused. When she'd spread her legs, the undergarment had bunched up around her hips. In deep concentration, he said, "I must be very careful here."

Expectation thickened her throat, and she swallowed loudly. The blade cut through the folds like a hot knife through porridge and exposed her dampened skin to the cool air. She could feel his visual exploration of her most private place, and the knowledge set her elbows to quivering.

Lifting his head, he grinned like a man who'd accomplished a great task. "You're beautiful everywhere."

Agnes choked back a moan and held out her hand for the knife.

He looked at her askance. "Patience."

"But I want the knife now."

"You may have it in a little while." He put the knife out of her reach and opened the chemise completely. "But for now, I'd like to bask in you."

Words of protest failed, and she watched him slip a hand between her legs. His graceful fingers parted her and found her feminine core. Instinctively she tried to close her legs against the delicious agony, but he was too strong and too determined. She gave up the fight.

He worked her tenderly, touching a spot and bringing it keenly to life, then moving higher to stroke and circle the place that gave her the most pleasure. She couldn't bring enough air into her lungs or breathe fast enough to keep control of her wits, and as she surrendered to passion, she glimpsed true harmony. The elation crested, and she teetered on the brink of falling, until an instant later, with one touch, he brought her to rise again and again and again.

She felt the student to his teacher, for he seemed to know her body better than she knew it herself. When the last ripple of passion flowed through her, she felt cleansed and wanton and oddly empty.

He reached for the placket of his breeches, an apology in his eyes. "I must get inside you now, love."

An end to her emptiness was in the offing, but Agnes squeezed her legs together, trapping his hands. Their pleasure should be equally shared, and she knew what to do. "You dallied with me. Now I shall dally with you. Give me the knife."

He gazed at her lap, then looked down at himself. "You are primed, and I am at the ready."

"Still . . ."

"Later I shall be your willing love slave, but just now . . ."

"I insist."

His expression turned winsome, and his shoulders slumped. "You're a cruel woman, Agnes MacKenzie."

"Will you help me down or must I jump?"

He sighed, shaking his head. "I could make much of this moment, you know."

She opened her palm. "The knife, if you please."

"Must you?"

"I always keep my promises."

"You'll leave your robe open so I can see you?"

It struck her as funny. "Why not? I've nothing left to hide from you."

He jiggled his eyebrows and peeked quickly at her. "A beautiful sight, and a lure that brings out the beast in me."

"A great beast?"

"Does the word ravishment tell you how primitively my mind is working?"

"Yes," she said, as chipper as a lark. "It inspires my own. The knife, if you please, Doctor."

He grasped her waist, and his hands felt warm and strong. In a familiar movement, he set her on the floor. Reluctance shone in his eyes, but he retrieved the dagger and laid it across her palm.

"Must I sit for this exquisite torture, or may I stand?"

An idea inspired her. "Suit yourself."

"If I did that, you'd still be on the table and rushing toward paradise again."

She liked his forthrightness, among other things. "Is that the way it always feels to you, like paradise?"

He stared at the healing wound on her shoulder, yet his thoughts were elsewhere. At length, he said, "No, I have not often found paradise, which is why I'm very eager to make love to you."

"You'll have to wait. But to help you endure this exquisite torture, I could find you a stick to bite on."

"I'd rather bite on something of yours."

Feeling confident and eager to test her skills of seduction, she knelt at his feet. Starting at the hem of the breeches, she slid the blade upward. When he told her to hurry, she slowed. When she told him to relax, he stiffened. At the bulging muscles in his thighs, the soft leather stretched as tight as skin, but she worked her fingers beneath it and cut the garment away.

At his groin she paused to look up at him. His gaze was fixed on her. At eye level with his jutting manhood, she glanced there, then at him. "I must be very careful here."

"And quick about it, lest we revisit that ravishment issue."

Holding one side of the fabric, she flicked the knife upward and sliced through to the waistband. He sucked in a breath and curled his fists around the edge of the table, but her attention was drawn to what the garment revealed.

Bold male beauty filled her vision. She let the knife clatter to the floor and peeled the other leg down to his ankle. When he lifted his foot to step out of the breeches, he was completely exposed to her, and her hands moved to the parts of him she had not seen. He felt heavy in her palms and strangely vulnerable until her fingers crept upward to cup him fully. He came alive beneath her touch. His hips jutted forward, and his manhood swelled, filling her hands and kindling her desire.

"No more." With a gentle tug, he lifted her and returned her to the workbench. The slate was still warm, and when he pulled her toward the spike of his manhood, she went eagerly. He positioned himself, then stared into her eyes. Joy and deeper emotions gazed back at her.

She smiled as he nudged inside her. He grinned and called her name. Then his lips took hers in a kiss of possession, of desire, and of soul-deep surrender. She clutched him tighter, and when he moved to join them fully, she cried out in pain.

He stopped, his labored breathing fanning her face,

indecision clouding his gaze. "Tell me that is not your maidenhead."

"And if it is?"

He glanced at the cot. "You should have a soft bed the first time—"

"Not if we have to move from here."

"You should have fresh linens."

"But I'm excited by silk and leather and you."

His eyes drifted shut, but his grip on her waist did not ease. Feeling his distress, she cradled his face in her hands. "I give my innocence to you freely."

He reached around her again and retrieved a small blue jar that contained a rose-scented salve. With a flick of his thumb, he sent the lid flying. Leaning down, he spread the folds of her womanhood and slid his longest finger inside her. Deeper he pushed. When he stopped, his smile turned to a leer. "Very nice, this maidenhead, but much too intact for our purposes."

Dipping that same finger into the salve, he parted her again and anointed her maidenhead.

"Thank you."

"Your sweetness unmans me," he said.

"You?" She stared at his engorged manhood. "If you call that unmanned, the king is a bloody Turk."

"Then I shall try to make you mine without too much discomfort."

"The thought of waiting distresses me more, Edward."

A lopsided grin was his reply, but the lightheartedness was short-lived. Joining their mouths again, he kissed her with purpose and claimed her for his own.

She shifted to deepen his possession, but he would not allow it. "Go cautiously, love. We've time aplenty."

The wanton in her ruled. Holding his gaze, she slowly scooted closer, drawing him more fully inside.

He sucked in a breath and a heartbeat later said, "Chivalry is much overrated, aye?"

"Very much so."

He enveloped her, one arm around her back, the other tunneling beneath her bottom to lift and draw her closer. She felt wedged into his loins, pressed into a union so powered by lust that her wanton soul rose to meet him. He groaned, deep in his chest and throat, and the vibrations hummed against her breasts and belly.

"Slowly, now," he said into her mouth, and began a steady rhythm of thrust and withdrawal.

From that instant on, he varied the depths of the strokes, but never the cadence, and with each movement he brought her closer and closer to ecstasy. When it danced before her, shimmering like the very essence of life, she begged him to go faster.

He stilled and broke the kiss. "I should not, not yet."

Through a haze of delirious wanting, she said, "But you must."

His chest heaved and his eyes were glassy with need. She raked her fingernails down his chest and willed him to get on with it. Again his gaze dropped to where they were joined. His hair fell over his brow, and he swallowed hard. As if entranced, he watched himself move in and out of her in a roundabout stroke. Then he looked up at her and smiled. When she returned the smile and purred, his expression changed.

"Lift your hips and move with me." He clenched his jaw; his nostrils flared. He quickened the pace, and she followed his lead, pressing and pulling, gasping and moaning. Lust churned in her loins, demanding release, until she could think of nothing save the true harmony that awaited her. When she reached the rapture, she went weak with the wonder of it, gasped, and cried out her pleasure.

As the final wave washed over her, she felt his release begin. Sealing their bodies and the union, he pulsed within her until the last of his passion was spent. Weakness curled her spine, and she reclined on the cool slate. Equally exhausted, he rested his forehead on her breast. Her oversensitized skin tingled at the silky touch of his hair.

When their breathing slowed, he withdrew and lay full upon her. Against her leg she felt his manhood, now sated and soft. Employing a gentle touch and tender kisses, he brought her back to the present. She stretched, feeling gloriously complete.

"Rest awhile." He carried her to the cot.

Agnes closed her eyes. He extinguished the lamp nearest the cot, casting her into partial shadow. She languished, reliving every moment of his lovemaking.

She must have dozed, but not for long. According to the clock, it was almost three, and she was alone on the cot.

Gloriously naked, Edward Napier sat on a stool near the new engine, the leather breeches in his lap, a needle and pink thread in his hands. A stitch made, he stared at his machine. Stitch. Stare. Stitch. Stare. Then his focus turned inward.

The clock ticked once, twice, a dozen times. He put aside the sewing and moved to the end of the workbench and the repair of her necklace. Using the tips of his fingers, he manipulated the string and the clasp, but the jewelry did not hold his attention, for he constantly gazed at the engine.

His head came up, and he looked at Agnes's feet, her knees, her hips. She closed her eyes. Feeling sublime, she feigned sleep and watched through slitted eyes. He continued the pattern of stitching his breeches, repairing her jewelry, and watching her. But through it all, she knew he was thinking about his machine. Occasionally he'd rummage through the stack of drawings and consult a particular page.

Half an hour later, Agnes felt ignored. Still pretending sleep, she writhed languidly and rolled onto her back. Through the veil of her lashes she saw him look her way. His winsome smile pushed her to devilry.

The robe was belted, not tightly but enough to hold the garment together. That wouldn't do. So she waited until he settled into his routine, and when he walked to the workbench, she carefully tugged the knot from her belt. When he abandoned her jade necklace and returned to the stool, she writhed on the cot. The robe fell open.

Like a whip, his gaze lashed her. Then he ambled across the room and stood beside the cot. To her dismay, he sighed in resignation, closed her robe, and retied the knot. As he turned to go, she hummed a sleepy moan. He stopped, his buttocks high and tight with well-formed muscles, his manhood rising to attention.

Desire for her was not enough, for he returned to his stool and his stitchery. Twice more she untied the belt, twice more he came to fasten it. Neither time did she open her eyes. Years of training had heightened her perception. She could hear the familiar sequence of his actions: the dull rustle of leather, the clicking of jade beads, the shuffling of paper. The heady awareness of his desire. The silence of his concentration.

The stool scooted on the stone floor, alerting her to his next task—the jewelry. Secure in the knowledge that his back was momentarily turned as he moved to the workbench, she reached for the knot in her belt. A hand grasped her wrist. Her eyes flew open. He loomed above her, a very confident man, wearing leather breeches with a seam of pink thread marching down one leg.

When had he donned those breeches, and how had he moved the stool from across the room? The latter he'd accomplished by tying a string to the leg of the stool. The former was a mystery.

"You've been pretending sleep."

"Lot of good it did," she grumbled.

The scoundrel looked at his machine. "I was inspired."

"I had hoped for a more personal inspiration."

It was his turn to grumble. "I thought you would congratulate me. Your presence played a part in my success."

What was he talking about, and why did he keep gazing at that contraption? Unless . . . "Your engine will work now?"

"Yes, I think so."

Troubled by her selfishness, Agnes considered the ramifications of what he'd done. "You'll be free of Throckmorton."

"Not only the Napier Mill will be free of him. Every textile concern with money and a thought for the future will be free of him. The people of India will have to slave at something else besides spinning thread."

Captivated by the knowledge that she'd witnessed his greatness, Agnes couldn't contain her joy. "How? Tell me what occurred. Was it a revelation? Did it come upon you slowly?"

He demurred with masculine grace. "Nay, the curve of your hip was the catalyst."

She huffed in disbelief and rolled to her side. "Go on with you." He was teasing her.

"Truly. The irregular vacuum stems from the bulbous shape of the pressure chamber. Mechanically speaking, all that's needed is an angle iron of sorts."

She couldn't stop staring at the manly bulge in his mended breeches. "A what?"

"How can I explain it simply?" he said, more to himself than to her. "Ah, I have it. Imagine, if you will, that your body is the engine and your legs are the pulleys. You do know what a pulley is?"

"Like a windlass?"

Raising an arm, he exclaimed, "Precisely!"

She felt petted, praised.

Then he returned to business. "Now that we've established that part, add to the equation an angle iron." He touched her hip. "Roll over on your back again, and I'll show you."

She wasn't sure she trusted him, not with that lovely bulge pulling at the new seam in his pants and playing havoc with her concentration. But she did as he asked.

All attentive and bright male, he touched her leg. "You see, a perpendicular brace is the key."

"I thought 'twas the angle iron."

"Not on it's own. Bend your knee and turn it out a bit. That'll make it clear. Yes, like that."

Cool air teased her private parts, and the yearning in her belly grew. He leaned over her, sighted the engine, then checked the position of her leg. "Lift your leg a little more . . ." Again he followed an imaginary line between the machine and her. "No, that's not quite it."

Moving quickly, he returned to the pallet, picked up a short, stout board, and held it at a right angle to the engine. "This is your leg." With the same detachment he employed when doctoring her, he gauged the position of her leg with the stick. Frowning, he motioned for her to spread her leg more. "But keep it bent. That's the crucial element."

She complied, exposing her femininity. He was unaffected, save the thickness in his breeches. Growing more uncomfortable, she asked, "What's a perpendicular brace?"

As if he were addressing a student, he said, "It's a thrusting wedge, so to speak. You've really grasped my theory, haven't you?"

"I'm confused about two things. How can a piece of wood be likened to an angle *iron,* and what is the perpendicular brace?"

"Excellent questions, and completely understandable. The brace keeps the specific vaculation of the design in rigid compliance with the whole of the structure—" He scratched his head. "But at the moment, I'm baffled. It worked on paper."

Bewildered, she tried to make sense of his explanation, but failed.

"Unless . . ." He snapped his fingers. "Could you lift your other leg as well. But keep your right knee where it is. That's vital, else the pressure goes out the flue."

He resumed his hand signals, instructing her to bend her other knee.

"That's the solution?" she asked.

He nodded, checking her position against the machine. He blew out his breath and clucked his tongue in concentration. Then he strolled to the end of the cot, the piece of wood in his hands. "A definite sweet spot in the evolution of harnessing the power of steam." He touched her knee, but his gaze was fixed on the machine. With slight but insistent pressure, he flattened her other leg to the cot, effectively spreading her wide.

"Truly interesting," he mused. "I'm always amazed

at the correlation of the tabulae rasae to the restrained friction of an armature under pressure."

He could have been speaking Greek. And why wasn't he acting on the desire that raged in his loins?

The stick clattered to the floor, and his hand moved into her lap. "Oh, you have a speck of lint."

Before she could close her legs, he fell on her, his shoulders wedged between her thighs, his hands securing her arms.

"What are you doing?"

His grin turned sly. "I'm giving you what you've been begging for for the last half hour."

The troll had led her on with his talk of armatures and braces. "You wretch!"

He chuckled. "Spoken by one who purrs and writhes and taunts a man to madness. May I kiss you here?"

"Absolutely not!"

Disappointment captured him, and he said, "Oh, very well. If you insist." In the next instant his expression turned cunning. "I'll skip the kiss and proceed to the important part."

His lips touched her there. She panicked and tried to scoot away but couldn't gain the necessary leverage to move out of his grasp. An instant later she couldn't have moved, even if the castle were crumbling around them.

Spreading her completely, he wielded that wicked tongue again, laving and lapping in long, slow strokes. She shivered and clenched her fists, and tried to hold back a moan of pleasure.

"Tell me what you feel," he said against her most tender spot.

Through gritted teeth, she said, "Forming a coherent thought is not an option now."

"Good. I must be doing this properly."

Properly? Like starting a fire from kindling, he nurtured her desire with each touch, tended it, and turned it inside out. At some point he let go of her hands, and they found their way into his hair. The will to resist fled, and she held on to him, waiting for the harmony. When her release came, the force of it took her by surprise, and she couldn't control the jerky movements of her loins. His muffled words of encouragement vibrated against her, prolonging her pleasure.

Skin flushed, breathing labored, she untangled her fingers from his hair and patted his head. "You're very inventive."

The clever devil blew against her still-throbbing parts. "I've also just begun."

"Please, Edward. I want you inside me."

"No. It's too soon after your first time. You'll be bruised and sore."

"Get the salve."

"Absolutely not!"

She almost screamed that he could send his doctoring skills to England, for she wanted his loving now. But the next sounds she made were cries of passion.

When he at last lay beside her on the narrow cot, her robe belted again, her bottom tucked snugly against his naked loins, Agnes asked, "When did you know that I was awake?"

"Awake and teasing me?"

"Aye."

He pointed to the metal shade on the lamp above the workbench where her necklace rested on the velvet. "See that reflector? It works like a mirror."

"You watched me?"

"And planned my revenge."

"Sweet torture is more like it." On that thought, she drifted into the most restful sleep of her life.

Sometime later she was jolted awake by the sound of squealing hinges on the upstairs door and footfalls on the stone steps.

"Cathcart!" yelled a familiar voice. "Rouse yourself."

14

HOOTS!

Agnes recognized the voice of Captain Cameron Cunningham. Her longtime friend was on his way down the stairs. Glancing at the clock, she fought a groan. It was past eleven.

Over her slashed chemise she wore her robe; nestled against her back, Edward wore nothing. His leather breeches were crumpled on the floor. His tunic lay nearby. A Napier tartan plaid served as their blanket. His arm draped her; his hand cupped her breast. He wasn't snoring. Was he awake?

"Rouse yourself and light a lamp, Edward," Cameron shouted. "'Tis black as pitch on these stairs."

It wasn't black as pitch in the laboratory; a single lamp burned above the engine. But Cameron had reached the landing and couldn't yet see into the dungeon.

She had to get off the cot. Near panic, she grasped Edward's wrist. At her touch, his arm stiffened, as if to keep her beside him. Were they alone, she would have enjoyed his possessiveness.

Turning, she scooted free of his embrace and scrambled to her feet. Now what to do? Finding her shoes seemed paramount. As she spied them, her night braid fell over her shoulder. A memory flashed in her mind of Edward brushing her hair and plaiting it. A trail of kisses down her spine had preceded the braiding. Recalling the hours of intimacy they'd shared, she shivered with pleasure.

Cameron's intrusion dampened the memory. His presence presented greater problems. She would not cower. She was unashamed. Her gaze was drawn to the cot and the sleeping earl of Cathcart. Her lover. As she watched, he rolled over on his back and started to snore. The tartan plaid was too small. The man too large. The sight of his manliness so openly displayed brought a tightness to her belly. Just as she covered him, Cameron stepped into the chamber.

Extremely tall and dressed in a white linen frock coat and breeches, the fair-haired Captain Cunningham stopped in his tracks. The package in his hands fell to the floor.

"Agnes?" he said, gawking.

No wilting, she told herself. Talk about anything except the obvious. Stall for time. She'd think of a plausible explanation. With that in mind, she tucked her shoes under her arm and approached him. "Trimble said he expected you any day. How was Penang?"

Still in the throes of shock, he narrowed his blue eyes and glanced at the sleeping earl of Cathcart. "I had no idea you and Edward knew each other . . . so well."

A litany of weak excuses popped into her mind. Cameron had been at sea for months. She'd known him most of her life. Her business was her own. "You didn't expect to come home and find everything as you left it, did you?"

His gaze drifted to the cot. "Nay, but I didn't expect to find you and—"

"See?" Smiling cordially, she blocked his line of vision to the scantily covered earl. "Isn't that always the way it is when you're gone for extended periods of time? When we returned from China, your father had won a seat in the Commons."

Hesitancy crept into his normally confident demeanor. "Father is well? Mother and Sibeal, too?"

It was the first question he should ask. "Aye, I saw them at Sarah's wedding. They're all healthy and eager to see you." Then she broached the subject that formed the foundation of their friendship. "Any news of Virginia?"

"Nay. She is not in China, nor any of the islands I visited in between."

"I'll find her."

He leaned against the bench, but his gaze kept straying from her to Edward Napier. "When did you . . . ah . . . and Edward . . . ah . . ."

The snoring stopped.

Cold from the floor seeped into Agnes's feet, and her mind worked at a snail's pace. Two things were vital. She must get out of this dungeon before Edward awakened, and she needed time to think. "When did I meet the earl of Cathcart?" She sounded cavalier, which made the situation worse. More seriously, she said, "I met him at Sarah's wedding."

Cameron retrieved the package he'd dropped on the floor. "I'm sorry to have missed it."

Before leaving for China, Cameron had been aware

of Sarah's plans. Explaining the ill-fated betrothal to Henry Elliot, the earl of Glenforth, and Sarah's quick marriage to another would take too much time. "Sarah did not marry Henry. 'Tis a very long story. I'll tell you all about it later, and you can tell me about the voyage. How long will you be in Glasgow?"

"A day or two at most. I've a craving for my mother's scones, so I'm going home to Perwickshire. MacAdoo's taking the ship on to London tomorrow."

MacAdoo Dundas was Cameron's oldest friend and his first mate on Cameron's ship, the *Maiden Virginia*.

An ungraceful exit beckoned, but Agnes took it. "Then I'll have to get to the docks today if I want to see him, won't I?"

Although he made no sound, Agnes could feel Edward coming awake. She'd traveled the world. She'd faced assassins. But facing Edward Napier now worried her more.

Cameron put the package on the workbench and lighted one of the lamps. "Whom did Sarah marry?"

Amid a rusting of fabric, Edward yawned and said, "She married Henry's brother, *Michael* Elliot."

Agnes almost felt sorry for Cameron. A year her senior and a close friend of Clan MacKenzie, he was obviously confused about what he should do. Edward made the situation worse when he gathered the tartan loosely around his waist and joined them.

Mussed from sleep, his thick, wavy hair in wild disarray, and his eyes gleaming, he extended his hand to Cameron. "Welcome home, Cam."

"I apologize for not knocking, but Bossy said nothing about . . ."

"About why Agnes would be here with me?" All proprietary male, Edward gave her a lazy grin.

Cameron rolled his eyes. "That, and why Sarah married Michael."

"Michael and I have solved two of Lord Lachlan's problems."

Problem? Agnes took offense. "You're the one with a problem."

"Hum." He scratched his chest. "You took care of that rather nicely."

Agnes had to get away. She remembered her necklace! A perfect excuse for her presence in the laboratory. Chin held high, she marched to the end of the table and snatched her jewelry. "Oh, here it is, my lord. I'm so sorry to have awakened you." She waved it at Cameron. "Lord Edward was nice enough to repair my necklace."

Edward, the troll, threw back his head and laughed. The tartan slipped, and he made a show of securing it. As he did, his gaze met hers. He looked pointedly at the leather breeches on the floor. Cocking an eyebrow, he seemed to say, "Shall I put them on now, Agnes?"

The challenge in his eyes spurred her to desperation. "Lord Edward, perhaps you'd care to tell Cameron how it is that I damaged my necklace."

His expression cooled. He didn't like being reminded of her sacrifice on his behalf.

Cameron's frown deepened. "I *am* surprised to see her here in a robe."

"I recall mentioning that very thing to her last—"

"Aye, you did, my lord," she rushed to say. The blighter wasn't embarrassed that they'd been caught. Informing him of the consequences should change that. "I'm sure I needn't remind you of what my father will do if he receives the wrong impression of what has passed here."

Undaunted, Edward snatched up his breeches. If he dropped that tartan, Agnes would drop him.

Cameron said, "Lord Lachlan'll nail your hide to the city gates of Tain, Edward, if you've dishonored her."

Confidence settled over Agnes. "Not to mention what my mother will do." But she knew that the duchess of Enderley would push for a wedding, and if anything annoyed Agnes, it was being forced.

Hoping for a graceful exit, she fussed with her hair and tried her best to mimic her sister Lottie. "I had my heart set on wearing my necklace today, and we mustn't let this—" She twirled her fingers to include the people, the room, and the moment. "—unfortunate and innocent moment be misunderstood."

"Innocent being the functional word," Edward murmured ruefully.

"You do have a way with words, my lord," Agnes said with finality and moved to the stairwell.

"Aren't you forgetting something, Agnes?"

At Edward's ominous tone, she slowed. "Nay."

"What of your handsword and stiletto?"

Hoots. Retracing her steps, she gathered the weapons. "Thank you, my lord."

"In the event that you are curious, Cam, she seduced me both before and after I repaired her necklace."

Agnes almost dropped the weapons. "How dare you!" was all she could think of to say.

Looking too much like the sage he was not, Cameron nodded. "I suspected as much. Had she not wanted you, you'd be dead, Edward."

She rounded on Cameron and hissed, "When did you become a soothsayer?"

Cameron's smile was tender and thoughtful. "I know your skills, Agnes. But talents aside, you have a love bruise on your neck, and Edward has scratches on his back."

"What the devil does that have to do with anything?"

"You marked me?" In mock surprise, Edward contorted to see his back. "I don't recall that we rutted like animals. We were aggressive, but—"

"Haud yer wheesht, Edward Napier. I made you no promises."

"Nay? You gifted me with your innocence."

Cameron said, "We call that a promise in the Highlands."

"It is so in the Lowlands as well, Cam." Then Edward had the nerve to crook his finger and beckon her.

More old-fashioned males. Agnes had had enough of them. "I will not be forced."

"It doesn't look as if he forced you, Agnes," Cameron said.

"Truc, Cam," Edward admitted. "She was unable to resist me, and I actually did the seducing."

"You did nothing of the sort."

Into the fray, Cameron said, "Do you think Lachlan MacKenzie opines for an alliance with the Napiers?"

In a low growl, Edward said, "He'll have it whether it pleases him or not."

She stepped between them. "Cameron Cunningham, if you even hint to my father that I've—"

"Been seduced?" Edward chirped.

Phrasing it that way, he made her sound weak. Agnes fumed but didn't spare him a glance. "Cameron, if you tell on me, I'll tell *your* father that you seduced Sorcha Burke."

"They know about Sorcha and me. She's married now and happy."

His debauchery didn't end there. Agnes had sailed the world with Cameron. "What of that girl in Calais?"

Cameron blanched. "That serving wench?"

Agnes had him. "You served her right enough. We stayed in port an extra day because you couldn't bring yourself to leave her bed."

Edward turned away from them, dropped the tartan, and pulled on the breeches. "Agnes. Are you comparing a night with me to a seaman's tumble with a dockside sally?"

She'd gone too far; his angry expression said as much, but she could not retreat now. "You likened me to a milkmaid."

His jaw tightened. To Cameron he said, "Trouble yourself not. I intend to tell his grace of Ross exactly how his daughter came to be here and what has occurred since then."

Drilling him with a stern gaze, she said, "While you're playing the gossipmonger, don't forget to tell Cameron the real reason why I am in Glasgow."

"Very well. Someone's trying to kill me."

"You?" Cameron said. "Why would anyone want to hurt you?"

With the short sword, Agnes pointed at the engine. "That."

As Agnes edged toward the stairs, Edward told Cameron about the attack in Edinburgh.

"Trust Agnes to find your culprit, Edward. She can follow the wake of a dolphin through the Minch."

The last thing Agnes heard as she climbed the stairs was Cameron saying, "Edward, is that pink thread in your breeches? Your tailor's a bit odd."

Angry and confused, Agnes slammed the heavy door. Edging through the tapestry, she paused. The doves had been removed and the blood cleaned from every surface. Mrs. Johnson must have worked all night.

Just as she touched the handle on the tower door, the shrill sound of Christopher's whistle rent the air. Edward wouldn't hear the noise, which was just as well. If the assassin thought to reach Edward through Christopher, he might succeed. Instead, he'd face Agnes MacKenzie. But why hadn't the other alarms sounded?

Pitching her necklace, stiletto, and shoes onto a chair, and tucking her short sword under her arm, she dashed for the new wing. Heart pounding, legs pumping, she unsheathed her weapon and raced through the corridor to the formal parlor. Not slowing, she burst into the portrait gallery and barreled into one of her father's messengers. This man she knew.

Beside Rabbie stood her sister Mary and a confused Christopher. Behind them stood a baffled Mr. Boswell.

"Please tell this lad," Mary wailed, her hands over her ears, "that we are not the angels of death come to murder his father."

Agnes almost wilted with relief. Between labored breaths she reminded Christopher that he'd met Mary in Edinburgh. "She drew a picture of you, don't you remember? Lady Juliet begged you to give it to her so she could remember you."

Embarrassed to his polished shoes, the lad flapped his arms. "Well, we didn't go to church today. Hannah fretted until Auntie Loo put her back to bed. I couldn't find you and father. I've been as bored as anything. Then Captain Cunningham arrived." His bottom lip quivered. "Nothing's as it should be anymore."

Immediately attentive to his distress, Agnes took his hand. "'Twill be better soon, Christopher. I give you my word."

"Cameron's here?" Mary asked, removing her spectacles. "Good. He'll help me."

"Help you what? Why are you here?"

Her critical gaze moved to Hogarth's depiction of Edward's grandfather. "I followed Rabbie."

Their father's messenger huffed. "Blackmailed me, she did. Fooled the duke and Wiltshire. Caught up with me in North Hampton. His grace'll banish me to the Orkneys or worse when he gets wind of it."

Eager to speak to both of them, but not at once, Agnes set her priorities. She told Mrs. Johnson to take charge of Christopher and Rabbie and asked Boswell to take Mary's bag to the room next to hers in the new wing.

When she turned to Mary, she wasn't surprised to hear her sister say, "Someone should have whipped Hogarth for putting parti-colored spaniels in this painting. He might as well have painted festoons on the subject's waistcoat and furbelows in his wig. Spaniels," she spat. "Wretched for the image of a Scotsman."

"I thought you would covet the frame."

With hands as graceful and talented as God could create, Mary touched the wood. "'Tis truly fine craftsmanship."

Smiling, Agnes hugged Mary. "How are you, sister dear?"

"Wait!" Mary stood back. "Your shoulder."

Agnes had forgotten the wound. "I'm fine, truly. And you?"

Her auburn hair glistened with dampness, and her dress was wrinkled beyond easy repair. Tears pooled in her hazel eyes. "Papa tried to force me to wed

Robert Spencer. He doesn't want *me,* Agnes. He made a wager with his friends in the House of Lords that he could seduce Contrary Mary."

Agnes's heart ached for her. "And he succeeded."

Mary nodded so vigorously, her hair came unbound. "His courting of me was a jest. I was such a fool. Papa doesn't understand. I had no choice but to flee."

"Oh, Mary." Agnes embraced her again, and as Mary cried in earnest, Agnes said, "I'll make certain he doesn't seduce anyone else."

"I knew I could count on you, Agnes." Mary dashed her tears. "I'm so tired, and I'm . . . I'm . . ."

"Pregnant."

"Aye. Oh, Agnes. What's to become of me? Papa's so angry, and he's actually taken a liking to Robert."

The earl of Wiltshire would pay, and Agnes knew some very inventive ways to seek retribution, but Mary needed her now. "Come," she said. "Forget about men. I'll send for a bath, and you can rest. It'll all look better in a while."

"You sound like Lottie."

Agnes made a funny face. "Heaven forbid!"

Mary lifted her chin in imitation of Lottie and said, "I insist on having a room to myself."

Agnes sketched an elaborate bow. "Your wish is my command, Your Highness."

Laughing, they climbed the stairs. As soon as Mary was resting quietly, Agnes changed her clothes and went in search of her father's messenger. She found him in the foyer with Edward and Cameron.

"Going somewhere, my lord?" she asked.

Edward's gaze traveled over her in proprietary fashion. "Yes. Sunday is wages day at the mill."

He couldn't go out alone. "Wait. I'll get a few things and go with you."

His cool demeanor spoke volumes about his mood. "Cameron will accompany me. You stay with Mary until your father arrives."

Mary had said nothing about Papa coming to Glasgow. "Where is he?"

With a glance, Edward deferred to Rabbie. "His grace and Robert Spencer, the earl of Wiltshire, are at most a day's ride behind us."

Oh, Lord. As if Agnes didn't have enough to deal with. But Edward's safety was foremost on her mind. "You'll not go anywhere else?"

Engrossed in pulling on his gloves, Edward chuckled. "Only a dockside sally could prevent me from returning to you, Agnes."

She winced at the cruel remark but knew she deserved it. "Edward—"

He held up his hand. "Save it for later, my lady."

That formality said, he marched out the front door. Cameron followed him.

Rabbie gave her a letter from her father. Unfortunately, the message had been penned before her letter had reached him.

According to Lachlan, the earl of Wiltshire had indeed made the awful wager that Mary had spoken of, but during the course of the seduction, Robert Spencer had fallen in love. Lachlan had penned his message before Mary's flight from London, so no mention was made of a journey to Glasgow.

Heaven help them when Papa arrived.

Agnes went to the kitchen and informed Mrs. Johnson that more guests were expected. At the cook's frightful look, Agnes sent Bossy to the orphanage for extra maids. Then she ordered Edward's mount and went to visit Trimble.

* * *

When she returned several hours later, Edward was waiting for her in his study. His first words frightened her all over again.

"A Dutchman visited the mill today. He thought you were my wife. Of course, I did not tell him how silly that notion was. He sent you this."

"What is it?"

"I do not know. It was not mine to examine."

Agnes took the small box from Edward's hands. Her own were shaking. The time would come to broach the problems between them, but not now. "I don't remember meeting a Dutchman."

"You haven't. He said that he saw us in passing in Trongate that day we visited Saint Vincent's Church."

A Dutchman. Even before she opened the gift and examined the velvet pouch inside, Agnes knew what it was. The pink rook from the chess set in the common room.

Hefting the bag in her hand, she said, "Tell me about him."

Edward made a slow inspection of her, but the hunger in his eyes had dimmed. "Prosperous fellow and honest to the teeth." Strolling to the firescreen, he touched the Napier shield. "The Dutchman admitted to knowing nothing about textiles, except the return to be made on his guilders. But I doubt you're interested."

Ice wouldn't melt on Edward's tongue, so cold was his tone. A chill went through her. How close had Edward come to death that day in Trongate, and later at the mill? The Rook had followed them there and left the golden badge of the MacKenzies in the carriage.

Thank God, Cameron had been with Edward today. But soon it would be over. At this very moment

Trimble's best thief was waiting for Throckmorton to take his family to tea. As soon as they left, the thief would search their rooms for proof of Throckmorton's part in the conspiracy.

Shoring her courage, she said, "The man who gave you this is the assassin."

His eyes widened; then he relaxed and toyed with the alphabet blocks he'd brought home for Hannah. "He's a businessman, Agnes."

"Nay, he is not. The Dutchman is the assassin. He goes by the name of the Rook." She fished the chessman from the pouch. "He took this from the common room last night. This is his way of taunting us."

"Sweet Saint Columba." Edward plopped down in a chair.

But thanks to Trimble, Agnes now knew where to find the Rook.

Clutching the game piece, she knelt beside Edward's chair and lied. "I'm going to visit Trimble. I shan't be long. When I return, we'll talk."

"Talk?" he taunted. "The way friends talk? How delightful. I seem to remember that you have an interesting way with words."

She couldn't hold back. "You told Cameron that you seduced me."

"So?"

"You made me sound weak."

"Weak as in purring like a kitten in my arms? Weak as in asking me to braid your hair because you were too exhausted from our lovemaking to lift a finger? Weak because your heart is filled with love for me?"

"You're being unfair."

"By accepting the consequences?"

"Consequences?"

"Ask Lady Mary. She knows about the lingering effects of passion."

"I cannot be with child. Not after only one night."

Turning away, he finished with, "Give my best to Trimble."

Agnes deserved his scorn, and later she would apologize. But she welcomed his anger, for it had blinded him to any suspicions about her upcoming mission.

Rising, she patted his arm and hurried up the stairs to change her clothes.

Then she went after the assassin.

15

HER STILETTO TUCKED INTO HER SLEEVE, AND HER SPECIAL tools in her vest, Agnes left her mount behind the Drygate Inn, hurried past the dovecote, and stepped into the kitchen. A robust cook worked at the stove. The oily odor of kidneys and leeks hung in the air.

Agnes cleared her throat.

The heavy woman turned and gasped. A wooden ladle fell from her hand. Wide-eyed, she stared at Agnes's manly attire.

Agnes pitched her a guinea. "I'd like some information on one of your guests." Trimble had told her where to find the Rook. Agnes hoped this woman could provide the details. "'Tis the Dutchman I seek. Which room is his?"

"Upstairs in the corner." The woman pulled a rag from her cleavage and mopped her brow. "Faces the mews, but he don't mind the stench. He asked for the room special. Keeps the window open, and none but the innkeeper has another key."

So he could slip in and out of the inn with a crossbow, and no one would notice. "Is the Dutchman about?"

"Oh, aye. Sleeps in the day, he does. Locks his door."

A minor impediment. "Have you some grease?"

The cook reached into a crock and slapped a handful of drippings onto a towel. Agnes took the cloth. "Where are the servants' stairs?"

She pointed toward a storage area across the room. "Behind those barrels. Door'll be the last on your right."

Agnes spied the kegs. "You haven't seen me here."

The cook waved the guinea. "For this, I'd deny seeing the Second Coming."

Agnes climbed the worn stairs. At the top she spied three doors and headed for the last one. Sunlight streamed through a window at the end of the hall, and wagons rumbled on the street below. Crouching, she peered through the keyhole.

The Rook slept on a bed against the wall, but in her narrow line of sight she could only see him from the chest down. The crossbow rested atop a table in the center of the room—blessedly out of easy reach. The remaining quarrel, its distinctive fletchings pale against the dark wood, lay nearby. A pair of knives was also visible on the table. His empty hands were folded over his belly.

She found him surprisingly small in stature, his feet almost an arm's length from the end of the bed. She thought of Edward, so tall his feet lapped over the cot. She remembered his powerful legs, the strength in his loins. Warmth crept up her neck, and her vision drifted out of focus.

Somewhere below, a door slammed, and someone yelled a greeting.

Troubled by distracting thoughts of Edward Napier, Agnes put him from her mind and oiled the iron hinges.

Taking a moment, she closed her mind to everything save the harmony. Like a rainbow of thought, it embraced her, and as she relaxed, she breathed deeply. Choosing the proper pick from inside her vest, she went to work on the lock. As it sprung, the lever made a dull thud. Quickly, she looked again through the keyhole. His chest rose and fell, but other than that, he had not moved.

But she did. Easing open the door, she slipped inside and hurried to the bed. In a movement she'd practiced thousands of times, she unsheathed the deadly blade. Then she pressed it to his neck.

His eyes flew open.

"Move and you're dead."

He had not moved. Blue-eyed and fair, he wore his hair close-cropped, and his complexion was pitted and dirty. He'd shaved off the beard he'd worn in Edinburgh.

"Do you know who I am?" she asked.

"Ya."

The Dutchman. She could smell his fear. "Who was the nanny?"

"Mrs. Borrowfield?" His speech was flavored with the guttural tones of his homeland.

"Aye, the woman who fled the church in Edinburgh."

"Hired out of London to report on the earl's progress on the engine."

"Hired by whom?"

His throat worked, and he swallowed loudly.

Agnes put gentle pressure on the knife. "You've begun to bleed, Rook."

"Throckmorton. Same as hired me."

"You did not kill the guard that night at the fountain at Napier House."

He shook his head, but winced when the knife cut deeper. "The inventor is my mark. Please do not kill me."

A fortnight ago she wouldn't have thought twice about slitting this villain's throat. But she couldn't summon the old ruthlessness. She knew the reason, a brilliant earl with magical hands and a heart-stealing smile.

"I beg of you," said the Rook. "I haff a family."

Agnes cast off thoughts of Edward Napier. "What were you looking for?"

"I am not a thief."

"But you wanted something from Napier House."

"Machine and its plans."

"Both are lost to you, as is your life."

He beseeched her with his eyes. "Please."

"Why did you slaughter doves and leave them at Napier House?"

"To frighten you."

The birds had not been chosen for any particular reason, except that they were convenient. "Should you move more than an eyelash, I'll put this knife through your jugular."

His fearful expression eased. "If you do, I will put mine through your belly."

She glanced down and her breath caught. He held a knife to her abdomen. The blade pierced her vest.

Damn! When had he pulled that blade and from where?

Keeping her knife taut to his neck, Agnes stepped

an arm's length back. In a blur of movement he pushed her out of the way and dashed for the window. Before she could cock her arm, he disappeared through the opening.

Shaken, she wilted on the bed. Trimble had warned her of the Rook's skill with knives. He'd had three— two on the table and one on his person. With an unsteady hand, she touched the puncture in her leather vest. A vision of the blade, jagged teeth on one edge, sent tremors of fear through her.

She took the remaining quarrel and went to Trimble's office to await the return of the thief sent to Throckmorton's rooms.

"I trust the Rook won't trouble us again," Trimble said.

Agnes told him what had occurred at the Drygate Inn.

"Didn't I say that he was skilled with a knife?"

"Aye, you did, but I forgot."

"How could you overlook that?" he demanded, his tone angry with concern, his face flushed with anger. "Have you lost your wits?"

In some respects she had. "I suffered a moment's preoccupation."

An hour later Trimble's man delivered a sheaf of papers. Among them were letters from Mrs. Borrowfield to Throckmorton, confirming the plot against Edward. In the hands of the magistrate, the writings were the proof needed to bring Throckmorton to justice.

"'Tis almost done," Trimble said. "Where will you go when it's over? What will you do?"

Agnes didn't know. She felt empty inside at the thought of leaving Napier House. "I'm not sure, but I'll let you know."

"Why not come with me to Maryland? Several

families who lost sons in the Colonial wars have engaged me to search for their young men."

Unwilling to share her true feelings, she shrugged. "A long ocean voyage holds no interest to me, Trimble. But I thank you."

"Then at least stay in Glasgow for a bit. That viscount has roses yet to pluck for you."

His attempt at humor warmed her a little. "Mary's here, and she needs me. I'm not sure where we'll go."

Trimble's kind features grew strained, and he touched her arm. "If I can help . . ."

Agnes put on a smile that she did not feel. "You can help. Find Virginia."

He smiled too. "We will. She cannot have vanished off the face of the earth."

Agnes knew it was true. Virginia was too bright, too plucky, even as a child. Agnes had been her mentor; she'd know if Virginia were dead. From a sailmaker Agnes had learned that a girl matching Virginia's description, albeit wearing boy's clothing, had boarded a ship that day. But Virginia had been wearing a new dress. When they'd found no trace of her a week later, Agnes had returned to the docks. Through the harbormaster she gleaned the names of every vessel that had been in port that day and their destinations. But crews and captains changed, and not all were honest in their manifests.

Finding Trimble had given Agnes new hope.

"Someone has knowledge of her," Trimble said. "We'll find the lass."

Agnes rose. "I'm certain of it."

Trimble walked her to the door. "Do not let down your guard again, Golden One."

"I will not. You can be sure of that."

"Promise me you'll tell Napier that the bowman remains on the loose."

With three knives, she reminded herself. "I'll consider it."

Agnes returned to Napier House. Boswell greeted her, saying that Auntie Loo was in the music room with the children and had asked for Agnes.

Hannah played on the floor with her new blocks. Christopher made war with his soldiers.

Taking Auntie Loo aside, Agnes told her what had transpired.

"Death's door is still closed to you."

But Agnes had peeked inside the room of death, and she remembered vividly the sight of that knife pressed against her. "If it's all the same to God, I'd rather not chance it again."

"I pray you do not, Agnes."

"I have the proof. Edward can take it to Constable Sir Jenkins."

"Lot of good that one's been."

"Let's hope he's better at bringing criminals to justice than he is at finding them."

Agnes found Edward and Mary in the Elizabethan room. Cameron had returned to his ship but was expected to join them for the evening meal.

A refreshed Mary was admiring the illuminated manuscripts.

"Will you excuse us?" Agnes said to her sister.

"Nay, Lady Mary," said Edward. "Stay. Your sister does her best work with an audience."

Mary glanced sharply at Edward. Picking up the ancient book, she approached him. "I may not have Agnes's skill with weapons, my lord, but I will defend her with my life, so have a care with what you say."

He looked from Mary to Agnes. "MacKenzie loyalty, I presume?"

"You are bright," Mary said much too cheerfully.

When they were alone, Agnes handed him the last of the five quarrels and the documents. "The constable can make good use of these."

He scanned the papers. "It was Throckmorton."

"Aye, he wanted to prevent you from perfecting your machine."

"But it doesn't work."

"He knows it will."

Putting the papers into his desk, he moved absently about the room. "You found the Rook?"

He needn't know that she'd held a knife to the man's throat or that her own life had been threatened. "Trimble found him and the letters."

"Good. I feared that you would go after him yourself."

He could have been discussing yesterday's rain, so detached did he seem. A part of Agnes wanted their former closeness, but with that intimacy came commitment, and she had already pledged her life elsewhere. The memory of their intimacy wouldn't leave her alone. If she looked at his hands, she recalled the tenderness of his touch. A glimpse of his mouth reminded her of the feel of his lips on hers. A stolen glance at his loins brought to mind his complete possession and the oneness they'd shared.

Regret thickened her throat. "I'm sorry about what happened between us last night."

He busied himself moving the standing mirror from the hearth to a spot by the door that led into the tower. "Didn't your mother ever tell you that a lady never apologizes for being attracted to a man?"

She'd said similar words to him after that first kiss in Whitburn. She wanted to say that she was more than attracted to him. Instead, she said, "Aye, but my mother never met a man like you."

Much too casually he said, "I suppose she didn't; her lovers were dukes."

He was speaking of her mother's affair with Lachlan MacKenzie and her later marriage to the duke of Enderley. No reply came to mind.

Edward adjusted the mirror. Their eyes met in the glass. "I am but an earl."

She could see his heartache, and heaven help her, she wanted to ease it, but she could not. "I was not referring to your position in nobility, and I am not my mother."

"No." He turned the mirror. "You're very much like your father. Even Lady Mary says so."

Reflected in the glass was the door leading to the new wing. "What is that supposed to mean?"

"That you do not take romantic entanglements seriously. With that in mind, I wonder if I imagined your maidenhead."

She deserved his anger. She had to bite her lip to keep from confessing her love. "I told you at the start that I would not—"

"Fall in love with me?" he challenged. "Oh, do not think I harbor any hope of you loving me."

"Even if I did—"

"Do you?" His voice cracked like a whip.

She winced. "Aye, but I cannot forsake Virginia."

Softly, he said, "Have I asked that of you?"

"Nay, but word will come, I know it in my soul, and when that moment arrives, I must be free to go after her." Choking back tears, she turned to face him. "But my loyalty will not end when she is returned. What if she has suffered during the separation? There could be adjustments, reunions. 'Tis a part of God's purpose for me."

Nodding, he strolled toward her. "I will not argue that."

She'd ended romantic entanglements before without remorse, but her heart had not been engaged. Her convictions were strong, but for the first time, she felt torn. She loved Edward Napier, and there was nothing to be done about it. Family came first. "Then, you understand?"

He cradled her face in his hands and lifted her chin. When their eyes met, he said, "I understand. But please consider this. God has given you a worthy cause, but not at the expense of your own happiness."

Never before had anyone delved so deeply into the events that ruled her life. Never before had the touch of a hand moved her to tears. "Finding Virginia is my happiness."

His smile was sad, bittersweet, and with his thumbs, he dashed her tears. "God is not as selfish as that. I believe that he has given you to me, for I cannot imagine another sunrise without you beside me."

Pain squeezed her heart and forced her to beg. "Please let me go."

"And lose what we feel for each other? Oh, nay. Let me help you find Virginia."

She searched his face, looked deeply into his eyes for any sign of artifice. The kindness and sincerity she discovered brought lightness to her soul. "Do you believe she is alive?"

"I believe what you believe, my love." He hugged her fiercely. "If you say you think Virginia is in Edinburgh, I shall beat a path to the stables and ready the carriage myself."

"You would do that?"

"I would do that and more. Should you suspect that your sister is in New Holland, I shall book our passage to Botany Bay tomorrow."

Our passage. Others had supported Agnes's cause, but none, save Cameron, had truly shared in the search or experienced the cruelty of the disappointments. A new kind of hope blossomed inside her. "But what about Christopher and Hannah? You cannot abandon them."

"Nor will *we,*" he insisted. "We shall take them along or leave them in the care of your kinswomen."

Hope sprang to life within her. "Not Juliet, lest my father spoil them."

He must have sensed her surrender, for he slid his hands to her arms and tightened his grip. "Then one of your sisters."

Years of disappointments nicked her confidence. "I am unprepared to make such a decision."

"Hear me well, Golden One. You are not alone anymore, and nothing will change what I feel for you or what you feel for me. My children will be safe with the countess of Tain."

"Aye, Lottie's the best of all of us at mothering."

"*That* I will argue, for I think you will be a wonderful mother, and when we find Virginia, perhaps we will have children of our own to present her."

The old guilt returned. "She will think I have blithely gone about my life without a care for her."

"Ha! Only a fool could think that, and I have yet to meet a foolish MacKenzie. Marry me, Agnes."

The words held both a promise and a solution. "I will when the Rook is dead."

After a meal that became a celebration, Agnes and Edward said good night to their guests and walked with Auntie Loo and the children to the old wing. After tucking the children in and telling them a story, Edward and Agnes found Auntie Loo in the common room. As she bid them good night, Auntie Loo gave Agnes a pointed look that said, "I'll keep watch." Agnes hugged her friend and whispered, "Leave the door unbolted. I'll be back to spell you at two o'clock."

At her friend's agreement, Agnes preceded Edward out the squat door. The mirror beside it reflected the door to the new wing.

Edward pulled her into his arms. "You're mine."

Into his mouth she breathed the word "Aye."

The kiss was long and tender, and as passion stirred to life, Agnes felt a sense of belonging. Napier House would become her home. She'd conceive and give birth to her children here. She'd grow old with Edward Napier.

"Much more of that," Edward said, "and I'll whisk you behind that tapestry and show you a very inventive way to make love."

"It must be inventive, if you thought of it."

He gave her a quick smack of a kiss and drew the tapestry aside. "Downstairs with you, my lovely."

The lantern still sat in the niche and cast good light. Mrs. Johnson must have told one of the maids from the orphanage to fill the lantern. Later Agnes intended to hire several of the girls on a permanent basis.

As she preceded Edward down the steps to the laboratory, Agnes felt a sense of unease. She stopped at the landing. Behind her she heard him bolt the door.

"Let's not go down there," she said. "Let's stay in the new wing tonight."

"No." He nudged her until she started walking again. "I intend to make love to you until you are too exhausted to move." His grin turned to a leer. "Then I'll watch you and think about my engine. You inspire me."

She wagged her finger at him. "I give you fair warning. I'll not fall for any of that 'your leg is like an angle iron' nonsense a second time."

"I'll be much more creative, I promise."

They entered the dungeon, which was dimly lit. Edward said, "That's odd. I left the lanterns burning."

The Rook stepped into a pool of lamplight. "There is enough light."

"Get down," Agnes shouted, even as she pushed Edward.

He hit the floor beside her. She pointed to the workbench, silently urging him to crawl beneath it. With her other hand, she fished under her petticoats for her stiletto. Finding it, she cut away her skirt. She must be free to move without impediment.

Crouched on the floor, she could see the Rook's legs as he walked around the table. He made not a sound. Three, four more steps and he would have them in view. Sighting the lamp, Agnes threw the small scabbard. It shattered the glass, and the flame dimmed, but did not go out.

Edward pointed to himself and indicated that he would circle around and come upon the assassin from behind. She nodded, and the instant he moved, a knife whistled through air. Her heart stopped. The blade hit a spot on the table no more than an inch above Edward's head. When the knife clattered to the floor, Edward picked it up.

"Poisoned," she hissed, and edged closer to him.

Anger blazed in his eyes. Another blade sailed through the air. Agnes ducked. The knife landed in the folds of her discarded skirt.

How many weapons did the Rook have? Scooting sideways, she nudged Edward farther beneath the shelter of the table.

The clock ticked harmlessly. The Rook stopped. If he knelt down, he would have them in plain view. Agnes stole a glance at her skirts and the hilt of the second knife. Catching the fabric, she pulled slowly.

Whoosh. Ping. Another knife thudded into the skirt. She snatched the blade. The tip was blunted. Nudging Edward again, she showed him what she intended to do.

He mouthed the words, "I love you."

Grasping the assassin's blade, she tested it for balance. It was heavier than her stiletto, but the haft fit her hand, and from this distance she knew her aim would be true.

With a flick of her wrist, she let the knife fly. "Have a taste of your own poison," she yelled.

It found a home in the Rook's calf. He made a soft grunt and pulled the blade free. Blood seeped through the leg of his breeches.

Edward started to stand. "No." She dragged him down.

The assassin dropped the knife and ran for the steps. Agnes rose to give chase, but Edward held her. "Let him go, love."

She moved close to him. "Listen to me. He will not stop until you are dead, and he will not kill me."

"How do you know that?"

Time was wasting. "I simply know it. Stay here."

"No. I'll go."

Knowing he would, she doubled her fist and socked him in the jaw. His eyes widened with shock, and he teetered. Seizing the moment, she ignored her aching knuckles and scurried from beneath the table. The hinges on the door squealed as the assassin ran for freedom.

The trail of his blood showed her the way. At the landing she paused, but only for a heartbeat. She pulled open the door. The tapestry fluttered into place.

She extinguished the lantern, then stepped into the old wing. The door to the tower opened. Thinking it was Auntie Loo, Agnes almost shouted a warning. Then a shape moved into the portal. It was the Rook. He ran into the tower. A moment later Agnes heard the eerie sound of the deadly backsword renting the air.

Edward rushed up behind her. "What happened?"

"He's dead. 'Twas the mirror you moved that confused him."

The cheval mirror reflected the entrance to the new wing. In his haste to flee, the Rook had gone the wrong way and met his death.

Flint struck steel in the common room, and light illuminated a grisly scene. Blood pooled in the rug beside the body of the Rook. His head had rolled to the foot of the stairs.

As calm as ever, Auntie Loo stepped into the doorway, the white copper sword dripping blood.

Edward hugged Agnes close, and in the pale light she could see tears twinkling in his eyes. "I thought we were dead."

Auntie Loo said, "Death's door is closed to the Golden One and to those who believe in her."

Held securely in Edward's arms, Agnes said, "And the door to home has opened for you, Auntie Loo. Your debt to me is paid."

She nodded solemnly, turned, and bracing her foot on the body of the Rook, she drew the blade of her sword across his shirt to wipe the blood away.

Agnes gazed at the man she loved. "Summon the guards to clean this up and dispose of the body. Mrs. Johnson doesn't need to see this."

"I will, but now I'd like to hold you and forget what has occurred here."

Returning the sword to the scabbard, Auntie Loo

joined them. "Spare Mrs. Johnson this carnage. Lord Lachlan's man will help me. I'll fetch him."

As she walked away, Edward said, "Will she truly return to China?"

"I hope so." Agnes hugged Edward. "Her mother is old and Auntie Loo is her only child."

"Hum, that feels good. Shall we name our first daughter for her?"

Gazing up into his face, Agnes thanked God for the gift of Edward's love. "Aye. May I suggest that we adjourn to a private place and beget her?"

Just before dawn Agnes questioned that decision. Amid the blaring of alarms and the shrill sound of whistles, her father and Robert Spencer charged into Napier House.

Dressed in her robe and standing beside Edward, who wore only the mended leather breeches, Agnes stared blankly at her father.

"Where the hell is Mary?" he demanded. "And get your hands off my Agnes."

Edward pulled Agnes closer. "Begging your pardon, my lord, but she's *my* Agnes, now."

As the subject of her father's intense scrutiny, Agnes could think of nothing to say. His clothing was soiled from the long ride, and he'd braided his hair at the temples. A thousand childhood memories came flooding back.

"You seduced her?" he asked Edward.

"Aye."

A grin as big as Scotland blossomed on Lachlan's face. He held out his hand in gentlemanly fashion. "Congratulations, Napier, she's yours."

"Papa!" Agnes yelled, as indignant as could be.

Lachlan sighed and shook his head. "You're a lucky man, Cathcart."

"I know that, my lord, and I promise you that she'll want for nothing."

"Nor will you," Lachlan said. "If companionship and loyalty are things you prize, Agnes Elizabeth has them to spare."

From the stairs Mary said, "Why thank you, Papa."

Robert Spencer, the dark-haired earl of Wiltshire rushed to the bottom of the steps. "So there you are," he said.

Mary planted her feet. "Don't you come near me."

"I'll do more than that, Mary Margaret MacKenzie."

"I want nothing to do with you."

"You've said that before."

"You plied me with Italian drink."

"You were as sober as a nun, but that was your only virtue."

"You took any other I had."

Edward moved away from Agnes and stepped between the English earl and Mary. "Wiltshire, we offer her shelter and you our hospitality, so long as your behavior merits it."

"Well put, Cathcart," said Lachlan.

Looking elegantly bedraggled, Robert Spencer slapped his plumed hat against his thigh. "She carries my child. She will marry me."

Mary hissed. "Note which of the two holds greater importance to his lordship."

Lachlan extended his hand. "Mary lass, please be reasonable."

"Reasonable?" Her eyes blazed defiance. "He forced me."

"Ha! You wanted me. You still do. You're too thick-headed to admit it."

Lachlan turned to Edward and Agnes. After kissing her cheek, he said to Edward, "My lord, I'm certain you'd prefer the company of my firstborn to the coil that goes between these two unfortunate lovers."

"Indeed, your grace." Edward held out his hand to Agnes. "Shall we, sweetheart?"

Agnes knew that Mary loved the English earl; she'd said as much. But their romantic journey had been fraught with obstacles. Perhaps some time here in Glasgow, away from both her detractors and his supporters, would allow Mary and Robert to mend the rift between them.

"Go, Agnes," her father said. "Leave these two to me."

"Will you?" Edward asked.

Agnes gazed into the eyes of the man she loved. "Aye."

Arm in arm, they strolled toward the old wing.

Mary's angry voice echoed through the corridors. "I admit to this, you pig-headed Englishman. I pray that you fall into the Minch and freeze your puny ballocks off."

Edward whistled. "Pity poor Wiltshire. I think the Lady Mary is more dangerous than you."

Feigning innocence, Agnes fluttered her eyelashes. "Oh, she is. I'm a kitten at heart."

Laughing, Edward swept her into his arms. "Will you purr for me, my little cat?"

Agnes languished in his arms, her soul brimming with gladness, her mind filled with visions of bright tomorrows. "Always, my love. Always."

Epilogue

Five years later

AGNES RESTED ON THE NARROW COT IN THE LABORATORY. On the floor beside her, her new daughter slept peacefully in the refurbished wicker basket. Hannah had left yesterday with Michael and Sarah and their twin sons for a visit to Edinburgh.

Across the room Edward sat on the floor near his latest invention, a bilge pump. Looking on were Christopher and four-year-old Jamie, the son Agnes had borne eight months to the day after their wedding. The low-pressure steam engine, perfected and patented, had taken its place among the other archetypes.

Edward spoke softly to the lads, and something about his tone alerted Agnes. A moment later Jamie got to his feet and skipped over to Agnes.

"Mama, when's a lassie's leg like an angle iron?"

Choking back laughter, Agnes glanced at her husband. Mischief twinkled in his eyes.

"When, Mama?"

"When her husband is too big for his breeches."

He giggled. "Papa said you'd blush."

"As usual," Edward declared, "your father is correct."

Little Juliet, born two days before and named for Agnes's stepmother, began to fuss. Agnes reached for her.

"Nay." Edward scooped the girl from the basket. First he kissed the baby's brow, then he sat on the edge of the cot and kissed Agnes. "We had an agreement, if you will recall. Rest or I'll carry you upstairs. How do you feel?"

This labor had been blessedly short, and counting Juliet, Agnes and her sisters had presented Lachlan MacKenzie with ten grandchildren. Mary was expecting again, and this time her husband, Robert Spencer, was taking wagers that she'd give him a son. "I feel wonderful. Having the best doctor in Christendom helps."

Edward shifted the baby to his shoulder and held her there, his graceful hand supporting her tiny back. Speaking softly to Juliet, he said, "You're a lucky lass. Your mother is beautiful and intelligent, too."

Christopher leaned close to his half sister and whispered, "If you're nice to our mother, she'll teach you how to pick a lock with naught but a hairpin for a tool."

"Not if she doesn't rest," Edward said with finality. "Close your eyes, love."

"But I'm not sleepy."

"Humor your doctor."

The upstairs door opened, and footfalls sounded on the ancient steps. Agnes knew the identity of their guest, but when Cameron Cunningham stepped into the room his complexion was pasty white, and his eyes were haunted with shock. His words robbed her of breath.

"I know where Virginia is."

**POCKET STAR BOOKS
PROUDLY PRESENTS**

TRUE HEART
Arnette Lamb

**Coming mid-December
from
Pocket Star Books**

**The following is a preview of
True Heart. . . .**

Prologue

"You didn't for a moment think I believed you asked me into the stables to show me a new horse."

Even after all these years, Juliet brought out the rogue in Lachlan. He took her hand and pressed her palm against his cheek. "What I have in mind is infinitely more entertaining than a foal."

Her interest engaged, she lifted her brows. Her fingers traced his mouth. "Which is why you brought me to the loft."

Her familiar scent softened the robust aroma of freshly mown hay. Her touch did more earthy things to his sense of decorum. "Why I brought you up here is a surprise."

"I see." She licked her lips. "You *intended* to wrinkle my dress and muss my hair?"

"Aye. The first before I ravished you, the second *while* I ravished you."

Always the grand skeptic, she said, "A husband cannot ravish his own wife. . . ." She had more to say, but she'd make him wait. Juliet had helped Lachlan raise Agnes, Sarah, Lottie, and Mary. But respect and love for his four bastard daughters only scratched the surface of her generosity. She'd given him four more daughters and an heir. He loved Juliet more today than when she'd placed his son in his arms. At sunrise next, he'd love her more still.

Touching her was a pleasure he couldn't deny himself now that they were alone. "In the event you've lost the gist of the conversation, you were holding forth on the issue of whether a husband may ravish his wife."

"The word 'holding' distracts me." She glided her hand down over the placket of his breeches and made a carnal image of the ordinary word. "Tell me why there is a satin pillow beneath the hay." She flicked her very arresting gaze to the spot where roof met wall.

Lachlan chuckled. "If you hope to tease me with conversational detours, you'll go wanting for that, love. Not even a bolster of gold could distract me at the moment."

Her supple fingers began a dangerous rhythm, and her voice softened to an enticing purr. "Pondering two things at once is surely manageable for a man of your invention."

Desire thrummed in his chest, rang in his ears. On a shallow breath, he said, "You, on the other hand, are not completely captivated."

With her free hand she cupped his neck and pulled him closer. "I've been captivated since the winter of sixty-two."

The occasion of her entry into Lachlan's life and the genesis of his true happiness. For hours he'd anticipated this time alone with her. Their eldest,

Virginia, was betrothed this very day to Cameron Cunningham, a lad they favored. Their son Kenneth would foster soon with Cameron's parents, Suisan and Myles. Lachlan's elder daughters were seventeen years old and planning their own futures.

For now, time alone with Juliet was a luxury to Lachlan, but in a few years he'd have her all to himself. This afternoon's tryst was a gift he intended to savor. Teasing her was a part of their lovers' game.

He plucked a straw from her hair. "But coherent thought is ever your constant companion, no?"

"Not always."

"Let's see about that." Gaze fixed to hers, he kissed her. Her brown eyes glittered with pleasure and desire smoldered in their depths. A sense of belonging swamped him, and as he deepened the kiss, he wondered for the thousandth time what great deed he'd done to deserve this woman. With a sweetness that always thrilled him, she returned his ardor and fired it with her own.

In the distance he heard the happy sound of childish laughter. Juliet heard it too, but that was the way of mothering with her. Even in the crowd at Midsummer Fair she could discern the voices of her own children.

"Which of our brood is so joyous? Cora?" He spoke of their youngest daughter.

"Kenneth. Agnes must be tickling him."

"I'll be glad when his voice changes."

"Will you rejoice when Agnes flies the nest?"

"Aye and nay. 'Tis dear Sarah I worry over more."

"Not our newly betrothed Virginia?"

Juliet's first daughter was unlike any of his other children. She'd been strongly influenced by her four older sisters. From Lottie she'd learned grace and stitchery. At Mary's hand she'd perfected an artist's skill. From Sarah she'd gained a love for books and law. From Agnes she'd learned too much cunning and bravery.

"Now who's distracted?" Juliet teased.

Lachlan moved closer. She winced and shifted.

"Uncomfortable?" he asked.

She gave him a look of tried patience. "No. But a pillow would be nice."

That mysterious pillow again. An odd jealousy stabbed him. He couldn't own her every thought. She was curious about the pillow and wouldn't leave the subject alone. He reached for the item in question and held it so they could both inspect it.

Embroidered in satin thread were the words "We love you, Papa."

Juliet said, "Only Lottie's stitches are so finely done."

Lachlan eased the pillow beneath her head. "Never will I understand the female mind."

"We are cerebral creatures, even in our stitchery."

They'd plowed this conversational field often over the years. "Cerebral." He pretended to ponder it. "For a thinker you're doing some very earthy things with your other hand."

"Then I'll allow you a moment to gather your priorities."

"Gather holds great appeal." Which is what he did to her skirts, moving his hand up her thighs. He found bare skin. "No underthings? You're bold, Juliet."

She fairly preened. "The last time you lured me into the stables you took my underclothing and wouldn't give them back. Agnes made a show of returning the garments to me."

Two months to the day after Kenneth had been born, Lachlan had enticed his wife into the loft.

They'd spent the day loving, laughing, and napping in their pursuit of happiness. She was the sun to his day. The moon to his night. The joy to his soul. The love in his heart.

He pressed her back into the soft hay. "We were also interrupted that day."

The interruption had come when she'd asked him to give her another child. He'd refused. She'd respected his wishes.

"'Twas a rough argument 'tween us." She mimicked his Scottish speech, but beneath the mockery lay regret, for she'd carried his children with ease and birthed them with joy. Five babes of her own had not been enough for his Juliet. Counting his illegitimate daughters, nine children were plenty for Lachlan.

"You're wonderful," he said.

"I thought I was the moon to your night."

"Aye, you are."

"The rain in your spring?"

"And the skip in my step."

She pretended to pout. "The thorn in your side?"

He blurted, "The bane of this loving if you laugh like that again."

She giggled low in her belly, more dangerous than full out laughter. Still in the throes of mirth, she said, "Do you recall the morning I seduced you in Smithson's wood house?"

He did. "Hot house better describes it. Actually I was remembering the time you tied me to the bed at Kinbairn Castle."

"You made a delicious captive, except for that one request you refused me."

Had she been cunning, Juliet could have gotten herself with child that day, for she had ruled their passion. "I prevailed."

"A winning day for both of us, but—" Something caught her attention. "Look." She pointed to the ceiling.

Craning his neck, Lachlan saw a piece of parchment secured to the rafter with an arrow. Printed on the parchment in Sarah's familiar handwriting were the words, "We love you, Mama."

Fatherly love filled him. Knowing he'd bring Juliet here, the lassies had left the pillow so he could see the affectionate words. Mary, the best archer of the four, had secured the note in a spot where Juliet couldn't miss it. Even though she wasn't their mother, they thought of her that way. But the positioning of the messages left no doubt that the girls knew that Lachlan and Juliet were making love in the loft.

On that lusty thought, he burrowed beneath her skirts and feasted on her sweetest spot.

Too soon she tugged on his hair. "Please, love."

He growled softly, triggering the first tremor in her surrender to passion. The beauty of her unfettered response moved him to his soul. But when she quieted, he eased up and over her, wedging himself into the cradle of her loins. His own need raging, he entered her, but not quickly or deeply enough, for she lifted her hips and locked her legs around him.

Lust almost overwhelmed him. "Say you're wearing one of those sponges." The sponges were the second most dependable way to control the size of their family.

Her slow smile struck fear in his heart. She wasn't wearing the sponge. If she moved so much as a muscle below the waist, he'd spill his seed, weighing the odds that she'd conceive again.

With his eyes he told her no.

Juliet's smile turned to resignation, and she mouthed the words, no ill feelings, love. He didn't need to hear the sound of the words; he'd heard them many times in the last three years. She waited until he'd mastered his passion. Then she reached into her bodice and retrieved a small corked bottle. With a flick of her thumb, she sent the cap sailing into the hay. The smell of lilac scented water teased his nose.

To tease her, he plucked up the wet sponge. "Excuse me for a moment." He put the sponge between his teeth, leered at her, and again burrowed beneath her skirts.

Primed, sleek, and ready, she awaited him. In his most inventive move to date, he inserted the sponge, then brought her to completion a second time.

"I want you now," she said between labored breaths.

Obliging her came easy to Lachlan. Just when he'd joined their bodies again and began to love her in earnest, voices sounded below.

"You must let me go with you," said a very disgruntled Virginia.

Lachlan groaned. Juliet slapped a hand over his mouth.

He knew to whom Virginia was speaking: her betrothed, Cameron Cunningham.

Hoping they wouldn't stay long, Lachlan returned his attention to Juliet.

Praying for patience, Cameron followed Virginia into the last stall.

She stopped and folded her arms. "Why can't I go with you?"

The greatest adventure of his life awaited Cameron. Years from now, after they were married, he'd sail around the world with her. For now, reason seemed prudent. "'Twouldn't be proper."

"Proper?" Her dark blue eyes glittered with temper, and her pretty complexion flushed with anger. "We're betrothed. That should be reason enough. Papa knows you will not ravish me. I haven't even gotten my menses yet."

From another female the remark would have sparked outrage, but Cameron had known Virginia MacKenzie since the day of her Christening, ten years ago. His ears still ached when he remembered how long and loudly she'd cried. He'd been eight years old at the time. He'd fostered here at Rosshaven. He'd learned husbandry from Lachlan MacKenzie, the best man o' the Highlands. The announcement earlier today of Virginia's betrothal to Cameron had been a formality. Their marriage, five years hence, would mark the happiest day of Cameron's life. Their parents heartily approved, for the union would unite their families.

He told her a lie and the least hurtful refusal. "You cannot go with me to France." He was sailing for China. She'd learn that truth from her father on the morrow.

"But everything's formal now, and I've made us a symbol of our own. See?" From her fancy wrist bag, she produced a silk scarf.

Fashioned after the ancient clan brooches, the design on the cloth featured a circle with stylistic hearts and an arrow running through.

"The arrow is for your mother's people, Clan Cameron. The hearts are in honor of our friendship and love, which will be timeless. It took me ever so long to think it up and a week of nights here in the stable to stitch it. 'Tis a secret. I wanted you to see it before everyone else."

Cameron voiced his first thought. "'Tis feminine for a man to wear."

Her eyes filled with tears. "That's a wretched thing to say."

Immediately defensive, Cameron stood his ground. "I'm sorry. I was surprised is all."

"Then don't disappoint me again. Take me with you. I'll cancel the betrothal if you do not."

His pride stinging, Cameron tucked the scarf into his sleeve and headed for the door. "Cancel it if you wish. I only agreed to please my parents."

Virginia gave up the fight. He couldn't mean those hurtful words, and by the time his ship sailed tomorrow, she'd be tucked securely in the hold.

Chapter 1

Nine years, eleven months, and thirteen days later, Cameron swung the canvas bag onto his shoulder and stepped on the quay in Glasgow Harbor. Pain no longer accompanied memories of Virginia. Only a deep sense of loss. Since her disappearance, he'd learned to live with an empty soul. The image of the clan brooch Virginia had designed years ago rose in his mind, as vivid as the day he'd first seen the delicate hearts with an arrow running through.

Cameron stopped in his tracks and blinked. The picture became real. Before him loomed a wall of hogsheads. Burned into the wood of each of the barrels was the symbol created almost a decade ago by Virginia MacKenzie.

His heart pounded, and the ale he'd drunk with his crew just moments ago turned sour in his belly. No one else had seen the hallmark. Virginia said it had been her secret gift in honor of their betrothal. By candlelight, she'd embroidered the scarf for him. After her disappearance, when Cameron had relayed to her father the details of that last meeting in the stables at Rosshaven, the duke of Ross confessed that he'd never seen Virginia's hallmark.

Cameron had thought never to see it again.

He put down his burden and peered closer at the design. With only a slight variance, a common heraldic crown over the top, the symbol was the same.

From the ashes of certainty, a spark of hope flickered to life. Virginia could be alive. The thought staggered him.

Mouth dry, hands shaking, he leaned against the stack of tobacco casks. Past disappointments warned caution. But what were the odds of another person combining the arrow of Clan Cameron, his mother's Highland family, with hearts of love? No coincidence appeared before him; Virginia was alive and this drawing was her cry for help.

Stuffing one of the hogsheads under his arm, he located Quinten Brown, captain of the merchantman.

"From where did this hallmark come?"

Brown swept off his three-cornered hat and tucked it under his arm. "Why would you be asking, Cunningham? Ain't the brandy trade enough for you?"

In his place, Cameron would also be protective of his livelihood; any businessman would. To allay the man's worry and loosen his tongue, Cameron fished a sack of coins from his waistcoat. "I've seen this design, and it's very important to me. I've no intention of heeling in on your trade."

Satisfied, Brown pocketed the gold. "'Course you ain't. I'll tell you what I know o' the matter. The cooper at Poplar Knoll always favored the plain crown—even after the colonies was lost to us." He traced the design. "This girlish mark, the hearts 'n' arrow, on their barrels. I ain't seen it afore."

"Then how do you know this tobacco came from there?"

"The new mistress herself come aboard to pay her respects to me." Rocking back on the heels of his bucket-top boots, the seaman clutched his lapels. "Her husband, Mr. Parker-Jones, bought the plantation more'n a year ago. I tell you true, Cunningham, the slaves 'n' servants o' that place are praising God. The old owner and his wife were devils and more."

In his search for Virginia, Cameron had scoured every port in the British Isles, the Baltic, Europe, and even the slave markets of Byzantine. He'd searched Boston, the cities of Chesapeake Bay, and even the Spanish-held New Orleans. "Where is this plantation?"

"Poplar Knoll? The tidewaters of Virginia."

Cameron had sailed those waters, but not in years. With his father serving in the House of Commons, Cameron now favored the shorter European trade routes. "On the York River?"

"No. The James, just west of Charles City."

"The south or the north shore?"

"South, if I'm remembered of it. Fine dock with lovey doves carved into the moorings. Yes, south side."

At the least, the person who'd crafted this hallmark had some knowledge of Virginia. If she were on an isolated plantation, that would explain why he hadn't found her. The lost war with the colonies had limited shipping traffic, and little news traveled out of tidewater Virginia.

Anticipation thrumming through him, he thanked the captain and made his way to Napier House, home of Virginia's sister, Agnes. Now the countess of Cathcart, Agnes was the only family member who still believed that Virginia was alive.

Dear God, he prayed, let it be so.

POPLAR KNOLL PLANTATION
TIDEWATER VIRGINIA

Planting would be upon them soon. From dawn's first light until sunset or rain forced them to stop, they'd hunker in the fields. Virginia shifted on the bench, her back aching at the thought. In the corner of the weaving shed, the strongest of the slaves dismantled the looms used to weave book muslin, the fabric of necessity for slaves and bond servants. Everyone, even the pregnant females worked in the fields until harvest. At first frost, the looms would come out again.

Life would continue for another year. But three harvests hence Virginia's indenture would end. The old bitterness stirred, but she stifled it. She'd tried escape once, nine years ago. For penalty five years had been added to her servitude. Freedom would come. Three years from now, she'd have money in her purse, new shoes and a traveling coat, and passage to Williamsburg. From there—

"Duchess!"

Virginia started. Merriweather, the smartly dressed butler from the home house strolled toward her.

"Wash your hands and face, Duchess. Mrs. Parker-Jones wants to see you."

No one addressed Virginia as Virginia. They hadn't believed her story about who she was and how she'd come to the colonies. When she'd proclaimed herself the daughter of the duke of Ross, they'd laughed and named her Duchess. She'd been a frightened child of ten.

Merriweather cleared his throat. "You've done nothing wrong. The mistress hastened me to say so."

Virginia smiled and put aside the hat band she was tooling. She'd spoken only once to Mrs. Parker-Jones since the woman and her husband had purchased Poplar Knoll two years ago. Did this summons also involve the design Virginia had secretly branded into the hogsheads? Hopefully not, for she'd come away from the meeting with a small victory and an apology. She'd been assured the matter was ended.

Encouraged, she went to the table and washed her face in the bucket of clean water. Then she untied her apron and took the brush from her basket.

As they left the shed and made their way through the servants' hamlet, she brushed her hair and tied it at her nape.

"She'll not be seeing you in the front parlor, your grace."

No rancor hardened his words, and Virginia chuckled. She might be a bond servant, but never had she been a sloven.

She was ushered into the back parlor, where Mrs. Parker-Jones was reading the Bible. Putting the book aside, she waved the butler out the door. "Close it on your way out, if you please, Merriweather."

Although she'd never been in this room, Virginia

refused to gape at the fine furnishings. She'd seen better at Rosshaven.

"Tell me about yourself." Mrs. Parker-Jones indicated a chair. "How did you come to servitude?"

Caution settled over Virginia, and she stood beside the chair. "Three years remain on my indenture, Ma'am. I want no trouble."

"I want the truth. Are you Virginia MacKenzie, daughter of the sixth duke of Ross?"

Something in the tone of her voice alarmed Virginia, that and her knowledge of the specifics of Papa's title. She gripped the back of the chair. "Who wants to know?"

"Cameron Cunningham."

Images of her youth swam before Virginia. Then she saw nothing at all.

Look for
True Heart
Wherever Paperback Books Are Sold
Mid-December